TO SAY Goodbye

LINDSAY DETWILER

To Say Goodbye © 2016 by Lindsay Detwiler

To Say Goodbye is a work of fiction. All names, characters, events and places found therein are either from the author's imagination or used fictitiously. Any similarity to persons alive or dead, actual events, locations, or organizations is entirely coincidental and not intended by the author.

For information, contact the publisher, Hot Tree Publishing.

www.hottreepublishing.com

Editing: Hot Tree Editing

Cover Designer: Claire Smith

Format Design: RMGraphX

ISBN-10: 1-925448-27-4

ISBN-13: 978-1-925448-27-6

10 9 8 7 6 5 4 3 2 1

TO MY HUSBAND, CHAD

Prologue

SOPHIA

The rain pelted against the umbrella above her head, but a few rogue drops managed to slap against her chilled cheek. They intermixed with the tears streaming down her face, creating a sympathetic harmony of her sadness and of nature's seemingly melancholy mood. The weather befit the occasion, a punctuation to the sea of black circling the soggy earth around the casket.

She could feel her pointy-toed stilettos sinking into the mud. She knew by this point splotches of the sickly, sticky earth were probably all over her shoes, but she didn't dare look down. This was not the time to worry about her shoes, the weather, or anything else. It struck her as ridiculous that these thoughts were even swirling in her mind.

The rain continued to pound as the pastor droned on about salvation, faith, and heavenly things, but Sophia only heard a string of pointless words. She felt nauseous, felt hungover from grief. Faith did not exist anymore for her. Faith could not exist in a world without him.

She didn't know if she would be able to cry today. She'd cried so many tears over the past few nights, she thought she might be empty. Then again, she also didn't know if she'd make it through today standing. She wondered if—in fact, she hoped—she would fall to the ground, a heart attack panging in her chest from her grief. She wanted to lie in the gaping hole in the ground and bury herself beneath him.

She, quite simply, wanted to be dead too.

She could feel the gazes penetrating her, pitying her, gauging her reaction. She tried to look the prim and proper part of the solemn wife, flanked by her parents and in-laws, standing close to the casket. Inside though, something else was creeping in, something besides the skulking, downtrodden feelings.

Moments of rage began to infiltrate her, a silent warfare bubbling within.

How could this have happened to her? These sort of things didn't happen to women like her. Sure, like everyone, she'd experienced tragedy before. Grief had grasped her with its suffocating grip several times in her adult life, but this was a completely new level. He wasn't here this time. She couldn't lean on his shoulder, feel him wrap his arms around her, have him drag her out of the pit of sadness. She'd never been through something like this without him. She'd never endured a shredded heart without him there to help piece it back together. She wasn't equipped for an ordeal like this, wasn't strong enough.

Tim had been the pillar in her life for the past ten years. He'd been her best friend, her laughter, her teammate. He'd been the man to help her recover from disappointments and failures. He'd been the one who remembered her favorite drink at their favorite restaurants and who could order for her if she was running late. He'd been the one to embrace her on a bad day, to kiss her goodnight, to wrap her in his warmth as they fell asleep. He'd been her everything.

Now her everything was gone. How would she do this?

She wouldn't. She just wouldn't.

She would carry on through today for him, to honor his memory. She would say goodbye to the man who had been her foundation. She would honor his life. Then she would succumb to nothingness. She would sit and slowly watch her life fade away around her, watch everything blur by as she sat still. She would wait for death to come, for the end of her pain. Until then, she would just tick away the time.

She perused the crowd of mourners as another prayer started. Across the huddle, a man stood in a black suit. He wore sunglasses, probably to hide his grief-stricken expression. There was no umbrella to shield him from the weather. He stood unmoving, stoic, and rigid. He did not chant along to the prayer, did not wipe at his eyes like the other mourners. He stood, stubble marking his jaw, stone-faced, one hand clasping the other wrist. He did not move a muscle, his military training probably preparing him for a moment like this.

She hadn't seen him since an encounter they'd had months earlier, hadn't even thought about him. Of course he was here, though. He'd been Tim's best friend for years. Just because they'd grown apart didn't mean this loss wasn't impacting him. Fading friendships didn't make a loss any easier.

Before today, he'd been just a passing thought, a mere coincidence. Now, Sophia looked at him in a different light. Now, he was a relic of a life gone by, a memory of a man who was no longer here.

She stepped forward at her mother's prompting to say her final farewell. She felt herself breaking down, melting, falling apart. People crowded around her to help her through, to tell her it would be okay. She was tired of hearing it, even if they meant well. Things were not okay. The grief struck in waves, threatening to physically overpower her. The rain intensified. Her sadness and the cold, pelting rain were unbearable.

With her peripheral vision, she saw him approach. He shoved his sunglasses back out of respect to approach the grave. He gently tossed his white rose onto the coffin, and Sophia looked up at him. His face was still stone cold, stiff, but she detected something familiar—a tear streaming down his face. It was almost undetectable, mingling with the rainwater also running down his cheek.

He stood by her, not touching her, just staring into the grave.

Finally, he broke the silence. "What a shitty day."

Sophia's heart ached and her tears streamed. Her nose

was so stuffy she felt like she was suffocating. She felt like it was a physical chore to breathe, as though she had to remind her lungs how to work. Somehow, though, his words comforted her. It was hard to hear someone else say the words plastered on her heart, but in a strange way, it was a relief too. Finally, someone else was saying what she was thinking.

It wasn't going to be okay. She wasn't strong. She wasn't going to find her way without him.

A world without Tim was just a shitty excuse for a world.

It was over. Tim was gone. Now they were all left to pick up the pieces of a world forever changed.

Chapter One

SOPHIA

THREE MONTHS LATER

The alarm's ringing was an unfamiliar anthem to Sophia, and it startled her. She wasn't used to having to pay attention to time, to get up and be somewhere. She groggily rolled over to hit snooze, her head pounding from the incessant sound.

This had been a terrible idea. As she tried to fall back asleep, she thought maybe she could put it off for another day or two. Stella wouldn't begrudge her one more day at home.

Rolling onto her back and rubbing her eyes, though, she knew she had to get up. She'd given herself the much-needed time away. She had promised herself, had promised Stella, she would get back into the swing of things. Life was going on with or without her. She had to rejoin the land of the living. She swung her legs out of bed, her heart heavy as it always was in the mornings. She tried not to take note of Tim's side of the bed.

Tim's empty side of the bed.

She strolled to her closet, toward the back to get real clothes. She didn't even know if they fit anymore. Yoga pants and sweatshirts had been her uniform for the past twelve weeks.

Pulling on some jeans and a long-sleeved black shirt, the color of her life now, she headed to the bathroom to examine her hair. Her blonde locks were a frizzy disaster. Her own hairstyle was probably not going to instill much confidence in her clientele today. She couldn't bring herself to care, though.

These days, she didn't care about much.

She rustled her hand through her waves, deciding the messy look would have to do. Her alarm rang from the bedroom again, and she headed to shut it off. After fiddling with the buttons to stop the annoying sound, she saw a text from Stella.

Stella: I'm so glad you're coming in today. I've missed you so much! I only booked you for three appointments. We'll ease into it. Xoxo

Despite her apprehension, Sophia smiled. She'd missed her best friend. She was lucky to have such an amazing friend and business partner. Because of Stella, she'd been able to have the past few months to heal, or at least to wade through her grief.

Sophia headed downstairs to make her coffee. She

would eat a muffin at the shop for breakfast. As she sat at the kitchen table alone, heaviness rose in her chest. Today was the day. She would take a step away from Tim, away from the life they had. She had to start piecing together an existence by herself, a life without him.

These past three months had been excruciating. Despite her parents, in-laws, and friends, she'd sunken into a deep depression, a hermit-like state of existence. She wanted nothing to do with the outside world, believing if she could stay in the cocoon of their home, maybe she could stay a part of Tim's life. Maybe she wouldn't have to acknowledge he was gone. Most days were the same. She wrapped herself in the veil of silence in her house, her thoughts and memories ricocheting off the walls around her. It was maddening, but it was still easier than facing the world, facing the questions, facing the stares. She didn't want to pretend she was okay. She didn't want to hear fake words of encouragement. She wanted to melt into herself, to feel like crap, to mourn alone. She wanted to pretend she didn't live in a world without him. She wanted to lock herself away in their memories, surround herself with the familiar walls she had called home with him. She wanted to pretend he was just away temporarily and would be back any moment.

In short, she wanted to forget Tim had died, had gone, had left her.

This was silly, though, because everywhere she looked in their home, she saw him and, thus, felt his absence.

She saw the archway where he'd playfully flung paint in her hair as they touched up their new home when they first moved in. She saw his chair at the dinner table, saw the shelf in the fridge where five cans of his favorite beer still sat. There were places of slow dances, places of passionate kisses, and photographs all around. The house was starting to feel more like a mausoleum of memories than a sanctuary.

Her loved ones had tried to perk her up, tried to help her move on. There'd been dozens of casseroles and dinner offers, and many movie nights with Stella. Even though her in-laws were living in Florida now, they constantly sent her care packages. Tim's mom sent her favorite no-bake cookies and notes that said she hoped Sophia was doing okay. They'd even offered her a place to stay if she wanted to get away and soak up some sun.

Her parents and Stella had taken turns entertaining her, trying to make her smile. She loved them for it. But they weren't what she needed. They weren't Tim.

Sophia sighed, knowing this wasn't helping anything. She didn't think going back to work today was going to help either. But she had no choice. She needed to rejoin the world, practice surviving. It wasn't fair to make Stella keep shouldering the business. She needed to return.

Sophia checked her bag to make sure she had her keys and wallet, then headed out the door. The sun was shining, and neighbors were heading out to their cars as well. She gave a few brief hellos before jumping in her car.

"Here goes nothing," she said to herself as she started the car and headed down the road for the first time in a long time.

———————

"Morning, sunshine," Stella cheered as Sophia entered through the door of Pink Lemonade. She felt like an alien walking into the place that not long ago was her second home. The pink walls, the pink lemonade in the beverage dispenser, the magazines everywhere—it felt familiar. But being here for the first time since Tim's death felt strange. She wasn't the same woman who had walked out of here that fateful day. Everything had changed.

She shrugged off the thoughts. *I just have to survive today. I just have to focus on haircuts, perms, and nails.*

"I've missed you. I'm so glad you're back. It's going to be okay. We're going to get through," Stella said, heading from behind the register to give her a hug. "Come on over. Everything's exactly how you left it."

Sophia walked over to her station. A bouquet of flowers sat by her mirror. "Stell, what are these?" She touched the pink carnations and tried not to think about the funeral home, the bouquets there.

"Honey, I just wanted you to know I love you, and I know this is hard. I'm here for you."

"I know. I can't thank you enough for these past few months. I know it's been rough on you, running everything alone. I feel awful about it." She turned away from the flowers, closing her eyes and taking a breath.

"That's what friends are for. You needed some time. I think it's good you're back, though. You need to get into a routine again."

Sophia looked at her best friend with gratitude. Stella had been her best friend since right after high school when they met at the beauty academy. They'd been through bad dye jobs together, tears over failed tests, first jobs together at Opal's Salon, and eventually the chaos of opening their own hair salon. She'd been her maid of honor, her go-to for advice about everything. Now, though, her friend had proven she was truly one-of-a-kind. She'd helped Sophia through the worst moments of her life, and now she was about to help her through her first day of rejoining the world.

"I don't know what I'd do without you," Sophia said as she ran her fingers over her combs and plugged in her hot iron.

"Well, you're not going to have to find out anytime soon." Stella winked, tucking a piece of her hot-pink hair behind her ear.

The phone rang, breaking up their moment. It was back to busy, and Sophia was glad. She headed to the desk to answer the phone.

"Pink Lemonade, Sophia speaking, how can I help you?"

It was good to be back.

Eight hours later, two perms, a highlight job, six haircuts, five refills on the lemonade, and Sophia and Stella sat in their own chairs. They passed back and forth the box of Swedish Fish—they'd clung to the addiction from beauty school.

"Can you believe she actually thought gray looked good on her?" Stella squealed.

"Oh my God, it looked awful! I thought she was going to cry when I did the reveal. I surely would've. But the poor thing thought it looked trendy!"

"Wait until she's thirty. Gray won't be so trendy then, huh?"

The two women laughed, recalling the craziness of the day. A seventeen-year-old decided she'd jump on the trend wagon, dying her gorgeous blonde locks solid silver. It looked disastrous.

"How about Mrs. Joseph complaining about her cut?"

"Oh man. I thought she'd never leave. 'Just another one-sixteenth of an inch, dearie.' Such a sweet lady, but I'm glad you got her this time, Soph."

Sophia smiled, taking back the Swedish Fish for a few more. "It feels good to be back. It was nice to not think about everything, to be so busy I couldn't. I sort of wish I'd returned sooner."

"It was good to take some time. You needed to grieve."

"I think you were just worried my melancholy state would've transferred to my work."

"I was a bit concerned about you coloring everyone's hair black to match your period of mourning."

Sophia laughed. "Could you imagine Mrs. Joseph if I dyed her hair black?"

"We'd be mourning you when she killed you." After the words were out, Stella stopped, a sharp gasp escaping her lips. "Oh my God, Soph. I'm an idiot. I'm sorry." She reached over to pat Sophia's leg.

"It's okay. Really. I know Tim's dead. I haven't forgotten. You don't need to tiptoe."

"I know. I just... I... I don't know. I don't know how to do all of this. I'm terrible at this sort of thing."

Sophia smiled. "I don't think anyone *should* be good at this sort of thing. Trust me."

Stella sobered, looking off into the distance. "I can't imagine what you're going through. I really can't. I don't know how you're holding it together."

"I'm not."

"You look like you've got it together."

"I'm trying."

Stella looked at Sophia. "That's all you can do. Just keep trying, Soph. That's what he would want."

"Yeah, I suppose." Sophia stared at the floor in silence, the realization that a day's worth of work couldn't make everything go away.

"I guess I should get going."

"You want to do something? You okay?" Stella asked, standing now to take a load of towels to the laundry area.

"I'm okay, Stella. I'll see you tomorrow."

The two hugged as Stella walked her to the door.

"Soph?" Stella asked, and Sophia turned around.

"Love you. I'm glad you're back. I missed you. Plus, the customers have been complaining. My pink lemonade isn't nearly as good as yours."

Sophia smiled. "Love you back."

Then she headed to her car and home, or at least to the empty shell of the home remaining after Tim's death. She'd put in a day. She'd survived.

But how many more would she have to get through?

Chapter Two

JACKSON

The heavy liquid skirted down his throat, bubbling as it went. He pulled the glass bottle back and set it on the end table as his free hand flipped through the channels. One lonely lamp across the room gave the living area an eerie glow. He barely noticed, his eyes glued to the television, his feet propped up on the coffee table near the Chinese takeout containers.

Upstairs, a couple quarreled, someone stomping from room to room. He was already tired of his neighbors, tired of the apartment life. But what else did he have? The rent was cheap, cheap enough to afford on his wages at the restaurant. Plus, he was alone now. He didn't need much space. He was a bachelor, living the life some men dreamed of. It was a dream that had become his personal nightmare.

Some things about his life were good. It was nice to be living in one place, to not be at the mercy of the army, to not be constantly relocated. It was good to have a stable routine coupled with some freedom. It was nice to be back in his hometown, to be close to his parents again, to spend time with his family. His sister, Gretta, was only twenty minutes away with her husband and son. It was good to be in close proximity to them. This wasn't enough to cheer him up, though. Too much had been lost. First Chloe, then Logan. And now Tim was gone.

True, Tim hadn't really been a huge part of his life anymore. Life's business, the hectic state of their individual career paths kept them apart. Life had forced them apart. Now, death had permanently severed any chance of them restoring their friendship.

That didn't make the blow any less terrible. It seemed like Jackson couldn't catch a break these days. Everything crumbled around him, making him paranoid. He was on edge, wondering what would be next.

His cellphone rang, causing him to jump. Looking at the screen, he saw the name. It was Chloe returning his call. Finally.

"Hello?" his voice cracked. He hadn't used it in several hours, sitting in solitude after his shift at La Familia De Rinoldo. Now, it sounded broken.

"I listened to your messages. All six of them. Jackson, stop calling me. Everything's been settled."

"I know, I just, I thought maybe since it's Logan's birthday, we could make an exception."

Chloe huffed loudly into the phone. "You know it's not your weekend. The agreement gave me his birthday this year."

"I know, Chloe. But it's his birthday. I don't want to miss it. Please."

"Jackson, no. You know I'm not making any exceptions. The court made its decision. This weekend is mine."

"Please don't do this."

"I didn't do anything. You did it. You made the choice."

"I know I fucked up. But you can't keep my son from me."

"Yes, I can."

The phone clicked. It was done.

Jackson gritted his teeth, trying to quell the surging anger. He wanted to scream, wanted to drive the two hours to Chloe's new house and flip out. He wanted to hit the man who was now playing his role, who Logan was probably already calling Daddy. He wanted to take Logan and leave the country. Instead, he took another pull from his beer. As rational thought took over, he realized if he wanted to be mad at anyone, it should be himself.

Yeah, Chloe had messed up. She made her share of mistakes, burned him badly.

Jackson was the one to make the mistakes leading to the final loss, though, the worst loss. He was the reason Logan was gone from his life.

He was the only one to blame. His life was on a

downward spiral, had been for some time. And there was no one to turn to now, not really.

When he'd come back into town, he'd hoped to find what he'd been missing, to sort things out. He'd thought this town would allow him to reconnect with the person he'd once been. Now though, with all things happening as they were, he wasn't sure it was possible.

He finished his beer, turned off the television, and went to bed, hopeless and alone, wondering if life could possibly get any worse.

He'd left the army to settle into a life, the life he'd always dreamed about.

The only problem was the life he wanted to reclaim had collapsed around him. And he hadn't even known it.

Chapter Three

JACKSON

"Order up," Jackson yelled as he turned back to the Chicken Cordon Bleu he was making. He used his forearm to rub the sweat away from his brow as he busied his hands with the next task.

His father had thought he was crazy when he'd taken this job at the local gourmet restaurant.

"Son, you have over ten years in the army. You have experience with a construction crew. Don't you want to do something more substantial?"

"I love cooking."

"Hmph." His dad clearly didn't see a job as a chef as man's work. As a retired army sergeant himself, Louis Gauge, if he were being honest, held it against Jackson that he hadn't finished out his military career.

Nonetheless, Jackson had wanted to get away from his past. When he came home to Hollidaysburg, he wanted to get away from any ties to his previous life. Cooking seemed about as far away from the front lines as he could get.

He'd always loved the idea of taking simple ingredients and making something phenomenal out of them. If his dad hadn't pushed him into the military, he'd have probably gone to culinary school right out of high school. Those days were long gone, however. He was just glad the owners of La Familia De Rinoldo had given him a chance. He liked to work with his hands. He liked the chaos of the kitchen. He liked taking something ordinary and making an experience for the customers with it.

Life in the army had taught him to handle stress, to be organized, to be efficient. These skills translated well in the kitchen, which he was thankful for. However, other than that, his time in the army had offered him little satisfaction.

How could it when it had destroyed everything?

He slid the thought aside, focusing on the task at hand. The hours flew by with ease, and soon it was time to clock out. He should have been grateful for another day done. Instead, he was saddened. When your life at home consisted of takeout and television, there was little benefit to being done with work.

Figuring another night alone in his dingy, neutral apartment wouldn't do his psyche much good, he decided to visit his parents. His dad might not approve of his career choices, but he was still supportive of him. It would be good to see some friendly faces, to talk, maybe even to play a little poker with the old man. He would probably lose some money. After all, his dad wasn't called Lucky Lou for nothing.

Pulling into the driveway of his childhood home, Jackson took a second to glance around. Memories of being a boy flooded in. He saw himself as a six-year-old swinging in the tire swing, which was still in the front yard for his nephew, Jace. He could hear his mom singing him to sleep every night, could smell the aroma of the chocolate chip cookies she made every Sunday. He glanced to the back shed where he'd experienced his first kiss, saw the tree where he'd endured his first breakup. The home was filled with memories, memories of a time gone by. Memories of a time when he still believed life was fair, was something to be excited about. Certainly, there were bad memories too, especially after Wade. Looking at the house now, he didn't think of those. He thought of the warm memories, the memories that made him crave his youth, crave a simpler time.

Jackson turned off the engine, strolled to the front door, and glided his key in the lock.

"Mom, you home?" he yelled up the steps as he took off his shoes.

"Uncle Jackson!" a voice bellowed from upstairs. He heard his nephew jumping up and down. He smiled involuntarily, taking the steps two at a time.

"Jace, my man. What's happening?" he asked, extending his palm to give the boy five. Jace smiled up at him, giving

Jackson a grin that stopped his heart.

Jace was Logan's age. Seeing his nephew made him happy, but it also caused his heart to jolt, especially in these past few months. It killed him to think of all the smiles he was missing from Logan, to think about Logan's toothy grin looking up at another man.

Jace clung to Jackson's knee, and he ruffled his hair. Jackson's mom turned from the meatballs cooking on the stove, her Thursday night specialty. "Hey, honey. Are you hungry?"

"No, I couldn't look at food. Just came from work."

"You're getting too skinny. Sit down, eat."

"Mom, I'm stuffed."

"You look gaunt. You're not taking care of yourself. I can tell."

"*Mom*. I'm fine."

His mom always fussed over him, but now she was even more obsessive than usual. She was worried about him slipping into another depression like he had when he'd come home from the army. It was bad, he would admit. He couldn't blame her for worrying.

"Where's Gretta?" he asked, changing the subject as Jace ran to get his Legos to play with. Jackson leaned on the counter, his mother returning to the stove.

"Working late tonight. There's a huge bridal party coming in after store hours. Some highfalutin customers. I'm watching Logan because Jonathan is also working late. An important trial's happening."

Jackson grabbed a few Hershey Kisses from the candy

bowl, shoveling them into his mouth. His mother turned around at the rustling of the paper. "I thought you couldn't think about food?"

"It's just candy."

"Well, if you don't eat with us, I'm going to think you have something against my meatballs. Since you're a gourmet chef and all."

"You know I love your cooking, Mom." He walked over to give the sometimes-sassy woman a peck on the cheek.

"Well, I don't know. You haven't been around much. I've missed you. Are you okay?"

She looked at him seriously. He looked away. She could always tell when he was lying.

"I'm fine."

"Honey, how could you be? It's been a terrible time. What with Logan gone, and now Tim. It's been awful."

"I know." God, did he know. He didn't need a reminder of how tough things had been. He cast his gaze to the floor, trying to stop his mind from heading down the dark path it had traveled so many times lately. Mercifully, his mom's words snapped him out of it.

"Sorry. I didn't mean to bring up bad news." Jace mercifully returned to the room, forcing Jackson's mom to change the conversation. He quietly went to the corner of the kitchen, dumping his Legos all over the floor. Mrs. Gauge simply sighed, shaking her head at the mess. As one of her beloved grandchildren, though, Jace could easily get away with just about anything. The obsessively organized, clean-freak woman didn't say a word to him as he played.

"How's Sophia holding up?" she asked, turning back to their conversation.

Jackson shrugged. "Haven't seen her since the funeral."

"Why not?"

"I just thought it would be weird. What am I supposed to do? Stop by, chat her up? I barely know her."

"You were so close to Tim though."

"It was a long time ago."

"I just think she would appreciate it if you stopped by. Plus, it would be good for you. It would be good for you to socialize."

"With Tim's wife? You think that's a good idea?"

"I didn't say take her to bed, Jackson. Jesus."

Jackson covered his eyes with his hands. "I would hope not. My God. Do you always just say what you're thinking?"

"Pretty much. Which is why I'm also going to say it's time for a haircut. And a shave. You look like you're homeless."

"It's only been two days. Stubble is sexy."

"Not in my book," she said, turning to get the meatballs off the stove. "Go get your father. He's in the garage. Tell him dinner's ready."

"Will do."

Jackson traipsed down the stairs to the garage, beckoned his father to come inside, and returned to the kitchen. He smiled to see a plate at his seat at the table.

"Mom, I said I'm not hungry."

She ignored him, ordering Jace to his spot as she told Jackson to have a seat.

"Louis, please say grace," she ordered, and her husband complied.

———————

"Hey, man, come on in," Jackson said as he opened the door the following night. Evan was a few minutes early, as always. The punctuality engrained in their minds during their time in the army had never left Evan's personality, even though he too had ended up abandoning the career path in favor of civilian life.

They hugged the typical masculine, one-hand slapping hug, trying not to dismiss too much manliness or to let too much emotion creep in.

When Evan had called on Monday to say he'd be in town this weekend, Jackson had smiled.

"Of course I'll be home. Stop by, buddy. Can't wait to see you."

Each life stage was punctuated by different friendships, different connections. For Jackson, his twenties were marked by his friendship with Evan. Together, they'd been through boot camp, served two tours in Iraq, and survived a few close calls. Civilian life had taken them in different directions, but Jackson couldn't wait to see him again.

"How's it going, buddy?" Evan asked. Jackson gauged his appearance. It was strange seeing the spikey, gelled hair where the standard military haircut had once been.

"It's going. Working. That's about it. How about you?"

"It's awesome. Anna and I are getting married."

"Congrats. That's great." Jackson smiled as his friend beamed, obviously thrilled. A part of the words stung, though. Jackson didn't want to admit it, wouldn't let the cold emotion creep into his face. He sat stoically on the couch as his buddy animatedly discussed the details of his life—the engagement, the decision to elope next month, the new house.

Jackson was happy for him. He really was. He didn't begrudge his friend the happiness he deserved. But as Evan chattered on, Jackson's mind drifted away. He was taken back, back to a time when his life was in order, a time when he too thought marriage could fulfill him.

———

Beads of water still dripping from his closely shorn hair after his shower, he sauntered to the kitchen. He was shirtless, just as she'd always preferred him, his six-pack rippling. His army workouts had kept him in top condition, even in these past few months as he prepared for his return to civilian life.

It felt so undeniably good to be home. When he was away, he'd missed home like crazy. The past year had been the worst, though, knowing Chloe was home with their young son, alone, while he was off fearing death every moment. He hadn't wanted to miss a second, had been sick thinking about all the milestones breezing by. He'd hated leaving her alone with Logan, hated being away from his wife. His heart ached with every letter, every phone call.

But that was over now. He'd walked away from the family

tradition, walked away from the army life. He'd given up his combat boots and M-16 to return home to a traditional life. He was nervous about finding work, about fitting back in to the civilian lifestyle. Standing at the edge of the kitchen, taking in her brunette curls softly falling down the curve of her perfect back, watching her as she washed the dishes from dinner, he couldn't help but smile. He would give up anything to be here with her, his gorgeous wife.

She'd come into his life when he wasn't even thinking about love, had walked into the bar at the perfect moment. He'd been home on leave, had looked up from the bottle of beer he was having with Evan to see her coming in with a few friends. From the second he'd seen her bronzed skin, her perfect, chocolate locks, he been mesmerized by her.

Now, the woman who had stolen his gaze at the bar was his wife. Mrs. Gauge.

He ambled behind her now, wrapping his hands around her hips as she scrubbed a dish. He reached up to softly brush her hair to the side, his lips finding her neck. He waited for her customary murmur, the parting of her lips, the stretching of her neck to give him better access.

Instead, she'd shrugged him away. "I have to finish these before Logan wakes up," she said. He reached for the dish in her hand, ignoring the suds that were everywhere. He placed the dish in the water, reached for the nearby dishtowel, and dried his hands. He spun her around in his arms. Pressing against her, he leaned in to resume kissing her neck.

"He's sleeping. He's out like a light. I just checked. Forget about the dishes. I've missed you."

She stiffened, and his gut lurched. She'd been distant with him since he returned a week ago. He thought it'd just been the nerves of him returning, the stress of them adjusting to real married life. Maybe it was just awkward for her now that he was home. Maybe it was the stress of an almost toddler, the exhaustion of parenting alone. He couldn't blame her for feeling cold.

She sighed audibly and pushed him away. "Jackson, I didn't want to do this. Not now. But I'm going to be honest with you."

His stomach plummeted as he looked into the hazel eyes of his wife. Where once he'd seen love reverberating for him, he saw blankness, coldness. Something was wrong, and it wasn't just a lack of sleep.

"Okay," he said, not wanting to recognize the crumbling of the world around him. Not wanting to believe when he'd finally returned home, when he'd given it all up for her, it was going to amount to disaster.

"I've met someone else."

The words floated in the air between them, silence underscoring their power.

"What do you mean you've met someone else?"

"I've fallen in love with someone else. His name is Seth."

He waited for the laughter, waited for the telltale fine lines around her eyes to show as her smile widened. He waited for the "just kidding" line to come from her mouth, waited for her to pull on his hand and yank him upstairs for the hot sex he'd been craving.

Instead, she just stared, assessing his reaction.

"Jackson, I'm sorry. I didn't plan on this happening. I didn't."

"What are you talking about? You said a few months ago you couldn't wait for me to come home."

"I know. And I meant it at the time. But you were gone. You weren't here. It was lonely. And Seth came along. I met him at Logan's daycare. He has a little boy, too. We went for coffee one day, just as friends, and it all just happened so fast. I didn't plan to fall for him. It just happened."

"Jesus Christ, Chloe. We're married. We have a life together. A son. He isn't even two yet. And you're sleeping with someone else?"

"Don't be crude."

Anger boiled in his blood now. "I'm being crude? You're fucking cheating on me. I gave it all up, Chloe. I gave up my career for you. To be with you. I know it was hard with me away. So I quit, gave it up, abandoned my duty to be with you and Logan. I love you." He looked into her eyes, rage burning within him. Where once he saw eyes that only seemed to see him, he now saw regret. He saw distance. He saw screaming emptiness.

She didn't love him anymore. How could this happen? How could she fall out of love with him when things were finally back on track, when he was finally home? How could the spunky woman who had danced with him at the bar, whose kiss had made him come to life, not want to be with him? How could she change her mind so quickly?

Tears formed in her eyes. "I'm sorry. I just can't do this. I don't even know you."

"Yes, you do. You know me. You love me." He desperately clung to the façade, to the vision he had of her from the bar, the vision of her in the short white dress a few years ago. The vision of her in the photographs, of Logan in her stomach. The visions he had of them growing old together, raising Logan together, and sitting on their front porch with grandchildren at their feet.

Now, it was going up in a puff of smoke, blowing up like an artillery shell had just careened into them.

"I'm sorry. I really am. We'll work out a custody agreement. For now, Logan and I are going to move in with Seth."

"You're not taking my son."

"Jackson, I've already made my decision. Please don't make this harder."

"You can't leave. You can't." By now, he was pleading. He didn't care. He couldn't let his life fall apart like this.

"It's over. I won't fight you for the house. It's yours."

Tears now openly flowed from his eyes. He'd seen friends die, seen terrible sights of human suffering during his time abroad. He'd endured blazing heat, terrifying moments, hell on earth. Nothing, though, hurt as much as this. Nothing hurt as much as losing the woman he thought he would share forever with. More than that, nothing hurt as much as losing their son.

"Please don't take him."

"I'm going to get a bag. We'll get the rest of my stuff tomorrow."

With the confession made, she was gone, gone to pack up

for a new life with a man named Seth. Gone to take away his son, his whole life, his everything.

He was left behind in a house he no longer wanted, with half-washed dishes in the sink and an empty bed symbolizing a dream that had been destroyed. He was left to pick up the pieces of a life he could no longer have.

That night, it began.

The end of the beginning, the beginning of the end. The destruction of his life, of the Jackson he once was. The destruction of his belief in love, in happiness, in everything in between.

That was the night he'd started drinking.

He didn't stop until the gavel fell in the courtroom taking his son away, taking away every last remnant of hope. Even then, the booze kept soothing his veins, numbing him to the barbed-wire feeling in his heart.

———————

"Jackson? You hear me?" Evan burst into his thoughts, snapping him out of his memories.

"Yeah, sorry. Just tired."

"Hey, I'm sorry about the whole marriage thing. I shouldn't have said anything. Not with the whole Chloe situation."

"Man, I'm fine."

"It wasn't that long ago, and I don't think you're fine."

"I am. Listen, what do you say we get out of here? Go out? I haven't been to Chad's for a while."

"Are you sure that's a good idea?" Evan asked warily.

Jackson eyed him. "I'm fine. Really. We'll just have a beer or two."

Evan sighed. "I don't think it's a good idea."

"I've learned my lesson. Really. I know I've got to prove myself to Chloe if I want a chance to have Logan in my life."

"I don't think you should have to prove anything to that bitch, honestly. But you're right. You need to walk the line so you can appeal the custody ruling."

"A few beers aren't going to make much of a difference. It's fine."

"All right, but we're only having a few."

"Deal. Let's go."

They headed out the door and started walking down the street to Jackson's old haunt, and to the place that had haunted Jackson's life path as of late. Evan was probably right—it wasn't a good idea. But Jackson was never one to let past decisions or disasters scare him away. He liked to stare disaster in the face. So they trudged on until they saw the blinking sign for their destination. They headed inside the crowded bar, full of Friday night partiers and Friday night "I want to forget everything" drinkers.

I definitely need to forget, Jackson thought. *I need to forget everything.*

At the moment, it seemed highly unlikely that it would be possible.

Chapter Four

SOPHIA

"I don't think this is a good idea," Sophia urged as Stella pulled her out the door of Pink Lemonade after closing up shop.

"Oh, stop. It's just a few drinks. Come on. It's Friday."

Stella's studded high heels clicked on the pavement, making Sophia feel severely underdressed in her Converse sneakers. It didn't matter, though. Stella was still young and untainted, a believer in love. She could afford to dress the part of a woman looking for Mr. Right. Sophia had been there, done that, and lost the love of her life. Her heart was closed. Her wardrobe certainly reflected it.

She followed Stella down the block toward the sketchy bar Stella had raved about.

"I can't believe we haven't gone here before. It's so close to the shop," Stella announced as they pounded their feet on the pavement.

"From the name of it, I can. Desperate times, I suppose."

"Oh stop being a snob. It's going to be great. Cheap beer, quaint setting."

"So you're saying it's a dump."

Stella playfully hit her. "Don't be a downer. Come on. When's the last time you went out for a drink?"

Sophia didn't answer.

"Exactly."

"Stell, I'm just not in the mood. What's the point? I'm not ready to pick up some bar rat."

"Easy, cowgirl. First, no offense, but I don't think there's a fear of that in your apparel." Stella grinned, eying up Sophia's sneakers, jeans, and black T-shirt. "Don't get me wrong, you're gorgeous no matter what you're wearing. But your outfit doesn't exactly say come hither."

"I don't want it to."

"Okay, then. See, we're good. I'm not saying you have to jump into bed with someone. I'm not saying you're going to find the new love of your life. I'm saying let's go have a drink, celebrate your week back on the job. Just two friends kicking back a bit."

"You're right. I don't really want to go home yet anyway."

"That's the spirit. Look, Soph, I know these past few months have been unimaginable. I know it's going to take a long time for you to feel even semi-okay again. I'm here for you, though. It's going to be hard, sad, and awful. But

I'm going to make you smile. I'm not letting you slip away. Got it?"

Sophia smiled begrudgingly. "Got it."

The two women approached the slipshod building that was their destination. A florescent sign flashed in the window. The *O* in "Open" was burned out, so the sign just said "pen."

Sophia's hopes dissipated. So much for taking steps toward moving on. Chad's Chugs, though, quintessentially summarized the current state of her whole life—falling apart.

"Keep an open mind," Stella encouraged as she opened the screechy screen door to enter.

"I'm trying."

A stagnant, musty odor infused with alcohol wafted into Sophia's face, and she involuntarily coughed. "Just one beer, and then I'm out."

"Deal."

"Two Miller Lights," Stella ordered at the bar once they climbed onto the wobbling stools. A KISS song blared in the background, threatening to give Sophia a blasting headache. This wasn't quite the scene she had in mind. Of course, lately, her only scene was her living room.

As the bartender complied, Stella turned to Sophia. "Isn't it good to be out?"

"I guess."

"Oh stop. It's not so bad."

"How'd you find this place?"

"Larry brought me here last Friday."

"Who's Larry?"

Stella looked sheepish. "A guy I met a few weeks ago." Despite her attempts to hold back, Sophia could see she was busting to tell her more.

"Go on."

"He's great, Soph. Really great." Stella turned to her beer as the bartender set it in front of her. She pretended to be busying herself with the bottle.

"That's it? That's all you're going to say?"

Stella looked at her, unsure. Sophia sighed.

"Stella, you can talk to me about this. I'm not going to melt."

"I know. I just... I feel terrible talking about my love life. With everything. I didn't want to make you feel sad."

"Which is stupid. Because I already feel sad. You can't make it any worse. Trust me. Tell me about this guy."

"We met at Panera Bread a few weeks ago. I accidentally forgot my wallet in my car. He paid for my coffee and bagel, and we chatted. He's really great, Soph. He's an engineer. We went out twice already, and we have plans for tomorrow."

Sophia smiled, recognizing the telltale radiance in her friend's face. "You like him a lot, huh? I can see it on your face."

"He's perfect. Really. A great job, handsome, really sweet. I just feel so comfortable talking with him."

"I'm so happy for you. I am. I can't wait to meet him."

Sophia swigged her beer, turning slightly from the conversation.

Don't think about it. Be happy. Stella deserves this, she told herself as she fought back a stinging in her eyes. She didn't want to feel jealous, didn't want to feel angry that while Stella was out finding love and starting a new relationship, hers was gone. She wanted to feel happy, be selflessly happy for her friend's good fortune. It was unquestionably hard.

She turned toward the other side of the bar, pretending to be interested in watching a game of pool, so she could prevent Stella from detecting her true feelings. Stella had known her for years. Sophia's "I'm fine" lie would never work.

As she glanced around, she saw two men, both joking and laughing, sitting at a small table across the room. Through the hazy atmosphere and the low lights, her gaze fell on a familiar face. She was surprised when recognition clicked in.

Jackson.

Her mind instantly flashed back to the rainy day, standing by the grave, his sunglasses covering his eyes.

She tried to push the sickening memory back, tried to cover it, but she had few other memories of the muscular man to replace it with. There'd been pictures of this man as a boy, standing beside Tim at the creek or at family gatherings. There'd been stories she'd heard second-hand from Tim, memories he'd shared. She and Tim had seen him at the gas station a few months after they'd started dating. She'd been introduced briefly, hearing promises the two men would find time to get together.

Life, as always, got in the way.

Other than that, the man was practically a stranger to her. The only personal encounter she'd had with him was seven months ago, four months before her life went to shit. It had been a time she thought nothing bad could happen to her. The seemingly inconsequential moment now meant everything because it was a moment when Tim was still hers.

———————

Sophia trudged through the mall, shopping bags loading her arms. It was a Thursday night, and she was off from the shop. Tim was staying late for a meeting at work, so she'd decided to do a little retail therapy. Her summer wardrobe was lackluster, and she had some coupons to use.

A few hours into her shopping splurge, her stomach had been rumbling. She'd made the decision to head to the food court for a mall pretzel and a soda.

That's when she heard her name.

"Sophia?" the voice questioned behind her, and she spun.

In front of her stood a man dressed in baggy jeans and a gray T-shirt. Stubble grazed his chin, and he looked worn. Sophia took inventory of his body, her gaze traveling from his perfect jawline to his bulky arms. If she weren't married, she'd think he was...

"Sophia, is that you?" the man asked, and she paused, recognition taking a moment to click in. This man looked very different from the chubby-faced boy she'd known in the photographs. He was different even from the man she'd met over a decade ago at the gas station.

But the eyes, the steel-gray eyes gave him away.

"Jackson, right?" She didn't quite trust herself, didn't trust her memory, her eyes.

"Yeah, how are you? How's Tim?" He seemed genuinely happy to see her, and she reciprocated his smile.

She dropped her bags to rest her arms. "He's great. He's working late tonight. He was accepted into the law firm he had his eye on during college. Everything's good. How about you?"

It seemed like the right thing to ask, a natural follow-up. After she said it, though, she instantly regretted it. His face fell at the words. She didn't know what to do next.

"Oh, not as great, I'm afraid. Things are kind of shitty. I'm home now, though, for good. I'm done with the army."

"Oh, wait, so you're back in town? Here? I thought Tim said you were living up in Hastings?"

"I was. Things kind of fell apart with the wife. I decided to come back here, get a fresh start. I'm looking for work right now."

"I'm sorry." She could see the searing pain in his eyes. Her heart ached for him. "Well, listen, I know Tim will be thrilled to hear you're back. Let me give you his number."

Jackson beamed at the mention of Tim. "That'd be awesome. It's been so long. I'd love to see him. Let me put his number in my phone."

She told him the number and then asked for his. "I'll have him call you, huh?"

"That would be great. Sophia, it was really good seeing you. I hope to see you again soon."

"I'm sure of it. Tim has told me so much about you."

"See you around," he said before turning to leave.

She'd smiled on her way to the pretzel stand after reclaiming her bags from the ground. She couldn't wait to tell Tim about her encounter. Jackson looked so downtrodden. Maybe Tim could help turn things around.

Later that night, she'd told Tim about the run-in. He'd been happy to hear about Jackson too.

"That's awesome. I'll have to give him a call soon. Man, he was like a brother to me growing up."

She smiled, thinking how funny life was sometimes. A random trip to the mall had led to what was bound to be a reconnection. Life was beautiful sometimes.

But Jackson and Tim never got together. There was no reconnection. Jackson's number sat on Tim's phone, unused and undialed. There was no good reason, really. Life stood in the way. Long hours at the law firm, busy schedules. They had all thought there was plenty of time for reconnections, for visits, for meetings.

They had all been horribly, violently wrong.

Dressed in jeans and a black T-shirt, Jackson sat with a beer in the chaotic atmosphere of the bar, talking animatedly with his friend.

Stella followed Sophia's gaze. "Hey, there's Jackson." Sophia snapped back to the present, leaving the memories behind.

"Yeah. I haven't seen him since…"

"Do you want to go say hello?"

"I don't want to make things weird."

"I think it would be weird if you didn't say hello. He was Tim's best friend at one point."

"I barely know him."

"Stop being antisocial. Go say hello. Plus, his friend is pretty handsome." Stella winked.

"You're attached, remember?"

"Not yet." Stella grinned, nudging Sophia with her elbow.

Sophia plunged off her barstool, almost tipping it over. She'd only had a few sips to drink, but it looked like she had more. She walked casually over to the other side of the bar.

"Hey." It was all she could think to say.

Jackson turned in his chair, his knee bumping into her. She became acutely aware of how closely she was standing to him. This was awkward.

Stella was right behind her, smiling. "How are you, Jackson?"

"I'm great. This is Evan, my friend from the army. Evan, this is Sophia and her friend, Stella."

After pleasantries were exchanged, another pause

ensued. "Hey, Soph, I'm heading to the restroom. I'll be right back." Stella made her exit, apparently deciding Evan was nothing compared to Larry.

"How are you?" Jackson asked. "Sorry. Stupid question."

"I'm okay. Hanging in there. You? I didn't know if you were still in town."

He nodded. "Yeah, I've settled in since I saw you at the mall. Got myself an apartment and a job. It's not much, but it's a start I guess."

"I hate that Tim didn't call you before..." She didn't know why her thoughts were going there, didn't know why she'd insisted on bringing the mood down. It had just been on her chest, been on her lips.

Jackson looked at her with sorrow, with understanding. "I know. It's my fault too. I should've called. Things just were so messed up for me. I was embroiled in a custody battle and wasn't really in the mood for much."

"I didn't realize. I'm sorry."

"I don't have to tell you life's not fair. In reality, I can't feel too sorry for myself. I messed up big-time. It's my fault."

She found herself feeling his sorrow deep in her core, feeling the hurt on his face. She instinctively touched his shoulder. "Hang in there."

"You do the same." He offered her a grim smile before turning back to his beer.

So much for getting out and getting away, she thought as she headed back to her seat to wait for Stella.

But since Tim had died, she realized you never got

away from sorrow, from heartbreak. It was always there. It probably always would be.

Chapter Five

"Kara, honey, I love this picture, I do. The thing is, I can try to get your hair to do this, but with the wave in it and the thickness, it might not *quite* look like Reese Witherspoon's, just so you know."

"Let's just go for it," the teenager said, rolling her eyes. Sophia took a breath to try to calm herself. This was bound to be a disaster.

Stella gave her the knowing look, shrugged, and turned back to Mr. Peabody, the ninety-year-old in her chair. He was a bit of an easier client since he couldn't even hear what Stella was asking. He just nodded in agreement. Sophia wondered if he would even be able to see his final reveal.

Forty-five minutes later, the teenager, to Sophia's surprise, was gasping at how wonderful her hair looked and how it was just like the picture. Sophia smiled, glad to see a happy client but doubtful if she actually would be mistaken for Reese anytime soon. She'd done her best with the next-to-impossible task. Clients often expected her to be a miracle worker with a magic hair wand. If only it were true.

It felt good in some ways to be back to her routine, but in other ways, something was missing. Sophia was passionate about her work, loved doing hair since she was a little girl. She'd been the five-year-old caught chopping off the locks of all her Barbies because she needed to give them a "better" haircut. She'd been the high school girl obsessed with doing her hair in a different style every day of the week. She did her prom hair, did her friends' hair for prom, and changed her hair color at least once a month. There'd never even been a question about what she'd do with her life. This was what she always wanted.

These days, though, she often found herself internally mocking some of the clients who were obsessed with their hair color and the shade nuances. She found herself getting frustrated when her client complained about split ends or an awkward layer. She believed in beauty, knew a haircut could change everything. But after the past few months, something in her had changed, and not in a good way. Suddenly, she found herself thinking about how superficial it all was. Who cared if your hair was golden brown or chocolate brown? What did it matter if you had a few frizzy ends? In the scheme of things, did it even count for anything at all? Everything could change at the turn of a hat, in the blink of an eye, or any other stupid cliché that meant your husband could die and leave you all alone without warning.

She knew she had to quell these thoughts, or they would burn and rage inside her until they destroyed her. She couldn't begrudge people their normal lives, their happiness. A few months ago, she was one of them, obsessing over every eyelash and curl on her head. The most tragic thing that happened to her was a bad hair day.

Tim's death had put so much in perspective, but that perspective wasn't always a positive thing. She craved a day when she could again worry about the trivial aspects of everyday living. She just didn't know if the day would ever come.

After the teenager paid for her services, Sophia quietly tidied up the salon. Stella finished Mr. Peabody's haircut and style, and then, after shouting the total of the bill nine times, the shop was empty.

"Hey, Sarah's hair looked good, despite the obvious difficulties. Good work," Stella complemented her.

"Thanks. I tried."

Stella sang to herself as she jauntily carried some towels to the back room. She practically skipped around the shop.

"So tonight's the night, huh? You and Larry are going out on the town. Do you want me to do your hair?" Sophia offered. It had been their tradition. On date night, they treated each other to a signature style.

"Um, no, I think I'm just going to run the flat iron through it. I don't have much time. Does it look okay?"

"Looks awesome, as always." Sophia meant it. Stella always looked amazing. She wished she had the guts to pull off pink hair like Stella did. She managed to make it look simultaneously badass and elegant. That was Stella for you—a perfect contradiction. Sweet and sassy. Rational and bold. Tactful and tactless all at the same time.

"Thanks, love. So Larry is picking me up here in fifteen minutes. I wanted you to get to meet him."

"Oh, great! Fifteen minutes, though? You better get moving. What are you wearing?"

"I have a change of clothes in the back room. I'm going to go get ready. Be right back."

Stella scurried off to change into something that would probably look magazine-page worthy. Sophia smiled, excited for her best friend. She glanced in the mirror, something she tried not to do these days. Her own blonde locks looked haggard, frizzy, lifeless. Her face was devoid of makeup as it had been all week. She looked like she felt—bland.

Sophia headed to the schedule area to flip through and verify some appointments. She emptied the jug of its last cup of pink lemonade, sat in Stella's styling chair, and spun aimlessly around, waiting for the reveal of both Stella and the mystery man named Larry.

A few moments later, Stella reappeared, wearing a simple black dress. Some crystal jewelry classed it up, but the lace-up knee-high leather boots added a touch of Stella to the classy outfit. Her pink hair popped against her porcelain skin, and the look was completed with dramatic winged eyeliner. She looked gorgeous.

"You always look killer, you know that? You'd think you worked in the beauty industry or something." Sophia smiled, standing to approach her.

"You think it's not too trashy looking? Too teenage-like? Larry's sort of a more laid-back kind of guy. I don't want to scare him away."

"If the pink hair didn't scare him, I think you're golden."

Stella showed her perfect teeth. "I don't want to mess this up. I like him."

As if on cue, the bells on the door tinkled, and a tall, handsome guy strolled in. So much for time to straighten Stella's hair. He carried a bouquet of daisies in his arms. He wore a red-collared shirt, some trendy jeans, and simple shoes. His chocolate brown hair matched his perfect beard. He looked clean, put together, reliable, and sexy in a not-trying-too-hard way. He was a wonderful compliment to the edgy, wild Stella.

"Larry, I want you to meet my best friend and business partner, Sophia. Sophia, this is Larry."

Sophia amicably extended a hand. "I've heard great things about you," she offered, and Larry looked her in the eyes.

"Same here. It wasn't five minutes into our conversation that Stella started talking about you. In a good way, of course."

"So where are you two headed?" Sophia asked as Stella took the daisies and arranged them in a vase on the front counter.

"We're heading to Mama's Diner for some Italian first and then to a late movie."

Sophia brushed off the feeling of her cringing heart. She could feel Stella appraising her reaction from across the room. "Sounds lovely. Have a wonderful time." She sounded stiff, no matter how much she tried not to.

Stella approached her after the daisies were carefully resting in the vase.

"Soph?" She put an arm around her friend's shoulders, not saying anything else, not needing to.

"I'm great. You two have a wonderful time." Sophia managed to scrounge up a genuine smile, genuine enough to convince her friend she meant it.

"Okay, honey. I'll see you tomorrow."

Stella put her hand on Larry's arm, gave Sophia one more hesitant glance, then headed off into the night.

Once they were out of sight, Sophia let go of the fake smile on her face. She slumped to the floor, her back against the front desk. Tears formed in her eyes. She tried to fight them off.

Larry couldn't have known. It was bound to happen. She couldn't avoid Mama's forever, even if she wanted to.

Such was the hazard of living in the town where you had met your late husband.

Sophia tugged gently on her miniskirt, trying to magically extend the hem. Stella had promised her she looked amazing, but she felt uncomfortable. Scandalous wasn't an adjective she'd ever use to describe her style—except for tonight. She was afraid to move too quickly for fear she would reveal too much. This skirt was a terrible idea.

Stella had looped her arm through Sophia's as they strolled toward the restaurant. It was a muggy July night, and she could feel sweat beading on her forehead.

"Are you sure this is where you want to celebrate?" Stella asked as they approached the tiny building, the light-up sign teetering on the pole out front.

"The contractor said it's awesome, and I'm so hungry for some lasagna."

"Are you twenty-two or one-hundred and twenty-two?" Stella teased. "If I'd have realized this was what you had in mind when you said going out to celebrate, I wouldn't have loaned you my miniskirt."

"Sorry, Ms. Club Animal, but I thought we should do something a little bit more mature to celebrate since we're soon-to-be entrepreneurs and all."

"Ew. I hate that word. It sounds too stuffy. I prefer Business Diva."

"Whatever. Let's go have dinner. We can always go out somewhere more exciting later."

It had been a long, wonderful day. Sophia's dreams were coming true. Her beauty shop was under contract, and in a few short months, she would be co-owner of the hip, trendy shop in Hollidaysburg. What was even better was her best friend would be by her side.

The two had always talked about this day when they studied chair by chair in beauty school. Through their crazy perm disasters to perfecting ombre, they had promised each other they would work hard, save money, and open their own shop. They had dreams of working for themselves, of building a business, of someday catering to the celebrities.

The shop they'd just signed for wasn't in New York City or Los Angeles, so the probability of Angelina Jolie being on their clientele list was slim. They'd settled on Hollidaysburg, Pennsylvania, where Stella had grown up. Stella had convinced Sophia it was a nice starting point, offering a cheap lease and a low cost of living, something appealing for the two just into their early twenties. They still had loans to pay from beauty school, and a huge business loan was frightening. Plus, it afforded Sophia the luxury of only being about two hours from her parents and her own hometown. There would be time to expand to the big city. For now, she would celebrate the fact they had accomplished their dream—or would soon.

Entering the restaurant, they were serenaded by authentic Italian sounds and smells. Music played softly in the background, and Sophia looked around. Yep. As usual, they were underdressed—figuratively and literally—for the atmosphere. It was somewhat of a classy place. She probably should have thought about that before they came. However, the low-key sign and the dated exterior hadn't really given them any clues, in all fairness.

She held her head high, trying to ignore the stares from the slightly older crowd waiting to be seated at Mama's Diner. She told the hostess two and then slinked to a back corner with Stella.

"Fancy, schmancy," Stella teased. "You do know we aren't raking in any cash yet, right?"

"Hey, we deserve it. It's been a long road to this point, and there's a lot of work ahead of us."

"True. But it's so exciting. Now we just need to come up with a name."

A few minutes later, the hostess led the two to a table complete with more silverware than either were used to.

"Lord, this place is fancy," Sophia said. "Sorry, the contractor didn't specify."

"Welcome to Mama's," a deep voice urged as a tall, smooth-faced waiter approached. Sophia glanced up from her menu to see the warm, brown eyes and spikey hair. Her stomach involuntarily fluttered as she made eye contact with him, finding herself staring a little too long.

He beamed at her, seeming to not even notice Stella. She could feel his gaze carefully, almost imperceptibly moving down her body, inventorying her. She felt herself blush.

"What can I bring you ladies to drink?" he asked, his smooth voice wrapping itself around her. The music faded as she focused solely on him, his arms bulging as he pulled a notepad out of his apron.

Stella kicked her under the table, and Sophia startled. She muttered, "Oh, pink lemonade please."

The waiter grinned softly. "Sorry, we don't have pink

lemonade. I think we just have regular."

Her face burned even hotter.

"We'll just have some water, please." Stella jumped in, saving Sophia as she had so many times.

"Right away." The waiter walked away from the table slowly, barely moving his eyes.

"Pink lemonade? Really?" Stella teased once the waiter was out of earshot.

"It's our favorite."

"Yeah, but not at a fancy restaurant."

Sophia grimaced.

"Your face is so red. Get it together."

"It's hot in here."

"Pretty sure you're just obsessed with Tim."

"What?"

"The waiter, idiot. It's Tim. He went to my high school. He was a few years ahead of me. Ask him out."

"Stella, stop. He's our waiter. He's probably married or something."

"Nope. No ring."

"Will you stop scoping him out? I don't think he's interested in his customers. He's just doing his job for God's sake."

"Trust me, he's interested. He couldn't stop staring at you. You're welcome. If I'd let you wear that god-awful turtle neck, you'd have only been catching gramps's eye." She motioned toward the table beside them where an eighty-year-old man carefully chewed on his spaghetti, slurping the noodles every few moments.

"Shh, he's coming back."

Stella smiled, giving Sophia a mischievous look.

When the waiter set down their waters, Stella turned to him. "So, Tim, you went to school here, didn't you? I graduated a few years after you I think."

"Hollidaysburg High?"

"Yep."

"Yeah. Sorry, I didn't recognize you."

"That's okay. What are you up to these days?"

"Law school. I'm just working here to make some cash for tuition. How about you?"

Left out of the conversation, Sophia fiddled with her place setting.

"My best friend, Sophia, and I are back in town for good. We're in the process of starting a hair salon."

"That's awesome." Tim glanced from Stella to Sophia. "Where's it at?"

"Allegheny Street."

"Cool. What's it called?"

Stella eyed Sophia from across the table. They hadn't gotten that far yet. She smiled.

"Pink Lemonade," Stella said with an air of confidence. Sophia raised an eyebrow.

"It's a unique name."

"Yeah. Well, we wanted it to be memorable. Plus, as Sophia demonstrated, we have a thing for pink lemonade."

"I don't think you have to worry about being memorable," Tim said, turning slightly toward Sophia, his gaze wandering. Sophia averted her eyes to the table.

The dinner continued, Tim checking back on the table over and over. Sophia stayed silent, not knowing how to handle the situation. Flirting was never her strong suit.

When they left after dinner was over, Sophia figured she'd never see the waiter again. Walking back to their apartment, Sophia said, "So, is that really what we're calling the place?"

Stella nodded. "Yeah. I think it fits. You?"

"It's different. But we do love pink lemonade. Oh, we could paint the place pink and serve lemonade."

"Love it. Plus, it goes with my hair."

"Now we just need to start building a client list." Sophia had refocused on the business, trying to push the thought of the encounter at the restaurant out of her mind.

"We've already started."

"I mean other than family."

"Done."

"Oh yeah? Who?"

"Your soon-to-be boyfriend."

"What are you talking about?"

"Tim."

"Okay, first, he was our waiter. It's not as if he was trying to jump my bones over the lasagna. Second, he was more interested in you."

"Not true. His eyes were all over you. The chemistry was blatant. Plus, ew, he's not my type, and I'm not his. Too boring for me. Lawyer? Not going to work."

"Okay, wild child. It's not like he has my number or anything. I probably won't see him again."

"Yeah, you will."

"How do you know?"

"I wrote your number on the check. He'll probably call after his shift."

Sophia pretended to be mad, but she couldn't. There was something about the handsome man, something about his mannerisms, the way he looked at her. From the moment she saw him, there was a palpable chemistry, a connection. She'd never believed in love at first sight. Sure, she'd had a few boyfriends in high school, but they had been slow burns, friendships turned smoldering. This had been an intense wave of heat on sight, a ridiculous conflagration too strange to believe in.

A few hours later, Tim called her, and they sealed a first date. Over the next few years, Pink Lemonade would get off the ground, and everything would fall into place. There were the months of dating, the building of the business, and the graduation from law school for Tim. There was the proposal—at Mama's, of course—the purchase of the house, the wedding. There was the moving out, the moving on, the love flowing freely.

It had all started in a skimpy, scandalous miniskirt over some celebratory lasagna.

They just had no way to know it would end all too soon, the fire still burning, the ashes swept away to an unreachable area.

————

Sophia picked herself up from the floor, reaching for a tissue to sop up the tears saturating her cheeks. A headache surged, and her nose was stuffy. She felt hungover from her grief. She hated how these beautiful memories were now tainted by the knowledge of the ending. It was like trying to reread your favorite book. The moments weren't as magical, as special the second time around because you already knew how it all ended, how it all worked out. In her case, it ended with the destruction of a love that had marked her adult years.

Before Tim had come into her life at that restaurant a decade ago, she had herself situated. She knew how to maneuver life by herself, knew how to fall asleep alone. She even enjoyed it. Now, though, she'd been lulled into a comfortable routine in his arms, had fallen in love with the idea of having someone to walk through life with. She'd grown accustomed to falling asleep beside him, coming home to him, making decisions with him. He had been the one who sang to her in the car on long rides, who remembered they were out of trash bags when they were at the grocery store. He had been the one who reminded her about her oil needing to be changed. He had been the one who remembered to clean the furnace filter regularly.

It was so much more than the practicality of Tim that she missed. She missed the way his cologne wafted down the steps after his shower, the way he looked at her even when she was just wearing sweatpants and a T-shirt. She missed the way "I love you" rolled off his tongue, the way he would sneak up behind her and wrap his arms around her. She missed how he was drawn to every dog in the park, crouching down to pet it roughly as he turned to beg her for one of their own. She missed their inside jokes, their playfulness. She missed how he would sing Nelly's "Grills" into the spatula every time he fired up the grill like a total cornball. She missed how he could make her laugh her head off when she felt like crying. She missed the feel of his hands stroking her hair, rubbing her shoulders, easing her into a state of calmness.

She craved the feel of his hand brushing hers in bed when they were making love, or the easy laughter they shared afterward. She missed him, all of him, every single part of their life together. She would do anything to go back to being the twenty-two-year-old just meeting the man who would change everything. She would do anything to have those moments back, to not know how fleeting everything was. She wanted to go back to being the naïve girl who thought they had a lifetime of memories ahead of them.

But she couldn't. Now it was Stella's turn to start fresh, to experience new love at Mama's Diner with this handsome man named Larry. It was her turn to share first kisses, first fights, and first I love yous. It was her turn.

Because Sophia's turn was over.

Everyone told her she was young enough to move on eventually. How could she? Why would she want to? She'd had a once in a lifetime love, a love at first sight over lasagna kind of love, a knock her mismatched socks off kind of passion she couldn't find anywhere else.

Grabbing her jacket from the closet in the back room, she headed out of the shop, locking the door and shutting off the light on her way. She headed to the only place she felt safe these days, the only place where someone understood her. It was a short walk, but it was a painful one. She trudged on, alone, all alone, the new status of her life.

Ten minutes later, she stood, feet aching, staring at the only thing left of Tim in this world. She ran her hands over the smooth stone, her fingers tracing the letters as they always did.

She crumpled to her knees, her head on the stone. She wanted to bash her head against it, to keep bashing it until she was gone. She wanted to lie here on this ground until she too was dead.

She wanted to be with him, to feel his arms around her, to hear him tell the story of when they first met as he had so many times. She wanted to hear him talk animatedly about the new *Call of Duty* game coming out or the new Mexican restaurant in town or the new deposition he had to work on. She wanted to hear him chatter on mindlessly about the weather or about dinner or about his new pair of shoes. She just wanted to hear his voice, hear it saying anything at all.

Instead, only silence greeted her. A long, drowning silence swept around her, the streetlight nearby casting an eerie beam of light on the area. Water seeped into her jeans from the damp grass. It didn't matter. All that mattered was that he was dead, and with him, a part of her was dead too. In truth, it was more than just a part of her that died with him—she felt like her whole being had died. She was simply an empty shell mindlessly clattering through a semblance of the life she once had.

As she thought about how unfair life was, a soft sound of footsteps caught her attention. She turned from the stone to see who was nearby.

"Sophia," the familiar voice said, and she rose to greet him, happy to see she wasn't alone, at least for the moment.

Chapter Six

JACKSON

He wrapped his arms around her as she quite literally fell into him, tripping as she scrambled to reach him. Both her presence at the grave and her reaction to seeing him there surprised him. He hadn't expected to see anyone here, had expected just to wallow in the sight of his old friend's grave in solitude. He'd had an instant, inexplicable urge to come here. He hadn't been here since the day of the burial, had been avoiding it in some capacity. He felt like coming here was just acknowledging what he didn't want to recognize—Tim was gone, and he hadn't said goodbye. No one had.

He'd since realized what a blessing it was he was here. Sophia was clearly a train wreck. Who could blame her? She'd been trying so hard to hold it together. It was apparent at the funeral and even more obvious at the bar. Now, he saw the true state of her, the state that was to be expected.

She buried her face against his pecs, and he instinctively stroked her hair, comfort radiating through his fingers. They stood, two people grieving, holding onto each other. There was nothing sensuous about it, nothing inappropriate. They were two people, one from Tim's past and one from his present, finding solace in their mutual loss. Holding her, he realized now he too had been holding back, had been pretending Tim's death wasn't affecting him.

But it was.

It was another loss in the string of a life falling apart. It was also guilt. He hadn't made time, had been so absorbed in himself he hadn't made room for the friend who'd been his rock as a child. Tim had been there so many times for Jackson. He'd helped him through everything from failed classes to the death of Wade to breakups. He'd been there to encourage him through boot camp, to send letters and care packages when he was off in Iraq. Tim had never forgotten him, not really.

Jackson couldn't say the same thing.

Time had thrown a wedge between them. Time had been hard on Jackson and had tossed him off his path. He'd become absorbed in his own life. Now it was too late to tell Tim what he had meant to him.

"I'm sorry," Sophia finally said, pulling back. "I'm so sorry. It just all crept up on me, and then you were here, and I know you understand. I'm sorry."

"Don't apologize," he whispered, his voice breathy and crackling. "You don't have to apologize. You don't have to pretend. I know how much he meant to you. He meant a lot to me too. It's so hard. It sucks."

She looked at him, and even with the darkness, he could see recognition. They understood each other. They didn't have to pretend this was easy.

They stood for a moment side by side, staring at the grave.

"I miss him," she said.

"I know. Me too. I feel awful I didn't get to see him."

"I guess it's normal when someone dies. Having regrets. I have so many too. I think of all the times in those last weeks I ignored him or blew by him because I was running late. I think of all the pointless fights we had. I hate how I wasted so much time. But I didn't know. We couldn't have known."

Jackson sighed, debating whether to say what he was thinking. He felt like he could, though. He felt like he could be honest with Sophia, which was absurd because he didn't know her, not really.

"Everyone thinks time is what you need to deal with death. If only I'd had more time. If only I'd known. But Sophia, honestly, I don't think it really helps. When my brother, Wade, died, I'd known it was coming for a year. We'd been through all of the prognoses, heard the news, had time to prepare. It didn't help. Because when his time came, it was still the worst day of my life. I still couldn't say goodbye. My family still fell apart. I don't think death is ever easy."

Sophia looked at him. "I'm sorry. I didn't know. Tim never told me about it."

"I tried not to talk about Wade after he died. I sort of closed that part off. Tim followed suit out of respect for me."

"How old were you?"

"Thirteen."

"And Wade?"

"He was seventeen."

"What was it?"

"A rare blood cancer."

There were a few more moments of silence as each weighed what to say next.

"How'd you survive it?" she finally asked, staring at Tim's headstone.

"I almost didn't. I wanted to die too. But it was Tim. He pulled me through. Pulled our family through, really. We'd been friends before that. Wade's death just made me realize what an amazing friend Tim was even more. I just wish I could've been there for Tim at the end like he was there for me."

"That's what's so hard. No one was there for him. He died alone. In his office. *Alone.* That's the part that kills me." She choked on the last words, choked back tears. He pulled her close.

"He knew you loved him. He knew it. I could see it when I saw you two that first time together. He was crazy about you, Sophia."

"I don't know what I'm going to do. Everyone's trying to help. My parents, Stella, they all mean well. But no one gets it. How could they?"

"They can't."

She swiped at her tears for a moment, before breaking the silence. "I should probably get going, give you some time alone. I'm sorry again."

"Don't be sorry. It was good to have someone to talk to."

She started walking away.

"Sophia?" he asked. She turned around. "Can I give you a ride?"

"No, I'm fine. It's not a far walk."

"Please? My truck's right over there. It's the least I can do."

She hesitated, clearly thinking of turning him down. She shrugged. "Okay."

He nodded to Tim's grave, saying a silent goodbye. *I'll take care of her, buddy. I'll make sure she's okay,* he promised silently.

It was the least he could do. After all Tim had done for him, it was the very least he could do.

———

The next week passed with a perfunctory quality. Jackson spent his days going to work, coming home, and sleeping. It was the existence he'd acclimated to.

He'd considered calling Sophia after the night at the

grave, but he thought better of it. She had a network of family and friends. He didn't want to intrude. He was a part of Tim's past, a part of Tim's life Sophia barely knew. Besides, he couldn't really do anything for her. How could he make things better? He didn't want to start rumors around town, didn't want to be known as the widow stealer of his best friend.

On Saturday morning, Jackson felt better. It was his weekend with Logan. He jumped in his truck bright and early to get on the road by seven. He was driving the hour to meet Chloe for the pass off. He would have two days with his son, two days he hoped would rejuvenate him.

He hated that it had come to this. He hated that he was a weekend father—or more accurately, a two weekends a month and a few court-appointed holidays a year kind of father. This wasn't what he had planned.

He'd wanted to be the father his dad hadn't been. Sure, his dad had provided for him, had given him so much. He hadn't been abusive or anything like that. Still, his dad had been the cold, emotionless, authoritative father Jackson didn't ever want to be. Jackson couldn't remember his dad ever telling him he loved him, couldn't remember a single hug. His father was a no-nonsense, respect-your-elders kind of father.

Things had only worsened after Wade died. His already rigid dad had tightened up even more, afraid to show emotion, afraid to show the world the hurt that most certainly had been his over the loss of his eldest child. He shut down completely, shut them out completely, cocooning himself in an unbreakable wall of stoicism. The wall had shifted slightly, allowing some glimmer of emotion to shine through, but for the most part, his dad was still the picture of sternness Jackson remembered all too well.

When Chloe found out she was pregnant, Jackson promised himself right away he wouldn't be Louis Gauge. He would tell his son he loved him every day, would give him more hugs and kisses than he could ever want. He would smother his son in love, teach him something every day. He would be the Dr. Seuss-reading, picture-painting, cookie-baking father he'd always wanted. He would be the kind of loving father he'd secretly always wanted.

More importantly, he would respect any career choice Logan wanted to pursue. He wouldn't force him into the family business.

Now, though, things were so different. Jackson couldn't be the father he wanted to be. He wasn't showering Logan with love every day. He wasn't the one teaching him new words or how to tie his shoes or how to use manners. He was hours away, clutching only a picture of the son he loved more than anything. He was left hoping the new man in Logan's life was fair and loving, was the kind of father figure Logan could look up to.

Driving down the highway, Jackson glanced at the horizon, still shaded in pink from the sunrise.

He'd been telling himself everything would get better if he just hung on. He'd told himself not to give up. Lately, though, he'd been feeling utterly hopeless. He'd been feeling like all was gone. How could things get better? He'd lost. There was no one left in his corner, either, other than his parents and sister. He was a lost man, a lost dad, a lost everything.

The pull of the booze was strengthening again, inviting him into its cool, plentiful ability to drown out the world. He'd been fighting it off, but ever since Tim's death, the pull had strengthened.

If things didn't turn around soon, he worried he would cave to its pressures and, tragically, succumb to the fact his life was doomed.

"Daddy!" The curly haired boy charged toward Jackson as soon as his mother lifted him from his car seat.

"My man!" Jackson proclaimed, ruffling the boy's hair as the child wrapped himself around his legs.

"I brought my dinosaur." He held up a stuffed toy, the one Jackson had bought him during their last visit.

"Perfect. Are you ready to have some fun?"

"Yeah. Bye, Mommy." He blew a kiss at his mother as Jackson loaded him in the truck. Once Logan was buckled in safely, his dinosaur in his lap, Jackson shut the door to the extended cab.

"I'll see you at exactly four on Sunday. His bedtime is at eight. Please don't screw up his schedule like you did last time." Chloe's voice oozed with coldness as she flipped her brunette locks.

Jackson eyed her as he stood, hands on the top of the truck door. "I wish it didn't have to be like this," he hissed, hoping to catch just a sliver of the woman he once knew.

The warm woman was gone, replaced with a cold version of her, an ice queen who felt nothing for him.

"Me too. I wish I didn't have to give you any visitation rights. If I had my way, you'd be gone from his life. But I don't. So just be sure you don't screw up. Because if I hear you were drunk around our son, it's done."

"Chloe, I won't. I love him. You know why I turned to the bottle."

"So it's my fault?"

"Let's not do this again, okay?"

"You made your choice."

"And you made yours. Need I remind you I came home to be with you, and you had been cheating on me?"

Chloe rolled her eyes and stomped away. Jackson closed his eyes and reminded himself to breathe.

It was so hard to imagine a time they had been in love, a time their relationship had been sparkling with hopes and dreams. How could love turn so cold so quickly?

It pained him they were at this point. It wasn't because he still loved her. Sure, a piece of him would always remember, would always love the woman he'd fallen for when they first met. But the fantasy was gone now. What devastated him was the hostility and how it was affecting Logan. He didn't want that.

He wished Chloe could understand it was a mistake. He hadn't meant to become a bad role model. It'd happened without warning. He'd been at such a low place, a place he thought was impossible.

I can't go back, he thought as he climbed into the driver seat. Looking in the rearview mirror, he saw Logan talking to his stuffed dinosaur.

No matter how much Chloe took away from him, no matter how little time he had with his son, he wouldn't mess it up. He would be the kind of father Logan would idolize, would look up to, even if it was only two weekends a month.

———

"That was fun, Daddy! Dinosaurs! Rawrr," Logan shouted, squeezing Jackson's hand as they left the theater that afternoon. Logan was skipping, holding his dinosaur in his other arm.

They'd gone to see the latest animated dinosaur movie, the one Logan had been talking about. Jackson had planned this for weeks, couldn't wait to see his son's face, couldn't wait to see the amazement in his eyes.

But after they bought their popcorn and sodas and found seats, after the previews were over and the movie started, Jackson's heart was stabbed again.

"Daddy took me to see this," Logan mumbled, looking at Jackson. "I sawed it."

"No buddy, we talked about seeing it on the way here. We haven't seen it."

"Yuh-huh. Me and Mommy and Daddy sawed it yesterday."

Jackson froze.

His anger seethed. He balled his fist in his hand, clenching his jaw.

He'd told Chloe he wanted to take Logan to see the movie.

So she'd taken Logan with Seth yesterday apparently.

Then his anger pressurized. He realized Logan had called Seth Daddy. Just like he'd suspected. He'd have to fight to stay in Logan's life.

He sighed, exhaling. *Let it go. It doesn't matter. Breathe.*

"Well, buddy, did you like the movie? Do you want to see it again?"

Just then, the dinosaur ran across the screen, causing a cascade of giggles from the kids around them. Logan looked at the screen and laughed too.

He was entranced. Obviously, the answer was yes.

Jackson tried to let the hurt roll off him, tried to wash it down with soda and popcorn butter. It was hard to know Logan was slipping away, a replacement daddy waiting in the wings. It was impossible to be okay with some strange man, some man who had stolen his wife, now stealing the most important thing to him.

As the weekend rolled on and their bi-weekly goodbye inched closer, Jackson felt his life floating into thin air. The gloom of the days without Logan crept back in, and the old Jackson seemed to be coming back.

"Daddy, why you no live with me anymore?" Logan asked Saturday night when Jackson tucked him in—at nine o'clock. Screw Chloe's bedtime orders.

"Well, buddy. Things are complicated right now. I want to spend more time with you. I do. I love you." Jackson hugged his son, held him close, and prayed Logan would never doubt those words.

Tears streamed down Logan's face. Jackson stooped down to eye level with him. There was a soft drizzle falling, and the air had grown chilly.

"Logan, listen, it's okay. I'll call you tomorrow, all right? And then, before you know it, I'll be back for you again. Next time, we'll go to the diner again and see another movie. What do you say?"

"Daddy, I miss you."

"I know, Logan. I miss you too. These next few weeks will go so fast. Now give me a hug and then get in the car with your mom, okay?"

Logan woefully nodded, tears still streaming. Jackson hugged his son tightly, clasping onto him. As it always did, Jackson's weekend with Logan flew by. He felt like he was just playing at the role of father, barely having time to settle Logan in before it was time to turn around and meet Chloe again.

Chloe glared from behind, her foot tapping, her hood up to protect her from the drizzle.

"Come on, Logan. Let's get in the car." She reached for her son's arm, tugging him toward his seat.

After a long moment, Logan followed his mother.

Logan's doughy brown eyes looked at Jackson in a way that made him want to crumple on the pavement. He didn't though, standing stoically, perhaps channeling the stance his own father had shown him so many times.

"I love you," he said to his son as Chloe shut the car door after buckling in their child.

"Goodbye, Jackson."

"Chloe, wait. You see what this is doing to him. Please reconsider."

"The court has made its decision. I'm not going to talk about this every time."

He reached for her arm. "Please. I know I made a mistake. I know. But I didn't hurt anyone. And I would never endanger Logan. You know that. I was just devastated about you, about us. I felt you slipping away. I was pissed you did that to me."

"I've heard this. It doesn't matter. The court heard your story. And they sided with me."

"Chloe, it's not like I murdered someone."

"You could've. You could've murdered our son. What if he had been in the car?"

"I would never do that."

"We're done here."

She got in the car, turning her back on him, as she'd done so many weeks now.

It was hopeless. There was no fixing this.

Chapter Seven

JACKSON

He knew he should turn the truck around, go back to his apartment, and watch television. This was a bad idea. A weird one. She would think he was being creepy, odd.

No matter how much he rationalized, however, he couldn't make himself turn the truck around.

November 14.

He'd been watching the date on the calendar, knowing it was going to be a rough day for everyone, especially for Sophia. The first year was always the worst. The first day without them, the first holiday.

Tim's first birthday since his death, and, thus, the first birthday he wouldn't be able to actually celebrate.

He'd thought about calling her, just to check in. He'd

thought about doing nothing at all, leaving it to family and friends. Then he thought about Tim, thought about the man who always knew what to do, who never worried about appearances when it came to helping someone out. He would want him to check on Sophia, to make sure she was okay.

He pulled into the driveway and noticed the parked red Corolla. She was home. Turning off the truck, he sat for a long moment, contemplating. He was just doing this because he was worried about her, because he had a connection with her through Tim. He just wanted to make sure she was okay.

Grabbing the bag on the passenger seat, he shuffled to the door. He wondered for a brief moment if she might be busy. Maybe she was with her family or Stella. Maybe he would be intruding.

He rang the doorbell, deciding it was too late to turn around. He'd just hand her the food, see how she was, and leave.

A moment later, the door opened, and a surprised Sophia stood in front of him. Her hair was pulled back into a disheveled ponytail. Her mascara was smudged, clearly hinting at the tears she'd been shedding. She wore loose sweatpants and a tank top. An unbuttoned flannel shirt loosely draped over her.

She looked the part of a saddened widow on the birthday of her late husband.

"Hey," she said, looking both surprised and relieved to see him.

"Hey. I don't want to intrude. I just thought today might be rough."

She silently nodded, stepping back and gesturing him in.

"Am I interrupting?"

"No. My parents were here, but I sent them home. I didn't want to see anyone."

His stomach fell. This was exactly what he was afraid of. "Listen, I can go. I just wanted to bring you dinner in case you were hungry."

She studied him, her blue eyes sparkling in the light of the kitchen. She paused, her face softening. She seemed to be thinking something.

Finally, after a long pause, she simply said, "Stay."

He nodded, ambling to the island in the kitchen with the paper sack. "I brought some hoagies from Wayne's Place down the street. Their food is good."

"It's the best. Tim loved that place."

"Sorry." Great. He was screwing everything up. He was making everything worse.

She shook her head, reminiscing. "No. I think it's good."

He sat down on a stool at the island, unfolding napkins and pulling out the sandwiches. She sat beside him, hugging one knee to her chest, looking at the food, looking at him.

"Thanks for coming."

"Why don't you eat something?"

"Not hungry."

"Me neither. But these subs are seriously awesome.

You're not going to waste it, are you? That's obviously a sin."

She shrugged. "Maybe just a few bites."

"Deal."

He handed her the wrapped sandwich, and she methodically, carefully unwrapped it. She took a bite, chewing slowly.

"God, that's good," she admitted, taking another bite.

"Damn right. Best in the state."

They chewed in silence, two lonely people sitting beside each other, alone in their worlds, in their problems. It felt weird being here, being in the home Tim once shared with her, a home symbolic of a life Jackson no longer recognized.

It felt right too. It felt, in a strange way, as if he could help Tim by helping her. He could do right by him by seeing to it Sophia didn't fall completely apart.

"Tough day?" he asked, knowing the answer.

"One of the worst so far. I didn't think it would hit me like this."

"The firsts are always the worst. It gets easier."

"Does it? Because right now, I don't believe it."

He set his sandwich down. "It never gets *easy*. It just gets easier. The suffocating stillness, the pain in your chest, it gets bearable. You'll see."

She nodded, accepting his words. "Jackson?"

"Yeah?"

"Tell me a story about him. Tell me something about when you two were young."

He paused, wiping his face with a napkin. "Are you sure?"

"Positive. I think that's what's killing me the most.

It's like people are afraid to mention him, you know? His parents, my parents, everyone. Everyone's afraid to bring him up. It's like they think I've forgotten. I want to hear about him. I want to talk about him. I miss him. It's bad enough he's dead. And now everyone is tiptoeing around even the mention of him like he didn't even exist."

He felt the tension ease. He was relieved to be given permission to talk about Tim because that was exactly what he needed, too.

"How about I tell you about the day he almost drowned?"

"Well that seems a bit melancholy, huh?" She grinned.

"You said you didn't want people censoring themselves."

"Go on."

"We were eight. I'd known Tim for about a year at this point. He was always the sensible one. I, as you probably have figured out, was a bit of the rash one. Always getting us into trouble, always coming up with crazy schemes. Well, it was his birthday, and I hadn't had a chance to get him a gift. His party was in the afternoon, but I decided since I didn't get him anything, I'd just take him fishing."

"Tim? Fishing?" Sophia smiled.

"Yeah, I know. Even at eight, it was pretty apparent he wasn't quite the fishing, hunting, hands-on kind of guy. He was happier sitting in our treehouse reading a book. I, on the other hand, liked getting dirty, liked being in the wild."

"A man's man." She put her sandwich down to wipe the dressing off her hands, her gaze still locked on him.

"You could say that. Anyway, I didn't want to tell him my idea. I just wanted to surprise him. So I told him to meet me at our treehouse at eight in the morning. I'd already hidden my dad's fishing pole out by the river and all of the supplies."

"Your parents let you go by yourself at that age?"

"I didn't say we had permission, did I?" He smiled at her, fully engulfed in the memory now. Her face had softened. "Anyway, he met me at the treehouse, apprehensive of course. The week before, I'd stolen fireworks from a neighbor's house and almost caught Tim on fire. But he trusted me, God knows why. I blindfolded him, deciding to lead him to the river as a surprise."

Sophia eyed him furtively, seeming to know where the story was going.

"Let's just say I wasn't the best guide. We walked down the pathway behind his house and arrived at the river. But I got distracted. Tim lost his footing. Before I knew what happened, he was screaming wildly in the river water, flailing about, still blindfolded."

Sophia covered her mouth. "He couldn't swim."

"Yeah, well I didn't know that. So all I saw was Tim sinking down. It took a minute until I realized what was happening. I ended up having to jump in and save him."

"What a great surprise."

"Yeah, obviously. To top it all off, he ended up getting bit by a snake on the way out of the woods. And I forgot my dad's fishing pole. We spent Tim's birthday party first at the emergency room and then grounded. He was pretty pissed at me for about a week."

"You were trouble."

"Yeah, I was. Still am, I suppose."

"Nah, I don't think you're half bad." She nudged him playfully with her elbow. "After all, you managed to make me smile today. And eat. My mom would be grateful."

"It's just hard, you know, to think about it all. To think how it all ended. It's not fair. He was a good man. He was always good. He didn't deserve to die."

"No one ever does," Sophia added rationally. "But you're right. He didn't deserve it. He had so much ahead of him. So many people to help. I always think if someone had to go, why him? He was the important one. He was the one doing big things. I cut hair. My life wouldn't be missed."

"Hey. Stop it. That's ridiculous. Of course you matter." He found himself getting angry by her words. They scared him, probably because he recognized them.

She shrugged. "It's the truth. Where's my life really going?"

He covered her hand with his. "It's going somewhere. That's all that matters. Sophia, I know this is awful, and I know you don't want to hear this. But this isn't it for you. There are big things in store for you. I just know it. I know we don't know each other very well, but I can see it in your eyes. You're going to have a full life. I know it's not what you had in mind, not what you planned. You're going to be okay, though."

There was a pause, a silence. He felt himself feeling more comfortable, more open than he had in months, years if he were being honest. He felt himself saying the things to her he needed to be saying to himself. In her, he saw a broken woman, a destroyed woman, who was going to resurrect herself from destruction. In her, he saw hope in an odd way.

He saw a will to survive, to keep moving. Despite her understandable succumbing to sadness, to pity, to depression, there was a fight in her, a determination to not give up. A determination to live the life she had planned, just in a different way.

"Thank you. I'm glad you came today."

He took this as his cue to leave, standing and clearing the garbage away. "Call me anytime you need me."

She walked him to the door, hanging on the oak doorframe as she said to him, "Same to you."

She smiled at him, waving him goodbye, and he turned to head toward his truck.

He had gone to visit her to help her through a rough day.

What he hadn't expected was that seeing Sophia would help him as well, help him see the hope he had thought was gone.

Chapter Eight

SOPHIA

She lay on her side, his Penn State hoodie in her arms. She'd told herself after the first month was up, she'd stop doing this. But she couldn't. She pressed the hoodie against her face, breathed in, and smelled the faint smell of Tim. She was probably imagining it, but it comforted her just the same. She fell asleep with the hoodie in her arms every night since he was gone. It was crazy, she knew, but it felt like a piece of him was still here. It felt like she wasn't in the bed alone.

Tears streaming down her face as the moonlight scattered the darkness just enough, she caught a glimpse of the empty pillow. She could tell herself the hoodie helped, tell herself she could feel Tim's presence.

It was a lie, though.

Here, in the darkness, his absence was most noticeable. The gaping hole on his side of the bed, the lack of a good-night kiss, the absence of his I love you underscoring the loss. Here, in the bed they shared, she was left with the reality of his departure. She was left to toss and turn, to ponder the life gone by, the life she lost, and the coming years of loneliness.

How many more years would she go to sleep alone? How many more nights would she lie here, drowning in tears of pity and sorrow? How many more nights would she agonize over the constricting feeling in her chest, the knowledge he would never smile at her, would never tell her about his day, would never whisper to her again?

It was torturous.

Rolling on to her other side to turn away from the physical sign of his absence, she thought about tonight. She thought about Jackson showing up.

It was a simple gesture, maybe even an awkward one. His blatant nervousness told her he'd second-guessed himself for showing up. She'd seen on his face the fear, the worry of what to say.

But once he'd settled in, they'd relaxed into a comfortable encounter. His presence, his voice, it soothed her. She knew a part of it was she felt a link to Tim when he was close. She felt like someone who also understood Tim on a fundamental level was there, someone she could talk to about his quirks and nuances.

Thinking about it, though, there was something else. It was in the way he looked at her, the way he seemed to know what she needed to hear before she knew herself. It was in his kind gestures, his calm demeanor. It was in his steel-gray eyes.

When she looked into his eyes, she saw a familiarity, an understanding. He wasn't afraid of her despair, of her hopelessness. He embraced it. He understood it. When she looked at him, she recognized another lost soul. And somehow, it made her feel more hopeful. It made her feel like she wasn't alone.

She barely knew Jackson. She only knew of his connections to Tim. A piece of her, though, wanted to know more. She wanted to know just Jackson, the man behind the friendship. She wanted to know what caused the ache in his eyes. She wanted to help him sort through the demons he was facing, the demons clearly written into the lines on his rigid face. She wanted to know how he got to who he was today, what he'd faced along the way. She wanted to help him the way he was helping her.

Her stomach fell, and she turned back over to face Tim's spot.

An unfamiliar feeling settled into her, and she set her jaw rigid.

Guilt.

She shouldn't be lying here, thinking about another man. Sure, the feelings were platonic. She would never feel something for Jackson. He was Tim's best friend. That would be ridiculous. Still, it somehow felt wrong that as her husband's side of the bed lay empty only months after his death, she lay here thinking about another man on his birthday.

She wouldn't do this, she couldn't. She could be friends with Jackson if she guarded herself. She wouldn't let anything grow between them that could be misconstrued. She would protect her heart from all men. She wouldn't let them in.

She couldn't, after all. She wasn't ready to say goodbye to Tim, the man who had been the love of her life, who always would be. Her heart was gone, given away to the waiter at Mama's Diner all those years ago. He'd never given it back, not even when he left this world, not even when she tossed the final white rose on his grave.

Her heart was six feet under, rotting away.

As she drifted off to sleep, she thought back to a memory of Tim, replacing her guilty musings of Jackson with one of her favorite dates with her husband.

———————

Sophia could feel the biting cold seeping into her skin, even through her hat, gloves, scarf, and ski coat. It was the kind of cold, snowy night where all was silent, where everything seemed preserved in a glassy cast. Her boots crunched in the snow as she followed Tim up the hill, her breaths coming in heavy pants from the exertion.

What had they been thinking?

He turned to look at her, his cheeks reddened from the cold. "Whose idea was this, anyway?" he teased.

She gave him a playful scowl.

"We'll be there soon."

The battle of boredom had usurped them for the past two days. The town was in a state of emergency, so everything was closed down. Tim had stayed home to work from their home office. Pink Lemonade was shut down, buried under two feet of snow.

The first day had been a glorious gift, Tim easily distracted from his work by her. They'd spent most of Wednesday tucked under their fluffy down comforter, basking in the warmth of their body heat.

The second day of the snow emergency, which brought another seven inches, had been relaxing. She had sat in her cozy socks and yoga pants binge watching Orange is the New Black *for a second time while Tim caught up on some trial preparations. She'd made a crockpot meal for dinner, and they'd enjoyed a few glasses of wine.*

By the third day, however, the prospect of another at-home day was maddening when an ice storm coated the already treacherous snow. Sophia wasn't the sit-still kind of girl. She was antsy, always fidgeting, and doing. It drove Tim crazy—she never sat still, whether they were watching a movie or eating dinner. A third day of laziness might, in fact, drive her over the edge.

"I'm going crazy! Can we please go somewhere?" she demanded earlier in the evening, stomping into Tim's office and plopping herself on the desk in front of him.

He smiled, shoving some papers aside as he put his hands on her knees. "Sorry, I left my team of sled dogs up North."

"I can't stand doing nothing."

"There's plenty to do. I mean, the filing cabinet needs to

be cleaned out, the curtains could be ironed..."

She playfully hit him. "Then why don't you do it, you sexist ass."

"I'm not the bored one."

"Yeah, because you're too busy being boring and doing work."

"I could take a break and spice things up with you if you want." He stood now, leaning to kiss her neck.

"While that sounds wonderful, I still want to get out of this house."

"Oh, we're getting really spicy now, huh?" He grinned the boyish grin she knew all too well.

"Stop it, you maniac. I just want to go shopping, go do something."

He kissed her cheek. "If you're not out spending money, you're not happy, huh?"

She was, admittedly, a bit of a shopaholic. Luckily, his salary combined with her money from the salon let her quench her consumeristic cravings frequently.

"I don't care where we go. I just need out of here."

He contemplated the situation, glancing out the window. "My truck is snowed in, and I don't feel like uncovering it yet. Plus, the roads aren't safe. How about we walk to the town center? We could check out the Chinese restaurant, get some food. Maybe some of the boutique shops will be open."

"Really? Have you seen the weather lately, genius?"

"The Chinese restaurant is always open. The owners live above the restaurant. Trust me."

"So you suggest we trudge through almost two feet of

snow, uphill, to get some Chinese food?"

"Hey, you're the one who can't stand being all alone in a house with a hunk."

She rolled her eyes, smiling. "Fine. I'll go get ready."

So here they were, traipsing through snow, sweating from the exertion of uneven steps. They followed the road, which was barren of cars, and finally made it to the center of town.

She turned the corner of the block and cheered gleefully.

"It's open! It's actually open."

Tim smiled. "Did you doubt me?"

"Yes. And the whole way up the hill, I was contemplating your murder when we arrived."

Tim reached in his pocket. "Oh, shit. Hold on to those murder thoughts."

She stopped, her heart sinking. "What?"

"I forgot my wallet. Shit." He put a hand up to his brow, scrunching his face in disbelief.

"Are you kidding me? Oh my God, so we walked this whole way, and you forgot money?"

"I'm so sorry, Soph. I think we're going to have to go back."

She was so disappointed and unreasonably angry. To have walked so far and to be so close. She was enraged.

"I'm going to kill you."

A smirk formed on his face. He tried to fight it, tried to push it back, but the angrier she grew, the more it surfaced.

"Wait a second. Let me see your pocket." She practically mauled him, reaching into his front pocket. Her fingers felt *the familiar leather. She pulled it out as he backed away, laughing.*

He was guffawing by now. "You should've seen your face. You looked like you were going to cry."

She had a new rage now, and she flew over to him, hitting him with his wallet. "You're such an idiot." By now, though, she was laughing audibly, too.

A playful fight ensued, which ended with her picking up a handful of snow, hurriedly forming a lopsided snowball, and hurling it in his face.

"You want to play?" He grabbed her around the waist. She tried to kick and claw, to fight away, but it was no use. With his free hand, he scooped snow off the ledge of the nearby business's window and shoved it down her back. She squealed, kicking free.

They both panted, exhausted from their ridiculous horseplay.

"Thank God no one is around to see us acting like children."

"Why? What's wrong with it?"

"Can we go eat now? I'm starving."

"After you, Mrs. Clawson."

He headed to the door, holding it wide open.

For the next hour, they had Great Wall of China to themselves. They feasted on their favorites, General Tso's chicken and chicken with broccoli. They joked about her client from hell on Monday and talked about his upcoming trial. They talked about the trip to Fiji they needed to plan and pondered over whether they were too young to retire to Florida.

They talked about going to see the adoption counselor next month and maybe getting the ball rolling on children.

"How are we ever going to be good parents? We're terrible adults ourselves."

"I like to call myself youthful," Tim argued as he shoved some chicken in his mouth.

Sophia averted her eyes. She tried to fight the familiar, ugly pang in her chest, but she couldn't. Tim, always perceptive, noticed. He put down his fork and slid his hand across the table, cradling hers.

"Soph, it's fine. We've got time."

"We're almost thirty." She bit her lip and sighed, frustrated at the words. Almost thirty. And no children in sight.

"Oh stop. It's just a number. It's going to be fine. We're going to be fine. Someday, you'll look back and realize it all worked out."

She smiled, feeling sentimental. "You're right. It's going to be okay." And she believed it. Despite what they'd been through, despite the sadness that had almost drowned her three years ago, she was okay. Tim made sure of it. Looking at him eating his meal, she realized they were lucky, despite everything. She spoke up, breaking the silence. "You know, I think the best thing I've ever done is marry the guy sitting across from me."

He smiled back, a genuine smile. "Oh man, does this mean I have to reply with a cheesy sentiment, too? Because I was going to say the best thing I ever did was trade my Chrysler in for my pickup."

She stabbed at him with her chopstick, but she laughed.

Tim was always the funny one, the teasing one. He was rational to a fault, logical. But he had the quirky side few people saw. She was glad their conversations were easy, playful.

Theirs was not the typical relationship. They both had a wild streak to them that only complemented the wild streak in the other. They were sassy and teasing, playful and restless. They were two spirited people, spirited in different ways, trying to settle into this thing called adulthood.

Now, they were getting ready to take a big step toward being grown-ups.

Adoption had been a word floating around their home for a few months now, a word that scared her but excited her. She was anxious to have children, but she was also fearful of how she would handle new responsibilities.

Looking across the table, though, at the goofy lawyer she called husband, her fears softened. Tim made everything possible. With him, she never felt in over her head. He was a true partner, a true comfort. They could do anything together.

"I love you," she said seriously, putting her chopsticks down.

"I love you, too."

They were such simple times, such simple words. In the moment, it had been just an average albeit cold date. Now, she would give anything to go back. She would give anything to talk about their work and kids. She would give anything to hear him say those words she'd heard so often but never really took the time to hear at all.

It wasn't so long ago she was the playful almost thirty-year-old eating Chinese food with her husband across from her, hitting him with his wallet for being mischievous. Now, though, it felt like a different life, a different couple, a different her.

That snowy, simple day, she had no way of knowing eventually, she'd be lying here, alone, all of their dreams of Fiji and Florida and children vanishing like a snowflake in July.

Chapter Nine

"How was your date with Larry?" Sophia asked the next morning as she sipped on her tall latte. It was Sunday, and Pink Lemonade was closed for the day. This had been their Sunday tradition since they opened the shop—breakfast at Christine's Coffee Company down the street.

A familiar look overtook Stella's face, and she looked up to the sky. "Perfect. Magical. Awesome. I think I'm falling for him. Which is crazy, right? I mean, I don't usually fall for a guy like him."

Sophia broke apart the cinnamon roll on her plate, smiling. It wasn't crazy Stella was falling hard and fast. She always did.

Over the years as Sophia went slow and steady with Tim, Stella had whirled through at least a dozen boyfriends. There was Jeremy, the guy she met when she tripped over his leg on the bus. There was Anthony, the nerdy accountant Stella had dated for six months in her late twenties when she decided it was time to mature her tastes in men. There'd been Carlos, the wild rocker, who had ended in an almost violent breakup when Stella found him in bed with another woman. There had been a man of every type.

Which was okay, Sophia thought. Stella was still figuring it all out. She wore her heart on her sleeve, wasn't afraid to fall in love, wasn't afraid to try and try again.

If she were going through this, she wouldn't be afraid to get back out there, Sophia thought and then scolded herself. She loved Tim. She still loved Tim, and she always would. She didn't need to move on.

Still, the thought of being all alone for the next several decades was frightening. She thought about the empty loneliness of their bed, the stark contrast from the warmth of lying beside a lover. She thought about facing everything from broken water heaters to snow removal to financial decisions all by herself. She thought about dying a childless, broken old woman. It was terrifying.

But moving on, well, that was terrifying too.

"Sophia?"

She snapped back. She had a habit of drifting off these days, and she felt terrible about it. "I'm sorry. I'm so sorry. I didn't sleep well last night. What were you saying?"

Stella just smiled. "You know, if you weren't my best friend, I might be pissed that I'm boring you so much."

"You're not boring me."

"I know, I'm just teasing. Anyway, I was asking how you are. I know it can't be easy. Sometimes I feel guilty for talking about Larry, especially after the whole Mama's thing."

"Stella, it's fine. It's not like I can close down Mama's just so I don't have to think about it."

"I mean, we could. I could claim food poisoning or something and get them shut down." Stella grinned as she moved the cup of hot chocolate to her lips. Her eyes were covered in a shimmery, loud purple shadow today. On Sophia, it would look garish. On Stella, it looked amazing.

"I'm fine. Really."

"Does this fine have anything to do with a gorgeous man named Jackson? One of my clients saw him stop by your house."

"He just stopped by to check on me."

"Oh, come on. He's gorgeous. You're gorgeous. I think there's more to it."

"Stella, stop." Sophia fiddled with her coffee, the conversation making her uncomfortable.

"Come on, Sophia. There's no harm in admitting he's pretty attractive," Stella prodded.

"Some might say he's good-looking, but it's irrelevant."

"*Everyone* would say he's good-looking unless they're sexually dead inside."

"Well, that would be me these days."

"Oh stop. You're not. I see the way your eyes light up when you say his name."

"Stella, seriously." Sophia felt herself shutting down, felt herself getting uncharacteristically angry with her friend. "He was just checking on me. He was Tim's best friend for God's sake. And Tim hasn't been gone very long. I'm not ready. Nowhere near it. I don't think I ever will be."

Stella softened, reaching over to grab Sophia's hand. "I know. Not yet. But don't shut down completely. Don't close yourself off. Tim wouldn't want that."

"Shut myself off to what?"

"Possibility."

"There is no possibility with Jackson. *None.*"

"That's not what I see. I saw him look at you at the bar. I see you light up when you talk about him."

"Because he gets it, Stella. He gets it. He knew Tim, as well as I knew him. He knows what this loss is like, at least better than most. I can talk to him."

Stella put her hands up as if to say she was done. "Okay. I'm glad you have him then. Cling to anything that makes this bearable. Anything at all."

Sophia returned to her cinnamon roll, trying to push the whole conversation, the whole concept of possibility out of her head.

———————

Sophia turned the radio to the classical station. She didn't want to hear any love songs, didn't want to be slapped in the face with words about lost lovers. She just wanted to drive, take in the sight of the fall leaves, and focus on her visit.

Her mom had been insistent she not come alone.

"We'll come to you, dear. It's okay. We like the drive," Clarissa had said when Sophia called yesterday about coming up.

"Mom, I'm fine. I want to get out of town. It'll be good for me to come to you."

"Sophia, really. Your father and I aren't doing anything anyway. Why go through the trouble of driving here?"

"Mom, I'm not a fragile flower. I'm fine."

Her mom had sighed, finally giving in.

Sophia loved her parents. Over the past few months, they'd driven the two-hour drive to visit her almost every week, making excuses to check in on her. It was good to have them there, good to be kept busy. But she needed to get out of the house now, away from the memories. She wanted to visit her childhood home, sleep in her childhood room, remember a time when life was simpler.

She had driven this drive so many times with Tim when they were dating, when they were married. She'd been blessed to have parents and a husband who got along splendidly. Tim was the son her father never had, and they always joked and laughed like old friends.

Pulling into the driveway, Sophia could see her mom in the living room window, peering out. She blasted to the front door, rushing down the driveway before Sophia was even out of her car.

"Hey, Mom," Sophia said as she grabbed her bag from the passenger seat and started getting out.

"Sophia, we were so worried! You're fifteen minutes late!"

"Mom, I stopped to get a coffee. I'm fine." She smiled at her mom's frantic worry. She was lucky to be so loved.

She followed her mom into the house, the familiar scent of the home taking her back. She reached down to pet Muffin, the twenty-year-old orange cat who just refused to give up on life. He hissed at her before recognizing her scent and then purring.

She ambled into the kitchen, where a feast was strewn about the counter. All of the traditional items were there—her mom's turkey, stuffing, mashed potatoes, homemade mac and cheese, vegetables. The only substitution was a raspberry pie for the traditional pumpkin.

"Mom, what's all this?"

"I just whipped a few things up."

Ever since her mom had retired from teaching last year, she'd been frantically trying to keep busy. Cooking had been her recent forte, and Thanksgiving dinner was apparently the perfect time to show it all off.

"Looks great. Where's Dad?"

"I'm coming," he yelled, heading down the hallway from the back library. Also recently retired, he managed to keep himself busy with the one thing he'd devoted his life to—reading. As a previous English teacher, he didn't seem like he'd ever give up his love for books.

"It's good to have you home," her dad said, approaching her for a hug.

The three sat down at the kitchen table, the same one Sophia had done her high school homework on, had painted her nails on for prom, had sat around when she told her parents she was engaged. It was filled with memories.

"So, honey, we're glad you're here. We wanted to talk to you about something."

Sophia perked up, looking up from her plate after serving herself some turkey.

"Oh yeah?"

"Your father and I have an idea."

They looked at each other, pausing, as if weighing whether or not to continue.

"Go ahead, guys." They were making her nervous.

"We want you to move back home with us."

Sophia stopped herself from laughing out loud. "Are you serious?"

They didn't laugh, didn't budge. Clearly they were serious.

"It's just, well, we hate you being so far away and all. All alone in that big house, surrounded by memories. We miss you. We're worried about you. It's not good to be cooped up alone. Come home. You can have your old room back. We'll find you a job at Maria's salon." Maria was her mom's friend from high school.

"Guys, you can't be serious. My life is in Hollidaysburg. I can't just leave my business, Stella, everything behind."

"We hate you being there, so far away. We know this is hard. And, honey, with the holidays, it's only going to get harder."

Sophia felt frustration mounting. She reminded herself they were just trying to look out for her.

"Guys, I'm fine. Really. I'm going to be fine. I love you, and I appreciate the offer. But I'm not going to just leave my life behind. Honestly. Today's a holiday, and I'm fine, aren't I?"

Her mom sighed. "Well, think about it. The offer still stands. One phone call, and we'll be there with a U-Haul."

"I'm sure you will." Sophia smiled, reaching to gently touch her mom's hand. "Now can we talk about something else, please? How's retirement? What have you been up to? Any exciting plans?"

They proceeded to chat about her mom's hope to travel to Paris over the summer and the new knitting class she was taking. They chatted about trivial things, which was exactly what Sophia wanted, what she needed.

The day passed quickly, just like Sophia hoped it would. Her parents mercifully tried to do everything to scoot around the fact it was a holiday. There were no holiday traditions in place—no "let's talk about what we're thankful for," none of Tim's favorite pumpkin pie. They pretended it was just a dinner, another day, and Sophia was glad for it. The less fanfare the better.

Sophia felt refreshed. It was a relief to be out of her house, away from the memories. Maybe her mom was right. Maybe she should consider the offer.

But when she thought about leaving it all behind for good, the sadness came back in. It wouldn't do her any good to run away. Sure, leaving her house, her town might be a temporary relief, might make her feel better for a time. Eventually, though, he would creep back in. The memories, the images, they would follow her. She couldn't forget.

In truth, she wasn't ready to forget.

She wanted to stay surrounded by their life, by her life. She needed Stella, the shop, the familiars of the life she'd built with Tim.

As she said her farewells to her parents, wished them a Happy Thanksgiving, and climbed into her car, she realized something else.

She'd survived the first major holiday without him.

Pulling out of her parents' driveway, headlights illuminating their smiling and waving bodies, she turned the radio down.

The soundtrack of their memories would accompany her on the way home. It was too loud, drowning out everything else, for her to even think about listening to the radio.

Tears were overpowered with a smile, though, as she thought about last year.

———————

"You're kidding, right?" she asked incredulously as he stood across from her in the kitchen.

"I'm dead serious. Come on, don't be such a killjoy. Let's do it."

"But..." All of the reasons this was a bad idea rushed to her mind.

Their families would be devastated.

They didn't do things like this.

It wasn't traditional.

It would be freaking cold.

He ambled across the kitchen, his eyes pleading with her. "Come on. Let's not be those boring, married people for once. We can see our families another time. Let's do this. You. Me. A bottle of wine. Some sand between our toes."

"Some snowy sand maybe. Have you forgotten it's November? As in the end of November?"

"So bring a sweatshirt. It'll be fun. It'll be peaceful."

She closed her eyes, shaking her head. "Okay."

"Yeah? You're in?" He smiled widely, the one she loved.

"On one condition."

"What's that?"

"You can be the one to break the news to our parents that we won't be attending the traditional family Thanksgiving."

"Do you want your mom to hate me?"

"She already does," Sophia winked. Tim poked her in the ribs, tickling her until she shrieked.

"Take it back."

Sophia just continued to scream.

"Take. It. Back."

"Okay, okay. I'm kidding." He finally stopped, and Sophia backed up to catch her breath. She shook her head. "You know my mom freaking loves you. I think she likes you more than me."

"Well, yeah. Obviously. I'm amazing."

"Okay, Mr. Amazing. You have some phone calls to make."

"Let me book the hotel first."

"You better make sure we get the hot tub suite. Guess I

should go pack my suitcase."

"Just a bikini will be fine," he shouted over his shoulder, heading to find his cell phone.

"Are you trying to kill me?"

He popped back in the kitchen, peering around the corner. "Maybe."

She rolled her eyes again. This was absurd. But she had to admit, she did kind of like the idea of breaking the mold, of doing something different.

They'd been married for years, had gone through all the ruts of typical married life. But they weren't bored. They weren't getting stagnant. Tim was making sure of that. They were still spontaneous, still a bit crazy.

They were crazy enough to head to Ocean City, Maryland, for Thanksgiving, to abandon their families and risk sheer chaos in order to get a romantic getaway alone. It was odd, probably not the wisest choice—the beach in prewinter. Who the hell did that? But it was them.

As long as she was with him, she didn't care if she was in Antarctica or Area 51.

That Thanksgiving, they snuggled in the whipping wind and thirty-eight-degree weather on a beach towel, Tim insisting he would feel sand between his toes. They snuggled together, nothing sexy or romantic happening because they were too damn cold to take off any layers of clothes. They listened to the rush of the ocean, smelled the salty air, and shared a sub from a shop a block back.

"This is the weirdest Thanksgiving I've ever had," she confessed, her face snuggled against his stubbly chin, her

cheeks rubbing raw.

"Weird but good. I'm glad we have this life, Sophia. I'm happy to be on the beach, alone, with you. I love you."

She leaned in for a kiss, her hood up, her hair whipping around. They kissed for a long moment, realizing how lucky they were to have each other.

Life wasn't perfect. Their families probably were still complaining about their absurd, semi-selfish idea to escape to the beach on a holiday. She didn't care. Sitting here, freezing her ass off, with the man she loved beside her was perfect.

They were the only two fools on the beach, no one else dumb enough to brave the cold. But she didn't feel lonely. She felt content, at home. They might not have children, they might not have the typical life, but she loved that. She loved how Tim made her want to go to their summer vacation spot in November, how he forced her to put her toes in the sand even though she was freezing. He made her life exciting and full. He made her see things, made her live.

"Maybe next year, we'll go to a beach closer to the equator, what do you think?"

"Yeah, in hindsight, that probably would've been smarter."

"There's always next year," Tim said, and he leaned in to kiss her again.

After a few moments, they picked up their sandy blanket, huddled together, and hurried back to the hotel, the hot tub, and some room service turkey calling their names.

———————

Stopping at the gas station about an hour into her trip home, she stumbled inside to get a coffee, to perk herself back up. She felt drained from the day, from driving, from her memories.

"I wish we were snuggled on a beach towel, Tim. I'd give anything to freeze my ass off again," she said aloud as she poured her coffee. A guy beside her gave her a glance. She felt her cheeks warm.

She was turning into that lady, the lady who mumbled to herself in convenience stores. If they knew, if they could read her heart right now, understand the pain suffocating it, they would know talking out loud was the least of her problems.

She had to keep trudging forward. Moving back in with her parents wasn't the answer. Abandoning her life wasn't the answer. She had to find a way to keep on, even if she didn't know how. Tim would want that. He'd want her to find her own beach trip, to find her own seashells, to find her own sunshine when the cold threatened to roll in.

Chapter Ten

JACKSON

Once, Christmas had been one of Jackson's favorite seasons. The smell of nutmeg, the promise of Santa, the collection of family by the tree, by the fireplace. It was a magical season when anything was possible.

Then his brother, Wade, died.

Then he went into the army.

Then his wife left him.

Then he lost his son.

Over the years, December became more of a gloomy, black month than a season of joy. Jackson felt more like an adherent to Krampus's camp than Santa's. He felt void, empty, nothingness instead of holiday warmth.

Especially this year.

"It's not your holiday," Chloe had argued on the phone

just last week when Jackson called to make arrangements for Christmas.

"Chloe, come on, it's Christmas. I don't even have to take him. Can I just come to your house for a few hours? Give him presents?"

"Mail them. I'll tell him they're from you, or give them to him on your next weekend. The court gave you Easter. I got Christmas. That was the deal."

"Please don't do this."

She had hung up, the click of the phone echoing in the silence. He'd been infuriated, heartbroken, angry, and depressed all within a single moment.

Jackson glanced around his apartment, the sheer blankness of the room only enhancing his non-holiday spirit. There was no tree, no cookies in the oven. Nothing to symbolize the season. Without Logan, what was the point? A part of him knew he was being childish. Logan was young. He wouldn't care if they celebrated Christmas a few weeks afterward. To Jackson, though, it was a reminder that things had changed, that he would be forever settling for any time he could get with his son. It wouldn't be the same, no matter how hard he tried to convince himself it would. It would never be the same unless he had Logan back with him, at least joint custody.

He would go to his parents' house for Christmas morning. Gretta, Jonathan, and Jace would be there, too. He would pretend to conjure up some merriness for a few hours before returning home to wallow in loathing, pity, and hurt at the absence of his son.

His son's Christmas would now be devoid of him. How many more until Logan had forgotten all about him? How many more until Logan was asking to cancel their weekend together?

He'd confided as much in Jonathan who had comforted him, trying to make him see reason. "Jackson, buddy, hang in there. Give it a few more months. Get yourself established. Show the courts you've settled yourself. We can appeal the decision, fight for joint custody. This isn't forever. Decisions can be reversed. Just give it time."

At the time, Jackson had nodded despite his inner rage. Time? He didn't have time. Every month that went by without Logan was like an inferno of sorrow. Every month without his son was a step closer to oblivion in his son's life. Every month was one step closer to Seth taking over his place.

On Christmas Eve, after a depressing phone call with Logan about Santa, Jackson found himself flipping aimlessly through Christmas movies, not really paying attention. He found himself thinking about previous years, good and bad, previous Christmases. There had been many characters in his Christmas scenes, but Tim had been a constant.

He thought back to another depressing Christmas when Tim had been there for him.

"You know, Jackson, you don't have to do this. You're an

adult. He doesn't make decisions for you." Tim sat beside Jackson on the sofa in Tim's parents' garage, their typical hangout. It was Christmas Eve, and they had just exchanged gifts. Jackson opened the new video game, pretending to be interested in the back.

"I know. But he's right. It's not like my life's going anywhere else. Construction work is good, but it's not what I had in mind."

"What about culinary school? You've always loved cooking."

"There's no money in it."

"It's not all about money, you know."

Jackson eyed him. "You're going to be a lawyer, and their paychecks aren't half bad from what I've heard."

"You got me there. But I've always wanted a law degree. It's not something my dad forced me into."

"It's not like my dad's holding a gun to my head."

"No. It's kind of worse. I know this isn't what you want."

When graduation had come two years ago, Jackson had felt elated with possibility. Everyone was heading off to achieve their dreams, Tim included. He hadn't quite pinned down what he wanted to do.

But his father had.

When he casually mentioned culinary school, his dad had shut down the idea. "That's not a man's job. I'll not support that."

"Dad, why? It's what I love."

"The military. That's where it's at."

Jackson had put off joining, had given up on his dreams

of culinary. He'd gone off to a construction job, a manly job, and worked for the past two years.

But he was miserable. It was hard work, thankless work. He couldn't see himself doing it forever.

So last week, he'd made a rash decision. His dad was right. The military was a respectable career. It was something to be proud of. He could do it. It would be good for him, a prudent choice.

Tim, however, didn't think so.

"I just think your father isn't seeing clearly. He's seeing what he wants to see. He's seeing what he wanted Wade to be."

"Don't." Jackson's voice was stern.

"Look, I'm sorry. I know you don't like talking about it, especially this time of year. But Jackson, you can't be Wade. You shouldn't have to be. I think your father puts that on your shoulders."

"Listen, this is my choice. It's an admirable choice."

"I support you no matter what, you know that. I just want you to be happy."

"I am."

Tim grinned. "All right then, soldier. Let's see what you're made of, get you ready for combat."

"Call of Duty 2? I don't think they use this at boot camp."

"You never know."

They laughed as they grabbed their controllers, Tim pushing the button on their garage game room Xbox. They rang in Christmas like they had for so many years—playing video games, shooting each other, and laughing.

Within a few months, Jackson knew he would be gone, shipped off to boot camp, to a life far from his life of Call of Duty, *Tim, and their hometown. Things would change drastically, and life would take a twisted turn.*

That Christmas, the Christmas before he changed his life course, Jackson felt blessed to have such an awesome friend in his life.

Jackson found himself standing in front of his gaming console, flipping through the games. There it was, the case beat-up, the disk probably scratched. *Call of Duty 2.*

Feeling nostalgic, wishing he could go back, Jackson did the only thing he could think to do on this lonely Christmas Eve.

He popped the disk in and warmed up his shooting skills once more.

Scattered hunks of wrapping paper littered his parents' living room floor. Jace, exhausted from the excitement, napped on the sofa. The whole family had eaten more ham, turkey, and green bean casserole than recommended.

Christmas was done.

It had been a relatively merry Christmas, all things considered. Jackson had spent the day with his family, watching the holiday through Jace's eyes, trying not to envy his sister and brother-in-law for their happiness. It wasn't their fault they had a functional family unit and he didn't.

He'd held it together, plastered a semi-genuine grin on his face for the day. He tried not to think of all those missing, tried to be thankful for what he had.

He'd laughed at all the right parts of *A Christmas Story*, a Gauge family tradition. He ate three helpings of dinner. He smiled graciously at the socks and underwear his mom bought him, thanked Gretta for the gift card to the gaming store. He passed on the wine, whiskey, and beer.

Driving home, though, his emotions started to unwind. The fake enthusiasm of the day peeled away, revealing the cracked, broken man underneath.

He was afraid to go home, afraid to find himself wallowing in sadness and, consequentially, in alcohol. He was afraid of hitting rock bottom again. He was afraid of being alone.

So he did something a bit rash, a bit crazy.

He turned his truck around and headed in the other direction, driving toward the one person he wanted to see, hoping she wasn't too busy or too depressed or too anything to spend time with him.

"Jackson?" She was obviously surprised to see him at the door ten minutes later, and he was surprised to find her alone. The television played in the background, and she was wearing pajamas.

"Am I interrupting?"

"Definitely not," she replied, ushering him in.

"Are you alone?"

"Should I be creeped out by that question?" she teased, smiling as she pulled her robe around her.

"Sorry. Let me explain. You see, I thought about going home and watching some lame Christmas movies or drinking myself into a coma. So I didn't have to think about my son, Tim, or Wade. But then I started thinking. You're probably having a pretty crappy night too, right? I mean, best case scenario, I figured your family was hovering around you, telling you it would be okay, buying you fuzzy socks and perfume hoping they'll make you forget about Tim."

She nodded, laughing. "That was my early evening spot-on."

"Okay. Then I figured worst case, you were here alone, wallowing in sadness, replaying your Christmases with Tim movie style to sappy music in your head, also drowning in a bottle of wine."

She sheepishly nodded, turning to eye the half-empty bottle of wine on the end table by the couch. "And that summarizes the rest of my night."

"I thought so. So on the way home from my family's overly festive Christmas feast, I realized something. Since both of us are having a shitty Christmas, why not spend the evening together?"

"Misery loves company?"

"Sort of. More like, commiserating while also keeping each other out of depression status."

"And what did you have in mind?"

"A walk?"

"A walk? That was your master, soul-saving idea?"

"Yep. A walk. In the freezing cold air. Two miserable friends walking on Christmas trying to abate the loneliness and shittiness of the season."

"Well, when you put it that way, how could I resist? Let me go change."

"Don't change. Just throw a coat on. You don't have to impress anyone today."

She eyed him like he was crazy, but the wine was probably dulling her rational thoughts. "Okay, then. Lead the way."

It's a stupid idea, really, he thought as she followed him into the brisk December air. The moon was out, lighting their path. It was cold but not completely unbearable. It was a good temperature to walk with Sophia, to let the pure state of their friendship coupled with a jaunt through nature numb him to his thoughts.

"Despite your lack of eloquence, I do appreciate this," she said, turning to him. Her hands were shoved in her pockets, and her hair was in its customarily messy ponytail. "I told my parents to leave, that I was fine. I really wasn't. I was in a pretty low place. You saved me from making a huge mistake, too."

"Oh yeah?"

"Yeah. I was contemplating putting in our wedding

video when you came to the door."

"What? Are you crazy?"

"Yeah, I know. Masochistic at least. I just, I don't know... I wanted to see him. You know?"

"Yeah. I get it. But please don't. Don't do it. Not yet."

"So from the sounds of it, your holiday wasn't much better?"

He stared ahead, eying the glassy road as they meandered forward. "Nope. My ex-wife refused to budge on the custody agreement. She gets Christmas this year with Logan. I wanted to just stop by, to just see him for a little bit. She refused."

"She wouldn't consider it at all? Not even for Christmas?"

"Nope."

"Jackson, I'm sorry. That sucks."

"Yeah, it does. I can't really blame her. Hey, do you want to sit for a few?" They had reached the tiny park at the end of the block. A bench illuminated by a streetlight humbly invited them in.

She nodded, parking herself on the bench. He sat beside her.

"So what happened? Tell me."

He hesitated, not sure if he wanted to open up. "Well, I came home from the military. I'd left to be with her, to be with Logan. I was tired of having to leave. It wasn't fair to either of them. So I quit. I'd been home a week when she told me the truth. She was seeing someone else. She was leaving me."

Sophia gasped, putting a hand on his arm. "I'm sorry.

That's awful."

"Yeah. It was. She took my son, moved him in with Seth, and left me with the house. Not the homecoming I'd planned. I was jobless, wifeless, and sonless. I was pretty low. So I started drinking. A lot. Alcoholic level a lot."

She looked at him, her eyes sparkling from the streetlight. She didn't gasp, didn't judge. She just listened. He tensed his jaw.

"One night, about a month after she left, I got really drunk. The booze gave me this crazy idea to get in my truck and drive to see Logan. I was on my way when I lost control of the vehicle and crashed into a tree."

"Oh my God! That's awful."

"Yeah. Luckily for me, I wasn't hurt, and I didn't hurt anyone else. It wasn't as serious as it could have been. But I had no one to call. A guy I worked construction with came and picked me up. I was lucky I wasn't caught by the police. It's a small town, though, and Chloe, of course, found out. She was pissed, especially since I'd been on my way to Logan. She filed for sole custody immediately. Her lawyer painted me out to be a basket case from my Iraq tours, and she won, leaving me with a few weekends a month and a few appointed holidays."

"That's not fair. She did this. She started it."

He smiled at her. It felt good to have someone on his side, deserved or not.

"Can you appeal?" she asked.

"I'd sort of given up on everything. But recently, I've been talking about it with my brother-in-law. He thinks we have a shot."

"Don't give up. You're a good man. You made a mistake. I think the court was crazy not to see that."

"I've had some shady moments in my past, some rock bottom moments. Being in Iraq took its toll. I'm not a saint, Sophia. Don't get the wrong idea."

"None of us are."

He looked over at her now, this woman who'd been through so much, yet she was comforting him. "How are you holding up? Really?"

"Honestly? I'm not. I mean, I put on a good show during the day, but it's awful. Some days, I don't even want to get out of bed. Some days, I feel like it's going to be okay, like I can be okay, only to have some other aspect of my life tell me otherwise. Most days, racking pain surges through my entire body. I don't know if I'll ever be okay."

He instinctively reached over, wrapping an arm around her, pulling her in to him.

"We're quite the pair, huh?"

She eyed him now, pulling back slightly.

"Sorry, I didn't mean it like that. I just meant—"

"I know." She settled back against him, and they sat for a few moments looking at the stars, wondering what the new year could possibly bring.

"I'm glad you stayed in town," Sophia murmured. He squeezed her arm.

"Me too."

"Thanks for making Christmas a little bit more bearable."

"Same here."

"And Jackson?"

"Yeah?" He turned to look at her now, her blue eyes gleaming up at him, her cheeks slightly pink from the chill of the night air.

"You're a good man. Chloe's a stupid bitch if she doesn't see that. You fight for Logan. You fight until you get him back. You survived Iraq. You can survive some stupid woman who has her head up her ass."

He smiled. "Tell me how you really feel, huh?"

"I don't like censoring myself."

"I see that. But thank you."

She did something surprising then, something that jolted him to life.

Under the moonlight on Christmas night, perhaps still emboldened by the contents of the wine bottle, she leaned over and kissed him on the cheek. Her lips felt smooth and shocking against the cold of his cheek.

"I can see why Tim thought you were such a good friend, even when you two lost touch," she said. She jumped to her feet then, before he had time to think about it. She pulled him off the bench and they headed toward her house in silence, the calmness of the neighborhood soothing both of them into a place of complacency if not downright peace.

Chapter Eleven

JACKSON

"Hey. I hope you like coffee." Jackson stood sheepishly holding two Dunkin Donuts large coffees at her door. She was dressed in leggings and a T-shirt and looked peaceful.

The holidays had been gone for a couple of weeks, and the two had fallen into somewhat of a routine. Once or twice a week, he'd show up at her door. She'd grab a coat, and they'd take a walk through her neighborhood. They'd stroll down memory lane together, too, talking about Tim, old times, and old dreams. They'd talk like two old friends who'd just rediscovered each other. Talking with her felt like talking with a piece of Tim. He felt close to him again by being with her.

It was more than that, though.

Sophia understood loss. She didn't try to tell him he

should cheer up or be thankful. She didn't begrudge him feelings of depression, hurt, or anger when he talked about Logan. She let him simmer in the grief, let him spew about it. She made him feel okay.

Jackson needed to be near her, not just for comfort, but also for a pull all too familiar. There was something about her, something about the way her hair frizzed a bit at the top, something about the way she aimlessly twirled the loose hair around her face. There was something about her delicate hands when they reached out to touch his arm, the way her blue eyes glimmered like she could feel his pain.

He shut down that side of his heart, closed off any lascivious feelings that were emerging.

She's your best friend's wife, he reminded himself. *She's off-limits. This is crazy.*

He promised himself—promised Tim—nothing would come of it. Sure, she was gorgeous; every man who came in contact with her was probably pulled in by her. Who wouldn't be? But she certainly didn't feel anything toward him, and he would never expect her to. It would be too weird.

"Thank you," she said, the smile lighting up her face. "Are you kidding? I love coffee." She helped herself to one of the cups in his hand and wandered back inside, not needing to lead him inside anymore. He knew the way. "What's up? You're earlier than usual."

"Yeah, I got off work early. I wanted to stop by, see how you're doing."

She smiled. "Better now. Who can resist a man with coffee?"

He felt his cheeks redden as he looked at the ground, fiddling with his coffee cup.

She reddened now, too. "Sorry. That sounded awkward."

He shook his head. "It's fine. I knew what you meant."

"You hungry?" she asked.

"Yeah. I planned on heading home for some frozen pizza after our walk."

"Frozen pizza?" She crinkled her nose. "That's sort of sad."

"Yeah, sort of is."

"So let's skip the walk today, huh? I actually have a roast in the crockpot that's about done. Stay for dinner."

"Sounds good." Deep down, he'd been hoping for an invitation, for an extension of their time together. Standing by Sophia, he realized how much he didn't want to go home to his gloomy apartment to watch reruns.

Sophia sipped her coffee before speaking again. "I'll warn you, I'm going to put you to work though. I hate mashing potatoes."

"Well, lucky for you, there's a gourmet chef in the house," he teased, raising his chin just a bit.

"Well then, what the heck am I doing getting anything ready at all? The kitchen awaits." She beamed at him, sipped her coffee, and gestured toward the kitchen.

As he sauntered toward the kitchen, he realized how good it felt to see her smile.

One hour later, they'd properly served the roast, mashed the potatoes—which were quite lumpy, to his chagrin—and set the table. They now sat across from each other, ready to dig in.

"This looks awesome," Jackson said. "But I will say, I think the potatoes clearly make the meal."

"Ha! Don't you wish. They look a bit lumpy."

"Questioning the master chef? Who do you think you are?"

She grabbed a fork and fluffed the potatoes, whipping them a bit before taking a bite. "Okay, so they don't taste too bad."

"Too bad? I'm insulted."

She grinned. "They're pretty damn good, I'll admit. Better than mine would be."

They ate for a few moments in silence before he spoke. "It's been so long since I've had a real, home-cooked dinner."

"God, me too. The grief books don't tell you how cooking for one is so much more depressing than cooking for two."

"Don't I know it."

"Yeah, but you're a bachelor. It's acceptable for you to eat takeout every day."

He nodded quietly, staring at the roast beef.

"Oops, sorry. Now who's saying the wrong thing?" she said, embarrassed.

"It's fine. It's not like I've forgotten."

"So was Chloe your first real love?"

"At the time, I thought so. I had a few girlfriends before her, but none like her. I thought it was the real deal."

"How'd you meet?"

"At a bar."

Sophia laughed a bit. "That's never a good sign."

He shot her a glance.

"Sorry. There I go again. I'm sure it was romantic."

"Not really. There was just something about her from the first second I saw her."

"Careful, soldier, or I might think you're a hopeless romantic."

"How do you know I'm not?"

"You? Muscular army man? It doesn't fit."

"Glad you can appreciate my muscles." He flexed, teasing her. Their banter was playful, easy, natural. It didn't feel like he was sitting down to a dinner with his late best friend's grieving wife. It felt like they were…

He stopped himself, exhaling as he put his bicep down. "I'm sorry."

She looked at him like he was crazy. "For what?"

"I feel weird, sitting here, at Tim's table, with his wife. Being flirtatious."

Her face fell. "That wasn't my intention, I'm sorry."

He looked up at her, her eyes swimming with confusion, with sorrow, with guilt. He smiled.

"Look at us, two wrecked souls, an awkward mess of potatoes and apologies."

She nodded. "We sure are. I bet Tim's looking down

laughing at us right now."

"Or he's pissed."

"Hey," she said, reaching across the table. "Nothing's going on. We're just friends, right? Just two friends helping each other through a rough time. I think Tim would be glad you came into my life. You make me smile, Jackson. I like spending time with you. But nothing's going on. We don't have to feel guilty."

He nodded, feeling better about the situation. She made him feel better about everything. She was right. They were just friends. It wouldn't do to tiptoe around each other.

They finished eating while talking about his work at the restaurant and about how she started her salon. They laughed. They smiled. It felt good to be carefree for a change.

After dinner, she cleared the plates. "It's too damn quiet in here." She found her phone, hooked it up to the speaker in the kitchen, and put on Pandora.

"What is this crap?" he teased as the latest pop song came on.

She scowled at him. "It's not crap. Maybe you're just old, soldier. What, you want some 1960s songs?"

Before he could even think, he charged across the kitchen, grabbing on to her arm, playfully poking at her. "Are you calling me old?" She screamed and wriggled to get away, both of them laughing and joking as they poked and tickled at each other, her shrieks filling the house with a warmth that certainly hadn't been there in a while.

When they both grew tired, he let up, his face actually

hurting from laughing. She wriggled back slightly, her wrists still in his hands. Her face was glowing with joy. It looked good on her.

The song changed, as if on cue. James Bay's song, "Why Don't You Be You," filled the kitchen, and her face softened.

"I *love* this song."

Before he could reconsider, rationalize, or tell himself it was wrong, he pulled her in, putting her hands on his shoulders, putting his hands on her waist. The move was smooth, easy, and as they looked into each other's eyes, the questions melted away. The guilt melted away. The fears, the rejections, the hurt, and the grief faded into the measures of the song. They fell into step, an easy sway, a silent dance on the ceramic tile. There was some tension between them. They were afraid to give in too much, to cross the line they knew was firmly planted.

He told himself they were just friends, again, just so his heart didn't get any ideas. People danced all the time. It didn't mean anything.

Looking into her face, he didn't see shame painted on it like he would expect. He didn't see regret or sorrow. He saw a softness that said she'd been missing this. A warmth radiated through his biceps, through his hands that were on her waist. The song lulled them into a quiet solace, something both had been missing.

When the song ended, they silently parted, neither knowing what to say. He didn't want to admit what his heart was feeling, didn't want to admit he could feel the friendship status between them threatening to become something more.

He wouldn't do that to her.

Besides, what would ever become of it? He would always be Tim's best friend in her eyes, and that would prevent anything from happening.

Not that he wanted anything to happen.

But as she pulled away, he could still feel her tight waist in his fingers, smell her perfume floating up from her neck. He could see those perfectly pink lips. He wondered what they would feel like...

"I should go," he said before he was swept away, before he ruined everything between them.

She nodded, the glow in her eyes slowly fading into confusion.

"Thanks for dinner. I'll call you?"

He rushed out the door, not looking back. The song had changed to a more upbeat song, and the moment was over.

Or was it?

———————

The night of the pot roast, of the dancing in the kitchen, had thrown him a bit. He'd managed to convince himself his visits were all about helping Sophia, all about his sense of duty to Tim.

Now, though, he couldn't stop thinking about her waist between his hands, about the way her eyes looked up at him. He silently asked the question he'd been avoiding, the "what if" question.

He stopped himself. This was madness. He wasn't this kind of man. Hell, he wasn't even a good enough man for Sophia, even if she weren't his best friend's wife. He was a broken-down excuse for a man, a lost man. He, as he had told Sophia, was no saint.

He was a wreck, flailing through life, trying to figure out where he was going. Sophia's life was already complicated and dilapidated. She needed a man who was settled, who was perfect. Not him.

Try as he might, he couldn't stop himself. Like his addiction to the feel of alcohol gliding down his throat, he was addicted to her presence.

He recommitted to his "just friends" theory, promised himself the night of the roast had been a moment of weakness. It wouldn't happen again.

So a few nights later, when Sophia called out of the blue and asked if he wanted to go out for dinner, he accepted. He tried to ignore the fact he was smiling from ear to ear at the sound of her voice, tried not to stress out over what to wear or what cologne to spray on.

He tried not to think about it like a date.

His heart, well, his heart was a different story.

———

"Well, I do hate when you turn down my dinner invitation, but I will let it slide this time," his mom replied. She'd called to invite him to dinner—meatloaf.

"Don't make a big deal out of this, Mom. We're just friends."

"Okay, whatever you say. But tell me, when are you

going to bring her over for dinner? Oh, maybe you could skip the going out thing and just come over for meatloaf?"

"No." In hindsight, he should've just told his mom he had to work when he turned down her dinner invitation. What the hell had he been thinking? He hadn't.

"Well, you can't keep this girl to yourself forever."

"She's not my girl, Mom."

"Bring her over. And soon."

"Okay. Gotta go. I'm picking her up soon."

"Flowers? Did you get flowers?"

"Mom…"

"Listen, friends or not, every girl loves flowers. Go get some. I raised you to be a gentleman, didn't I?"

He sighed. When he talked to his mom, he always felt like he was fifteen again. Perhaps that was her goal. "Okay, Mom. I'll get flowers."

"Is that Jackson? Does he have a date?" His sister's obnoxious voice blared in the background. His mom turned from her conversation with Jackson to fill Gretta in. While he was still on the phone.

"Mom!" he yelled, trying to get her attention, listening to Gretta and his mother plan and plot about what was not even a relationship.

"Sorry, honey. We're just so excited for you. Okay, you two lovebirds have fun. Don't get too wild. Or do. I mean, if she's gorgeous…"

"Okay, I'm hanging up." He clicked the phone, squeezing his brow, trying to shuck the idea his mom just hinted at sex from his mind.

He would never publicly admit it, but he did decide his mom was right about a few things.

One: Flowers wouldn't be a bad idea.

Two: Sophia was gorgeous. Absolutely gorgeous.

———

"Thanks, Jackson. You didn't have to do this," Sophia said when she answered the door. She was wearing skinny jeans, knee-high boots, and a royal blue sweater. Her hair was down, disheveled in a sexy way. She looked perfect.

Of course, his feelings were strictly platonic.

He shrugged, handing the white daisies to her. They were simple. Friendly. Non-romantic.

"So are you ready?"

"Yeah. Let's go."

"Where to?" She'd never really specified where she wanted to go.

"Well, I was hoping to go to Sean's."

"Really? Are you sure you don't want to go somewhere nicer?" Sean's was a run-down local restaurant, known for its basic bar foods and sometimes unsavory crowds.

"No. I kind of wanted low-key."

"That low-key?"

"I've heard they have good wings. And… well… to be honest, I've never been there. It's one of the places around here Tim never would take me."

He smiled. She wanted somewhere without memories. He could understand that.

"Okay. Let's go."

She paused.

"What is it?" he asked, waiting for her at the door.

"I'm sorry. This... I just feel... is this weird for you?"

He shrugged. "No. It's two friends going for wings."

She nodded, seeming to think for a moment. "Okay. You're right. I'm sorry. I'm being all crazy."

"You're not being crazy. Let's go have some wings."

"To the wings," she said, following him to his truck.

―――――――――― ‒

Three dozen wings later, they were laughing at the horrific entertainment—a biker gang band, by the looks of it, singing on the karaoke machine up front—and some of the sketchy patrons. They probably should've been terrified. The crowd was certainly eying them with suspicion.

"I feel like we're going to end up in a horror novel," Sophia laughed. "Guess this is why Tim would never bring us here."

"I mean, the wings are good. If we survive," he whispered, laughing. He was thankful for his military training and muscles at this point. Most of the sketchy patrons were either scrawny or really old. He felt like he could take them.

"This was a terrible idea," she said. "I'm sorry. I just thought... I thought if I went somewhere new, I wouldn't be thinking about him all night."

"It makes sense."

"Yeah. But we shouldn't have to come to some creepy place just so I don't bring him up."

"Stop being so hard on yourself," Jackson said, putting the wing down.

"I know. I just... I just feel like I need to be normal again. Do normal things. Go out. It's just so damn hard."

"It's always going to be. It's okay to struggle, Soph. I get it. Please don't feel like you can't struggle. You don't have to be perfect."

She smiled, nodding. "You're right. You're so right. Thank you. You want to get out of here? Go somewhere else?"

He looked at her, thinking. "No. I don't think I do." The biker gang had finished their final Sonny and Cher song, and the machine was empty. He wiped off his hands, and ordered her to do the same. She looked at him questioningly but complied.

He yanked her out of her seat, heading up front.

"Jackson, what the hell are you doing?" she hissed, her face paling.

"Come on. Let's do something crazy," he said, grabbing the mics up front. The rest of the bar stared at them like they were aliens.

"How you all doing tonight?" he said into the microphone. He handed the other one to Sophia. She refused.

"No way."

"Come on. You've got this. Plus, we don't know anyone here."

She sighed. "I don't sing."

"Me neither."

"Then what are we doing?" She tried to look dismayed, but he saw something beautiful on her face.

Excitement.

"We're doing something different, something crazy. Do you have a preference?"

She eyed him, probably thinking about turning him down.

But then, a fire sparked to life in her. He saw a glimpse of the girl she probably used to be, the girl who was spontaneous, spunky, and carefree. She headed over to the karaoke machine and made a selection.

Michael Jackson came on the system.

"Really? This is your pick?"

"Oh, don't tell me you don't like a little Michael Jackson? Come on. Who are you?"

He grimaced, looking up at the ceiling. The patrons of the bar glared at him, drinking their beverages and probably contemplating his murder.

"All right, I'm Jackson. But not Michael Jackson," he announced to the crowd, laughing at his own joke.

The patrons at the bar didn't budge, didn't give him a single laugh.

Sophia elbowed him. "Okay, no more comedian. Let's just sing."

Jackson would like to believe they made a perfect duo, singing on key to "Billy Jean" so well that the gruff men leaped to their feet and cheered at the bar.

In reality, the microphones' feedback blared. They forgot some of the words. He started to sweat.

In the middle, Sophia grabbed his hand, squeezing it. He finished out the song with her, holding on to the last note.

No one clapped or said anything when they exited the "stage" area, but it was okay.

"Oh my God, that was so fun," Sophia bubbled. "Can you believe we did that? We were awful. But it was fun."

He laughed, happy to see her happy. She was energized. She was having fun. She wasn't thinking about what she'd lost, at least for a few moments.

It was worth it. He'd take on every man in the bar. He'd sing Britney Spears' songs all night. He'd do the moonwalk if he could get her to smile.

When he dropped her off at her house an hour later, she was still beaming. "Thank you. I'm so glad we went out tonight. I haven't had so much fun since…" She froze, getting back into her head.

Jackson just nodded. He stood for a long moment outside her house, not sure what to do, how to act. He looked at her, her perfect skin, her bright eyes.

For a brief moment, he considered kissing her. She looked back, standing still, perhaps thinking the same thing. They stood in a moment of silence, gauging the situation, thinking about the night.

He stopped himself. He snapped out of it. He couldn't. He wouldn't ruin this night for her, wouldn't taint their good time.

"I had an amazing time, Sophia. Scary biker dudes and all."

"Maybe we could go out again sometime? You know, as friends."

"I'd like that. I like spending time with you."

She grinned, seemingly content with the outcome.

It was good enough for him. All he wanted was for her to be content. She went inside, and he glided back to his truck, back to his apartment to think about their night together.

He realized he wasn't lying. He had an amazing time. It wasn't the hot wings. It definitely wasn't the karaoke or the atmosphere.

It was her. She made everything better. She made his life seem better.

She made *him* better, he realized. She was making him into a better man, a selfless man, a man she deserved.

Life was complicated, and they were both dealing with so many demons. But he couldn't deny that together, nothing seemed so bad.

Chapter Twelve

JACKSON

"Can I please have another chocolate milk, Daddy?" Logan pleaded with his father from his high chair at the table, and the waitress smiled, looking to Jackson for an answer.

He should probably say no. Chloe would probably say no. But those eyes, the word "Daddy" coming out of his mouth. He just couldn't resist. "One more before we have to get going. We want to have enough time at the zoo."

"The zoo! Sounds awesome," a voice called from a few feet away. Jackson turned around to see a familiar pair.

Stella and Sophia.

He'd decided to bring Logan to Christine's Coffee for breakfast before their zoo adventure. He wanted to make the most of their day together before he was due back with Chloe.

"Hey, you two."

"Who's this?" Sophia asked as the two women crowded around the table. The waitress headed off to get the chocolate milk refill.

"Hey, this is Logan. Logan, can you say hi to my friends Stella and Sophia?"

"You have pink hair," the boy said, pointing to Stella.

She laughed. "Yes I do. And you have gorgeous curls."

"He's adorable," Sophia said, eyeing Jackson. Jackson beamed with pride.

"Yeah, he's pretty cute. Bad sometimes, but cute."

"I don't believe it," she said, smiling.

"Do you want to come to the zoo?" the boy asked Sophia.

"Sounds like fun. I love the zoo."

"Yeah, Logan loves animals. I figured since it isn't too cold out today, we would go walk around for a bit."

"Come with us," the boy implored, his toothy smile warming Jackson's heart.

"Buddy, I'm sure they're busy."

"Well, I am. I have a date with Larry. This one is free, aren't you?" Stella said mischievously, gesturing toward Sophia.

"I don't want to intrude," she replied bashfully.

"You wouldn't be. But I don't want you to feel like you have to come."

"Will you two stop already? You love zoo animals. It's a zoo, not a private wedding ceremony. You're not intruding. She doesn't feel obligated. You two make everything so difficult." Jackson and Sophia stared at Stella, who was shaking her head. "Honestly. She'll be over after we finish our coffees."

Sophia opened her mouth to say something. Stella just shoved her toward a booth. Sophia peered back, shrugged, and waved. Jackson smiled.

He knew the pink-haired girl would be a good thing.

The waitress delivered the chocolate milk to the table.

"Anything else?" she asked.

"Yeah. See those two women? I'll take their check please."

———————

"Squirrel!" Logan yelled as he raced to the enclosure.

"Buddy, it's a prairie dog," Jackson corrected.

"Squirrel!"

Jackson laughed, ruffling the boy's hair. "Squirrel it is."

Sophia smiled at him as the two walked behind Logan. Logan was entranced by all of the enclosures.

They'd gone to one of the indoor buildings to warm up. It was an above-average day for January, but a biting chill still hung in the air. It was a good thing Sophia reminded Jackson to bring Logan's hat and mittens.

They walked and laughed, eyeing the animals and smiling at Logan's amazement.

"This is fun. I'm glad Logan invited me," she said, her black sparkly hat making her blonde hair pop even more.

"I'm sorry if you felt obligated to come."

"Are you kidding? I love coming here. Tim would

sometimes bring me even though we didn't have kids. I love animals."

"You should have told me. It's so close to home."

"I didn't want you thinking I'd totally lost my mind."

"I wouldn't think that. I love coming here, too. If you love animals, why don't you have a pet?"

Sophia shrugged. "Tim always wanted a dog, but we were so busy. I was always busy at the shop, and he worked such long hours. I didn't feel like it would be fair."

"Is that why you guys were waiting to have kids?"

She looked away from Logan. "No. We were dealing with some issues. We were starting to seriously pursue adoption when... well, you know."

Jackson's stomach fell. "I'm sorry. I guess I have a knack for saying the wrong damn thing."

"Don't be sorry. It's okay."

They walked in silence, her hand on his arm as they chased after Logan. "He's adorable, you know. He looks just like you."

"Poor kid."

She nudged him. "Anything easing up with Chloe?"

"Are you kidding?"

"Sorry. Dumb question."

A zoo worker took Logan to a nearby enclosure, showing him the tortoise.

"Daddy!" Logan screamed. "Can I feed him?"

The zoo worker nodded, hinting that it was okay and that she would help him.

"Sure, bud. That's fine."

Jackson turned to Sophia, standing back and watching Logan with his peripheral vision. "I'm going to get the ball rolling on the appeal soon. I think I've shown the courts I've settled in, established myself. I'm working steadily at the restaurant. I'm making good money now. I've moved up to master chef."

"Really? That's awesome. Congratulations!"

"Yeah. I've decided I'm not ready to give up hope yet."

"What changed your mind?"

He stopped, turning slightly. "You."

She looked baffled. "Me?"

"Yeah. I see the way you haven't lost hope, the way you keep moving, keep going on."

"I don't really have a choice."

"Give yourself more credit, Sophia. You're such a strong woman. You've been through the wringer these past few months, and you still manage to flash that gorgeous smile. It's inspired me."

She looked away, embarrassed. Finally, she looked back to him. "You've inspired me, too."

"Oh yeah?"

"Yeah. I've realized Tim's death isn't the end of everything. I miss him like hell, I do. But you've made me realize life's still worth it. It's okay to be happy."

He looked down at her, the gorgeous woman whom he had found in the midst of tragedy.

He heard Logan chattering away to the tortoise in the background, could see the zoo worker out of the corner of his eye busy with his son.

It was a rash thing to do, really. A stupid thing. A foolish, selfish, guilt-ridden pleasure kind of thing. At the moment, however, Jackson wasn't thinking about the zoo or the fact the woman in front of him was his best friend's widow.

All he was thinking about was how her hair fell in soft waves down her back, how her skin looked touchable and soft. He was thinking about how her waist felt in his hands, how it felt to have her hand on his arm. He was thinking about her laughter, her pizzazz, her sense of humor.

So he did something he hadn't planned, something he didn't think he would do, especially after stopping himself the other night.

Leaning down, slowly, ever so slowly, he found her lips with his, tugging gently on them, hesitating long enough for her to pull away if she wanted to.

But she didn't.

For a single moment, everything faded away, all of the hurt, the sorrow, the grief.

For a moment, they were everything, linked together by a kiss neither expected.

Chapter Thirteen

SOPHIA

"Stella... Stella!" she screamed inside the doorway of her best friend's apartment. She heard voices from the bedroom, and suddenly she realized what a terrible idea this was. She couldn't just prance into her best friend's apartment. She was probably with Larry. This was ridiculous.

A moment later, Stella came running from the bedroom, wrapped in a robe. "Sophia? What's wrong?" Stella's hair was frizzy, ruffled in the signature look of a woman not wanting to be interrupted.

"Oh God, Stella. I'm an idiot. Larry's here, isn't he? I'm sorry. This is embarrassing."

Stella approached her. "It's fine. What's wrong?"

Sophia slumped to the couch, too upset to worry about

social niceties and the awkwardness of the situation.

"Everything."

Stella took a seat by her friend. "Spill."

"It's Jackson. We kissed."

Stella's face registered shock, but not *Oh my God, I can't believe you* shock—more like happy shock.

"Sophia! That's awesome. I knew it."

It was Sophia's turn to drop her jaw. "What? You knew what?"

"That you liked him."

Sophia sprang from the couch. "Stella, no, it's not like that. He's Tim's friend, and Tim hasn't been gone long. I'm not looking to move on."

"Calm down, it's fine. You might not be looking to move on, but maybe your heart is saying otherwise. You're young, Soph. No one expects you to stay in mourning forever."

"It's only been six months. It's too soon."

"Yeah, it's too soon to rush down the aisle. But a kiss? With a good man? Who could blame you?"

"Me. Tim."

"Tim would not blame you."

"Are you kidding? This was his friend."

"Soph, calm down. It's not like you had sex."

Sophia's heart stopped. "Oh my God. I'm such an idiot. I can't believe I did this. I'm a terrible wife."

Stella rose to hug her. "Hey, listen to me," she said, lifting Sophia's chin to look at her. "You're not a terrible wife. You're a good wife. You were the best. And you're grieving. There's no right or wrong to it. Seriously. Ease up on yourself. Jackson makes you happy. I can see it when you talk about him. I can see it when you look at him. There's nothing wrong with that. Stop shutting yourself off to possibility. Stop trying to grieve in the socially acceptable way. You're not cheating on Tim. You're not turning your back on him. He's gone, Soph. *He is gone.* And you're left here. He would want you to be happy, no matter what that looks like."

Tears rolled down Sophia's face now, a torrent of moisture dampening her cheeks. "I'm not ready to let him go. I want him back."

"I know. I know. But that can't happen, love. It just can't."

They embraced for a moment. Footsteps approached from the bedroom.

Larry stood before them, clad in his underwear and a T-shirt.

"Hey, Soph," he said casually, and Sophia shielded her eyes.

"Larry," she said, trying not to look.

"Larry Anderson, get back to the bedroom. This is private."

He pretended to salute her and headed back.

She shook her head. "Men."

"In his defense, I think what you two were doing was private, and I intruded."

"Stop, don't be ridiculous. We'll be spending the whole day in bed anyway, so we have plenty of time."

"I didn't really need to know that."

"Stop being a prude. Maybe that's your problem. You were only with one man, right? Tim was it for you? See, maybe that's why this is getting to you so much. You've been living the monogamous life too long. Now's your chance."

"Stella, you know people might call you insensitive for saying that."

"Look, I loved Tim, and I'm sad about what happened. But you need to be... satisfied... if you know what I mean.... You're only in your early thirties. So I say, follow this thing with Jackson where it goes. Enjoy it while it lasts. It's not like you have to marry him." She dramatically winked at the end.

Sophia grinned, shaking her head. She swiped a few tears. "I should have known better than to come to you for moral advice."

"I'll take that as a compliment. Now, before you go and I get back to, um, Larry... tell me about it."

"About our kiss?"

"No, you idiot. About the socks you knitted. Yes, the kiss. How was it?"

"It was by the tortoise."

"Um kinky, maybe?"

Sophia slapped her friend on the arm. "No. His son was nearby. He was busy feeding the tortoise and Jackson just, well, he just kissed me."

"And?"

"And it was phenomenal, okay? Like, I didn't want it to stop. Afterward, though, guilt tainted the whole thing. See, this is why nothing can come of this. I'll just feel guilty."

"So drink lots of wine afterward, wash away the shame, and you'll be none the wiser."

"Please don't ever go into counseling."

"Wasn't planning on it. Look, I love you. It will be fine. Stop worrying about how you're supposed to act and just act, okay?"

Sophia nodded, feeling strangely better after her chat with Stella. "I'll let you get back to Larry now, I suppose?"

Stella winked. "And I'll let you get back to Jackson. But please, no more tortoise stuff, all right? If you want to spice it up, I'll give you some pointers that don't involve creepy creatures."

Sophia shook her head. "You're ridiculous. But I love you. Thanks for helping me with my mini meltdown."

"What are friends for?"

And with that, she winked and turned to go back to her Sunday afternoon activities while Sophia headed home alone.

———

"Okay, Mrs. Snowson, what color are you thinking?" Sophia asked the next morning. An evening of Netflix and wine, as Stella had suggested, had done the trick. She'd come into the shop feeling much better about everything.

Stella, on the other hand, didn't look like she was feeling good about anything. Apparently she and Larry had too many activities last night.

"This golden red color is perfect," the elderly lady said. "But don't make it too red. And I don't want it orange. So be careful." Sophia nodded, silently heading over to mix up the color. Mrs. Snowson was a nice lady—although also very bossy. She wasn't afraid to tell Sophia if she hated her hair or demand her to redo it. It was going to be a long morning.

When she returned, she started carefully painting Mrs. Snowson's chin-length hair.

"So how is your boyfriend, dear?" The woman eyed her with a smug look, and Sophia's stomach dropped. Stella glanced over, appraising the situation.

"Um, Mrs. Snowson, I don't understand…" It was a small town. Everyone knew about Tim's death.

"The guy with the kid? Jackson, is it? Word has it you were locking lips at the zoo yesterday."

Sophia looked in the mirror, seeing herself blush. The pit of her stomach had the sinking feeling similar to when she was plummeting down a roller coaster. Except this roller coaster felt like it was lurching inconsistently toward her utter demise.

"Um, I… who did you hear this from?"

"My neighbor Jessie saw you two. She had her five-year-old girl, Veronica, there yesterday. Apparently they were in the same building as you and witnessed the kiss."

Sophia froze, looking to Stella. She didn't know what to say. This had been one of her fears. What should she say? Should she apologize? Explain?

She didn't owe this woman any explanation. Like Stella said, her husband was dead. It wasn't like she was cheating on her husband.

"What, Tim's only been gone, like six months now? Right? If it were me, I don't think I'd be able to move on so quickly." Mrs. Snowson's eyes met Sophia's in the mirror.

Tears started stinging her eyes. She saw the prideful, snooty look of Mrs. Snowson. The woman was clearly just trying to make her feel bad.

It was working.

Before Sophia could assess the situation or figure out how to proceed, Stella stomped over, a flat iron in her hand. She kneeled down into the old woman's face, so close they were almost nose to nose.

"Get the hell out." Stella's voice was barely a whisper, but it was punctuated with such rage, everyone froze.

"Excuse me?"

"I said get the hell out of our shop. And don't *fucking* come back." Stella punctuated the final line, her voice in a solid crescendo. Her own client sat stone-faced. Sophia's mouth fell open, her eyes widened. What was Stella doing?

Mrs. Snowson didn't say a word. She simply creaked out of the chair, her hair painted with a few streaks of color, grabbed her purse, and headed to the door.

Sophia awaited a rude remark or an angry threat from the woman, but none came. She couldn't blame her. Stella had been quite frightening.

Stella nodded at Sophia, headed back to her client, and continued working.

"So, did you say you wanted your ends flipped under or up?" she asked with a huge smile and a cheerful tone to her voice. The client, a middle-aged woman who was introverted on a normal day, just nodded. "Flipped under it is!" Stella proclaimed, spinning the chair cheerfully, acting as if she hadn't just flown into a rage and threatened a client.

Sophia marched to the back room to get herself together before her next client.

She couldn't believe the nerve of Mrs. Snowson. Then again, this wasn't really the woman's fault. It had been her own. Mrs. Snowson was right. It had been six months since Tim's death. Six lonely, lousy months. What kind of message was she sending? How much could Tim have meant if after all those years together, she only spent six months grieving for him?

She had to cool things down with Jackson. As good as his lips felt on hers, as good as it was to be with him, she had to put some distance there.

She had to grieve for Tim.

Chapter Fourteen

She looked around to make sure no one was nearby, and then she felt like an idiot. She wasn't breaking into someone's house, and she wasn't on a spy mission. This was just an adult, widowed woman going to a friend's house to talk. She had nothing to be guilty about.

Mrs. Snowson, though, had made her paranoid. She was worried about becoming the talk of the town—although apparently she already was.

She'd called Jackson a few hours ago, still having his phone number from their encounter at the mall.

"Can I come over?"

"Yeah, of course," he'd happily replied and given her his address. He'd sounded pleased, content to hear from her. He had no way of knowing how wrong things were.

He answered the door wearing a simple gray T-shirt and jeans, his signature two-day stubble accenting his jawline. His rugged hand extended toward his apartment, and she tried not to think about how firm, how strong his hands felt on her. She tried not to look at those lips that had expertly parted hers, or the gorgeous steel eyes that had made her feel like putty a couple short days ago.

"Come on in," he said, leading her in. The place was simple, bare. It was missing a woman's touch, only the basic essentials visible. It was clear he had probably tidied up because there were no signs of living. That, or he was a total clean freak.

"Can I sit down?" she asked formally. He scrunched his eyebrows, clearly detecting this visit wasn't a jovial one.

"Yeah, go ahead," he said, leading her toward the sofa. He sat a respectable distance away, obviously sensing she needed space.

She clutched her purse on her lap, fiddling with the strap as she talked.

"I wanted to talk about the other day, at the zoo."

He waited, not saying anything, apparently waiting for her to take the lead.

"It was a mistake. I'm sorry I was swept up in it. I feel awful."

"I'm the one who initiated it, Sophia. You have nothing to be sorry about."

"I do. I do have to be sorry. Because it wasn't right. Your son was there. Tim hasn't been gone very long, and he was your friend. We have no right to be kissing."

He inched closer to her now, reaching for her hand. She pulled away, looking up at him and wincing.

"Don't."

He pulled back, clearly wondering what had changed. "Sophia, I know this is hard. And awkward. But I'm not sorry about our kiss. Not at all. It was amazing."

"I know. And that's the problem. It *was* amazing. But my life with Tim was amazing, too. People are talking in town, and it's disrespectful. People think I didn't care about him, that I've forgotten him. That I've just thrown out our life together."

"What people are talking?"

"A lady in the beauty shop. She said some things about us."

"Who is it?"

"It doesn't matter, Jackson. That's not the point. The point is I can't go around kissing you in public like I'm a free woman. Because I'm not."

"But you are."

"No, I'm not! I still love him, Jackson. *I still love him.* We can't just rebound with each other."

"It wasn't a rebound, not for me."

Sophia didn't say anything, was afraid to admit the truth. It wasn't a rebound for her either. It wasn't. But she couldn't say that. What kind of woman fell for a new man after six months? What kind of woman fell for her late husband's best friend? She couldn't do this. She owed Tim more respect.

"Jackson, I appreciate everything you've done for

me these past months. You've made this bearable. I love spending time with you. But we can't anymore."

"Sophia, don't do this. Tim would want you to be happy."

"No, Jackson. Tim would want to be here with me if he could. He would want to be the one kissing me, and dancing with me, and holding me. But he can't. And I can't go off with his best friend. I can't do it, Jackson. Every time I look at you, I feel guilty." Tears were now flowing down her face. She tried to wipe them away. She stood up, walking to the edge of the living room to avoid his face, his eyes that would certainly make her lose her nerve.

"I can't spend time with you anymore. I'm sorry."

He leapt up to stop her, but she brushed by him. Tears flowing, she managed to make it to the door. She walked out the door, her resolve steadfast. Not stopping to hear his thoughts, she shut the door behind her.

She was doing the right thing. She was making the respectable choice.

It didn't mean her heart wasn't aching. For the first time in a while, she felt utterly, coldly alone, lost in a vast sea of dismal gloom and hopelessness.

———————

"Don't be mad."

"Why would I be mad?"

"Just trust me."

"What have you two done?"

"Close your eyes."

"Stella?"

"Just close them."

Sophia sighed, not truly wanting to comply. She was feeling more blue than usual after the whole Mrs. Snowson fiasco and the *I can't see you anymore* episode. She'd been doing the usual these days—watching Netflix. Alone. Stella was on a date with Larry.

Or so Sophia thought. Because now the two were standing in her living room, giddy as two children on Christmas morning. It was making her nervous.

"You two are scaring me."

"It's not scary. It's perfect. I should've thought of it sooner. Just don't be mad."

"When you say that, it makes me mad already."

Sophia sighed, peering at Stella first and then Larry. Finally, she succumbed to Stella's orders and closed her eyes.

"Now what?"

"Now we wait for Larry to go to the car and get your surprise."

"You do know I told you I'm not celebrating my birthday this year."

"You know I never listen. Besides, your birthday isn't until next week. We'll call it a 'yay, it's the end of January' gift."

"The 'yay, it's the end of January' gift better not be a blind date. Because I'm in my pajamas."

"Oh, he won't mind."

Sophia's heart stopped. She opened her eyes. "What?

Are you serious?" Panic ensued.

"Shut your eyes," Stella demanded, putting a hand over Sophia's face.

"I'm going to kill you."

"Not yet you're not. Oh, here he is!" Stella let out a squeal, and Sophia tried to move her hand.

"Can I open them yet?" Sophia was nervous as hell. Then she was even more nervous because something was sniffing her foot.

"Open them!" Stella proclaimed, clapping cheerfully as Sophia looked down to see her surprise.

A floppy, clumsy tan puppy with a black muzzle waddled around Sophia's feet.

Her jaw fell open and she eyed the two curiously. "A puppy? Are you kidding?"

"What? It's awesome. You're always sitting here, alone. Now you'll have a Netflix buddy."

"Guys, I can't keep it. No, no, no."

The puppy sniffed her foot, but she tried not to look at its fluffy cuteness. It tripped over her foot, and she almost laughed.

Almost.

She crossed her arms, staring Stella down. "This is a terrible surprise. I don't have time for a puppy."

"You have plenty of time," Stella said, not backing down. "Plus, he's adorable. And expensive. But mostly adorable. So you can't reject him. Look at him, he loves you already."

Sophia took a deep breath. "Guys, I appreciate it, but really..."

"Hold him," Stella demanded, picking up the puppy and placing it in Sophia's arms. "Love him. He just wants to be loved."

Sophia felt the big—and mighty heavy—bundle of fur in her arms. He was soft and warm, and he was giving her the doughiest eyes she'd ever seen. She felt her heart melt just a little bit.

"He's freaking heavy. How old is he? Like eight months?"

"Um, eight weeks."

Sophia froze. "What? What is he?"

"A mastiff. My best friend breeds them," Larry chimed in, reaching over to pat the dog's head.

"Wait, don't these things get really big?"

"Only about 270 pounds top weight. Not too bad, right?"

Sophia's jaw dropped again. She placed the puppy on the ground. "Okay, that seals it. No way. Not happening."

"Stop being a jerk. You're falling for him. I can see it. Give him a chance. It'll be good for you."

Sophia wanted to say no. Her head screamed nine million reasons why this puppy needed to get back in the car and go away.

But her heart, well, it was falling for him every minute. The face, those eyes, the clumsy steps.

Plus, it would be good to have a guard dog, right? Safety first.

"Fine. I'll keep him."

Stella squealed and clapped, jumping up and down. "I knew it! I knew you'd love him. Now what are you naming him?"

Sophia smiled, without hesitating. "Henry."

"Henry? Where'd that come from?"

"When I was little, I used to read the *Henry and Mudge* books."

"Wait, wasn't Henry the little boy?" Larry asked.

"You read those too?" Stella asked.

"Of course. But I'm pretty sure Henry is the boy."

"I think you're right. But whatever, I like Henry," Sophia retorted, picking the puppy up again now that she'd committed. She quickly shifted the puppy in her arms, his weight making her limbs go numb. The puppy playfully pulled on her shirt with its razor sharp puppy teeth, but she couldn't be mad. Looking into his eyes, she couldn't feel anything except sheer joy.

"Thanks, guys. You're right. This is perfect."

They stood, the three of them and the puppy, in a silent, beautiful moment worthy of a commercial. Sophia was just getting ready to tell Henry how much she loved him, how happy she was to have him.

And then, like so many things in her life right now, everything fell apart.

Sophia suddenly felt a warm sensation down the front of her shirt. She glanced down as a tinkling sound ricocheted from the hardwood floor. There was a lapse between the sound and her brain registering what was happening. Then she realized what the warmth was and what the tinkling sound was.

Henry had peed on her. As in all over her. Soaking, dripping pee. Sophia screamed, handing the puppy to

Larry. Henry peed on Larry who passed Henry to Stella.

Henry was, luckily for Stella, all empty. He licked her face.

Larry and Sophia glared at Stella.

"What? It's not my fault. Here, get together, let me take a photo for Instagram." Stella was laughing at this point as Larry and Sophia tried to fling the warm liquid off.

Stella just kept laughing, Henry's puppy barks only adding to the sound.

Chapter Fifteen

JACKSON

Jackson finished his shift at the restaurant, punched out, and headed home. Some of the crew were going out for drinks, but he didn't want to. It had nothing to do with his resolution to be a better man, although he wished he could claim that was it. He just didn't feel like socializing or being around anyone.

He felt like shit.

He felt terrible about the kiss. What was he thinking, putting Sophia in that position? She'd just lost her husband. She wasn't ready for a kiss, especially with him. She was off-limits. He'd promised himself he would keep her that way.

But those eyes. Her hair. Her laugh that was so rare

these days. He'd do anything to make her smile, to make her happy.

It wasn't something he wanted to admit or acknowledge. He'd tried over these past few months to reassure himself he was just helping her out as a friend, just doing what was right by Tim. In actuality, he was just being selfish.

He was falling for her.

Some would probably say it was just a rebound. He'd lost Chloe, who at one point had been the love of his life. Yes, he'd loved her, and it hurt like hell she'd been unfaithful. It was agony. He'd been crazy about her. But it was so different than what he felt now.

Chloe had been about passion, about rash decisions, about spur of the moment feelings. He'd barely known her when he'd said, "I do." He'd barely known her when they said goodbye.

Sophia was different. Chloe was a woman you raced to the altar with. Sophia was one you languidly strolled beside, not wanting to rush, not wanting to move too fast for fear of missing a single moment. She was the kind of woman who grounded him, who made him want to be better. She was the kind of woman he could see an entire future with.

She wasn't a rebound for him. She was a reawakening. He'd thought he'd known love with Chloe. Now he realized their relationship hadn't even been the tip of an iceberg.

Driving home in his dilapidated, rusty old truck, he shook his head, holding back tears. It didn't matter what he felt. *It didn't matter.* Sophia had walked away from everything. He'd messed everything up. He didn't even have a friendship to cling to anymore.

He didn't blame her. Love was scary, especially after what she'd lost. Plus, there was Tim to think about. He understood why she was racked with guilt because he was too. He knew why she was worried about the whispers, the stares.

Jackson felt like an asshole for not standing back. She was vulnerable. He should've been the rational one, the one to put a stop to whatever was growing between them. He should have protected her from himself, from their growing chemistry, from the uncertainty of their friendship growing into something else. He should be glad she walked away, glad he wouldn't have to resist anymore. It was out of his hands.

But he wasn't glad. He was miserable. He felt like he'd been lifted out of his despair, out of his lonely apartment where alcohol was the only thing that moved him. With Sophia, he'd seen a glimpse of hope for the future, of what life could be like, of what a real woman who completed him looked like.

Then, without warning, the glimpse faded, trashed by his mistake, by a feeling of betrayal toward his best friend and her husband. He was right back where he started, alone, depressed, and feeling like nothing was worth it anymore. Except it was worse now because he'd had a chance to see what happiness could actually look like.

It was crazy, but he *had* been happy. They had trodden cautiously from acquaintances to friends to... whatever they had been a few days ago. There hadn't been crazy, romantic moments and gestures because their relationship was one with odd rules. They'd shared some subs, an impromptu Christmas walk, a trip to the zoo. Regardless, he'd been happy. He'd felt more love, more romance in their encounters than he'd ever felt with Chloe.

At first, he'd wondered if the taboo status of her had been what attracted him so much. A suppressed rebel deep down, he never liked rules or lines in the sand. He always desired a way around them. But no, it was more than that. It wasn't just because he *wasn't* supposed to love her that his heart craved her. As he pulled into the driveway to his sad apartment, he realized with certainty it was because he *was* supposed to love her that he did. The more time they spent together, the more she tried to pull away, the more he realized loving Sophia was all he was meant to do.

The rest was unimportant.

———————

"So call her, you idiot," Gretta announced as she shoved some cheese and crackers in her mouth. Jackson sat at their parents' kitchen table across from Gretta and Jonathan. They were at his parents' home for a Sunday dinner, a monthly tradition. Jonathan was also going to review some appeal options with him. He hadn't planned on spewing about Sophia to his chatty, blunt sister. But she had caught on that something wasn't quite right.

"Why are you so mopey?" she'd asked over the

appetizers their mother had set out—he always knew when he came for Sunday dinner, he didn't need to eat for a week beforehand.

"Gretta," Jonathan prodded, giving her a look.

"I know, I know. Stuff sucks right now. But little brother, you look even more down than usual. What gives?"

"Nothing. Everything. I don't know." He'd readjusted his beanie as he'd said it, debating on whether or not to confide. It would be nice to get a second opinion on the situation.

"Gretta, stop giving your brother a hard time," his mother had chastised from near the stove, where she was putting final touches on the pot roast.

Gretta rolled her eyes. "You're in your thirties, and she still babies you. Good God, the favoritism."

Jackson smirked. "Not my fault I'm the baby of the family."

"Will you two stop?" Jonathan pleaded. "We have serious things to discuss."

"Yeah, like what's wrong."

Jackson took a breath. Then he confessed everything. He could feel his mom's ears listening in, could see Gretta's eyes twinkling.

Now she'd said what he'd been hoping she would say. She'd encouraged him to pursue Sophia, to at least call her. But he still wasn't sure.

"I don't know. It feels... wrong."

At this point, his mother paraded to the table with the pot roast, smiling wistfully at her son. She put the roaster down on a hot pad in the center of the ancient wooden table before placing a hand on his shoulder. "Your sister's right. Call her."

"Mom, don't you think it's inappropriate? Tim was my best friend."

"Honey, Tim's gone. You're still here. And you're wonderful, kind, and sweet. Tim would be crazy to want anyone except you with Sophia."

"See, what I mean? Favorite," Gretta teased as she hurried to finish her cracker, her bright red lipstick rubbing off.

"Oh, hush," their mother demanded as she walked back to the stove to get the rest of the food she'd prepared— which was enough to serve a family of twenty.

For the rest of the meal, Jackson's uncertainty eased. He didn't know if he'd call her, didn't know if he'd brave it. At least he had reassurance from his family he wasn't a creep or a jerk, and that he wasn't at fault for what his heart wanted. Coming from his mouthy sister, the woman who told him Chloe was a bitch upon meeting her, the woman who told him he'd never last two minutes in Iraq, well, it was something.

Gretta might be obnoxious sometimes and less than tactful, but she was honest. If she thought it was okay to call Sophia, well, then maybe it was.

Chapter Sixteen

JACKSON

On Wednesday, Jackson found himself with a rare morning off and decided instead of lying on the couch, he'd reconnect with the army body he'd once possessed. He snatched his running shoes from his bedroom floor, heading outside to jog off some nervous energy.

He'd pondered over his family's opinion for the past few days, thinking about their words of wisdom as he perused the television channels, as he went out on Monday with Evan, who was back in town for a few days, as he talked sports with the guys at work. He'd given it time, given her space, thought it would be good to think on it.

But he'd missed her. God, he'd missed her.

He'd missed the easy certainty of their walks in the evening, strolling together talking about anything they needed to get off their chests. He missed their playful banter, the jovial way she pushed him when he said something annoying. He missed the touch of her hand on his arm, the look in her eyes when he said something funny.

Still, he wasn't sure what to do with it all. It was such a weird situation, a guilt-ridden situation. Maybe he should just let it be.

Jogging down the block, he studied the sky. A thin fog lifted from the town, creating an eerie aura. The sun's rays crept through as the fiery ball began its great ascent. Snow at least temporarily melted, the morning was warmer than it had been in recent days. Still, a chill in the air bit into his bare fingers and slapped against his face, reminding him it would be a while until permanently spring-like weather took over.

He followed the path so familiar to him in childhood, dashing down Allegheny, up Maple. He ran until his chest heaved and his legs burned with exhaustion. He persevered, though, a destination in mind.

Before he knew it, he was there, standing at the edge of the park. Desolation marked the park at this hour and only a few young children played with their parents. Most of the town, however, was quiet and empty. It was refreshing to see the town devoid of people, the buildings and trees the only company.

He ran down the path into the park's entrance, deciding to head to a bench he'd once loved as a child. He'd spent a lot of time here with Tim, frolicking in the fields, playing on the jungle gym. A warm nostalgia of childhood permeated through him.

When he arrived at the spot, he bent over to catch his breath, hands on his knees. Wheezing, he realized how much he'd let himself go. Restaurant food, hours on the couch, and alcohol would wreck even the best military physique. He was slipping. He needed to make this a habit.

He sank down onto a shoddy bench, age weathering it to a state of utter ruin. He rested on its uneven slats, stretching his legs, taking in the misty sight of the empty fields before him. He shoved his hands in the pocket of his hoodie, leaned back, and stared at the sky.

Only the sounds of a few playing children interrupted his trance. It was soothing to be here, out of his apartment, alone. In his apartment, he felt lonely and depressed. Here, he was still alone, but somehow it was different. It felt like a good kind of alone.

Then it was all gone, disturbed by the screaming of a woman's voice.

"Dammit! Come back!"

He looked to his right to see a blonde woman in sweatpants, a hoodie, and what appeared to be yellow Crocs dashing after a floppy puppy. It took his mind a few moments to catch up, but eventually, recognition set in.

He smiled at the sight, at the coincidence, and at the fact that this was all coming together on a bench he used to visit with Tim.

Maybe coincidences weren't coincidences at all.

―――――――

"Gotcha!" he yelled once he snatched the ball of fur from the grass. The puppy licked his face, and despite his exhaustion and frustration from chasing the wild puppy for the past three minutes, he chuckled. Puppy breath never got old.

She came a few seconds behind him, heaving from exhaustion, her hair an utter mess. Her ponytail was falling out, she could barely talk, and her face was damp with perspiration, despite the chill in the air.

"Thank. You," she managed to punctuate as she took the puppy from his arms, her breath floating in ringlets in the biting air.

"You're welcome. What happened? Here, come sit down for a few and catch your breath." He led her to the bench, where she graciously sat, attaching a leash from her pocket to the puppy's collar.

"I didn't think he could run so fast. I took him outside to pee. I didn't have time to get a fence yet. And he must've seen a rabbit or something because—bam!—he was gone."

"He ran from your house?" It was only about six blocks away, but still, it was probably quite a feat when you were chasing a spastic puppy.

She nodded. "A car almost smooshed Henry. A car almost smooshed me. It was awful. I'm so glad you were here." After she said the words, she looked embarrassed.

"So I take it his name is Henry?" He didn't want to give her a chance to end the conversation prematurely, so he decided to pick neutral conversation territory.

"Yep."

"When did you get him?"

"I didn't. Stella and Larry bought him for me. I'm so glad," she said, sarcasm dripping from her words. He noticed, however, that there was a glimmer of a smile on her face as she eyed the puppy, despite the harrowing morning events.

"He's adorable. It'll get better. We all have our rough days, huh, bud?" Jackson said, petting the dog. He'd always been a sucker for dogs.

"Well, I hope so. So far, he's almost worn out his welcome. He kept me up all night last night, and then this morning, we had this escapade. I'm so sorry. You must've thought I'd lost my mind. Plus, I look terrible."

"Not true. About the looking terrible part."

She nudged him. "So you think I'm crazy?"

He made a gesture with his hand to say, "a little," and she laughed.

"You're probably right. I do feel a bit crazy sometimes."

"Don't we all?"

They sat for a moment as if neither knew what to say.

"Sophia," he started just as she stood to say she better get going. "Sophia, wait."

He stood, too, facing her, the dog's leash in her hand.

She shook her head. "Jackson, I can't."

He took a breath. It was now or never.

"Sophia, I know this whole thing is complicated. A train wreck even. Neither of us expected Tim to die. We didn't think there would be anything between us. But dammit, there is. We can't pretend it's not there or that it'll go away because we want it to. And the truth is, I've been thinking about it. I don't want it to go away, Sophia. You're the best thing that's happened to me since Logan. Seriously. I know I'm not the best thing that's ever happened to you. I know that was Tim. But he's gone. I wish he weren't. I wish he were here right now to kick my ass for saying this to you. He's not. He's not here, so we have to go on with our lives. The thing is, I miss you. I think I'm falling for you."

He exhaled, staring into her blue eyes, which were now watering. She looked to the ground for a minute, more tears welling, as he stood in agony, not knowing what he'd just done. He'd been courageous; he'd said what he wanted to say. Maybe it was too much.

Just when he was giving up hope, just when he was ready to apologize, she looked up. Her frizzy hair and tears punctuated her bewildered state, but to him, she was gorgeous, a radiant being.

"The thing is, Jackson, I think I'm falling for you too. And it scares me and it makes me feel like shit because of everything. But I miss you too."

He opened his mouth to respond, but before he could say anything, she was on her tiptoes, her lips moving on his, their bodies melding to each other. She kissed him hard, forcefully, like she meant it this time.

And he kissed her right back, pouring all of his fears and doubts into one kiss, pouring a lifetime of regrets and hopes and fears and dreams into the moment between them.

When they finally pulled apart, he noticed the misty fog in the background and the quietness of the area. It was as if time had stopped for them, and in many ways, time *had* stopped. They were no longer Jackson and Sophia from their past… they were the Jackson and Sophia who could carry each other into a new future.

She laughed then, looking down at her feet. "So that was all it took to bore him and wear him out?" she joked. Henry was curled up on her feet, dead asleep.

"Yep, write it down. All you have to do is chase him six blocks through traffic in yellow Crocs, find a hunky military man to stop him, make out with said military man, and presto. Henry's tired."

"Hey, what's wrong with my Crocs?"

"We just had a beautiful moment, I talk about myself being hunky, and all you're worried about is if I like your Crocs?"

"I work in the beauty industry. I have to keep a reputation for looking good, you know."

He wrapped his fingers around her wrist and pulled her back in. "You look good no matter what you're wearing," he whispered, and he took her lips with his again.

"I don't know where this is going, Jackson Gauge, and I don't even know completely if it's right. But God, it feels good," she whispered into his mouth as they kissed for a long time, only stopping to walk back to her house, his arm around her shoulders.

It was sealed.

Jackson Gauge was a new man once more.

Chapter Seventeen

Despite Henry's incessant crying and two impromptu potty breaks, Sophia slept better that night. Tim's side of the bed was still empty, and she still missed him like hell. Her heart still burned when she woke up and the realization of his absence sunk in.

Still, it was a little easier. She didn't feel the complete and utter debilitation of his absence. She didn't have a constant stream of thoughts rotating through her head about how long until her time here was done. Suddenly, she felt something she hadn't felt in a while—hope.

She'd told herself the kiss was not a big deal, that it shouldn't be a big deal. She told herself it was just two lonely adults turning to each other. In her heart, though, she knew better. When Jackson Gauge had kissed her, when she had kissed him back, everything had slipped away, all of the bad anyway. Suddenly, she saw so clearly what she'd been trying to ignore.

He was good for her, and she was good for him.

It still wouldn't be easy. She knew it was an odd situation, an awkward turn of events. She tried not to think about what others would say or how people would react. She tried not to think about the time frame of it or how it fit into the appropriate cycle of grief. For once since Tim died, she tried not to think at all. Instead, she focused on leaving her heart open to experience what it would, what it wanted to. She would worry about the logic and the rational thinking later, if at all.

The familiar whining stirred her from her dreams, but her head was still foggy.

"I'm coming," she croaked as she struggled to lift herself out of bed.

In the middle of the night, she'd been submerged in a wistful atmosphere of magic thanks to the kiss. However, at 6:30 a.m., Henry's ceaseless need for early trips to the grass was wearing on her.

"I'm too old for this," she mumbled as she went to the dog's cage to get him and take him outside. She leashed up the dog—she'd learned her lesson after yesterday— before stomping out the front door.

It was a much colder morning than yesterday, so

she wrapped herself tightly in her robe. Frost painted the grass, and the air warned of a coming storm. Henry yanked her toward the side yard, and she stumbled. As she glanced into the unnerving darkness, she caught sight of someone in the yard a distance from the back door. Her heart stopped, and she contemplated running back inside. Exhaustion prevented her from doing anything of the sort. She squinted into the darkness. Henry, peeing in the grass, woofed so weakly, it was laughable. So much for a guard dog.

Someone appeared to be stooping down in the backyard near the giant oak tree. She crept closer to the backyard to get a better view. Everything in her told her to go inside and call the cops, but she was just too damn intrigued. So she did what every ditz did in the horror movie, the ditz she often made fun of—she walked closer to the point of interest. Sophia figured she couldn't poke fun at the idiots in the movies anymore and ask why they would do something so dumb.

"Hello?" she whispered into the early morning air. The figure turned, still blurry in the blackness.

"Sophia? Did I wake you? I'm sorry."

Jackson. She breathed a sigh of relief. Then confusion set in.

"What the hell are you doing? It's 6:30."

"I'm sorry. I was trying to be quiet. I have to be at work at 8:00, so I had to come early."

She walked the dog closer, and Henry jumped on Jackson's leg, tail wagging.

"You're going to get the police called on you. Or shot." She peered at the yard near him, confusion eventually giving way to realization. "What are you doing anyway?"

He sighed. "Listen, I knew you needed an area for Henry. I couldn't install an actual fence with the ground frozen solid, so I had to make do." Jackson motioned toward a strong, fifteen-foot leash tethered around the base of the tree. Sophia grinned.

"I was going to leave a note on your door. This should make things easier for you. You won't have to worry about the guy running off. . . as long as you make sure his collar is secure."

Sophia gave it a try, buckling the hook to Henry's collar. Henry pranced around the tree, tangling himself up.

"Okay, well it seemed like a good idea," Jackson said, laughing as he tried to untangle the dog. Henry was so excited, he was jumping all over Jackson. Despite her grogginess, Sophia had to laugh.

"You do know you could have waited until later? You didn't have to come at the crack of dawn. Or before it. I feel awful."

"You should." He smiled. She was close enough to appreciate it now.

"Or maybe I should feel worried. Only a crazy man would be doing this."

"Or a man who doesn't want to see Henry get away again."

"You just don't want to chase him again."

"Maybe. Or maybe I just wanted to try to do something

to help out."

"Well, I appreciate it. Really. You shouldn't have done all of this." Henry was mercifully unwrapped and now peeing on the tree. He let out a gruff bark, and Sophia wrapped her arms around herself, the freezing air chilling her lungs.

"I'm going to go inside and make some coffee and breakfast before I freeze. Do you want to come in?"

"Sounds awesome."

Jackson unhooked Henry, following Sophia with the pup. On her way through the door, Sophia smiled to herself. Jackson was a good man, a damn good man.

———— ——

"Honey, you sound like you're in a good mood. It's good to hear you like this," Sophia's mom said when she called her after work that afternoon.

The makeshift tether was mercifully working well; Henry was actually playing in the yard right now as she watched from the window. Jackson had seemed to appreciate his payment, too—some waffles and scrambled eggs.

"Yeah, things are pretty good right now." Sophia twirled a curl between her fingers. She'd actually styled her hair today. Despite her exhaustion from Henry's resistance to sleep, she'd felt inspired after Jackson left for work. Things were looking different. She was feeling different.

She'd called to update her mom about Henry. Her mom had responded with plans to come over for dinner on

Saturday to see him. She was also a sucker for animals.

"Well, yeah, the puppy seems to be doing wonders for you."

Sophia took a breath. It was time. "Mom, it's not just Henry. The thing is, I'm seeing someone."

There was a pause as the news sank in with her mom. Then, her mom's voice bellowed through the phone, "Honey, that's great!" She could hear the genuine tone in her mom's voice, could picture the accompanying smile. She meant it. Her reaction hadn't been that it was too soon or that she was crazy. Maybe it was okay after all.

"Yeah. I mean, we are taking it really, really slow. But he makes me happy again."

"Is it someone I know?"

"Jackson Gauge."

"Tim's old friend?"

"Yeah. That's him."

There was a pause. Her mom hesitated. "Listen, Sophia, I'm thrilled for you. I am. But do you think it's a good idea to date someone who was so close to Tim?"

Sophia's heart fell. She'd feared this reaction, these words.

"We didn't plan on this happening, we didn't."

"Okay, honey. I just want you to be careful."

"I will."

"Maybe you could have him over on Saturday?"

"Will it be weird for you?"

"No, dear. Of course not."

Sophia agreed to talk to Jackson about dinner. Hanging

up the phone, she didn't feel as good about the situation as she'd hoped. That dangerous thing called doubt sidled in, and she feared she wouldn't be able to stop it.

———— —

"Jackson, you did not have to go overboard for this," Sophia scolded as she answered the door. She was dressed for the casual night she had planned in her home. He, on the other hand, wore a button-up shirt and a tie.

"I didn't know what to wear."

"It's fine. Come in. You look awesome."

"These are for you," he said, his hands appearing to be a bit shaky as he handed her a bouquet of roses.

"They're beautiful. Thank you." By this point, Henry was tugging on Jackson's pant leg. Jackson laughed. "How's little Houdini doing here? Did he break off his leash yet?" The simple solution was thankfully working, at least for now. With the ground frozen from the weather, she'd have to wait until everything thawed out this spring to get a real fence installed. She just hoped Henry stayed small enough for the tether to keep working.

"Nope. It's holding steady. Apparently a really skilled man installed it."

"Obviously," he teased as he sat on the floor to pet Henry. The dog loved him as evidenced by his wagging tail.

"My parents should be here any minute."

"Are you sure this is okay? This isn't weird for you?" he asked, eyeing her.

"No, I want them to meet you. Well, again. In this circumstance. Okay, I'm done talking." She reached for her glass of wine from the counter. "I'm going to check on the Cornish hens."

As she popped open the oven to verify they weren't burning, she took a deep breath. She was angry at herself for being so nervous. This was ridiculous. She was in her thirties. She'd been married. She'd been widowed. It wasn't like she needed her parents' approval of Jackson or like she had a huge announcement. This was just a dinner with people who were important to her.

But her stomach churned as if this were a big announcement, a big deal. In actuality, this was her first dinner with her parents and a new guy in years. In over a decade. This was her first event with Jackson. This was her first time hosting an actual dinner without Tim. There were, in fact, so many firsts with this dinner. She couldn't lie to herself, pretend this was nothing.

It was definitely something.

She shrugged off her introspection when the doorbell rang. She greeted her parents at the door, as did Henry.

"Honey, hey!" her mom exclaimed as she came in and shrugged off her jacket. She leaned in for a hug and a kiss, but it was short-lived. Henry was quickly jumping on her, and she happily obliged with his desire for attention.

"Oh my God, he's adorable!" her mother announced, picking up the puppy.

Her dad, lagging a bit behind, yelled, "Martha! Don't talk about Sophia's new man like that." He left out his signature dad chuckle, and Sophia groaned.

"Oh stop, Stuart. You know I was talking to the puppy," her mom scolded. The two always bickered. It was more than a little embarrassing.

Jackson played right in, standing up to walk over to her parents. "I mean, if we're being honest, I am pretty adorable," he said, laughing. Her dad grinned, shaking his hand. "Good to see you again."

"Yeah. Better circumstances this time." Her dad's face intensified, and Sophia noticed her mom shoot him a glare.

"Very true," Sophia said, trying to ease the awkwardness. "Mom, can you pull yourself away from the puppy for a few minutes to come eat? Dinner's ready. I just have to get it from the oven."

"I guess. But this face is killing me."

"It kills me, too, when he wakes me up at one in the morning. And two. And three."

"And when he goes for a morning jog, huh?" Jackson said, patting the dog's head.

"Well, sometimes that's not so bad," Sophia replied, winking at him.

She'd been so worried about everything, so nervous. But it was all falling into place. It felt like the four of them had been getting together for decades, as if this weren't the first dinner together.

Most days, it felt like Tim had only been gone a day, like these months had just been an eternally long day. Today, though, it felt like he'd been gone for a very long time, like Jackson and she were the ones with the long life together.

Her stomach clenched at the thought, just as she caught sight of her wedding picture with Tim across the living room. How could she think like this? How could she forget all of the time they'd had? How could she invite a new man into their home and pretend he'd never existed?

She told herself to breathe, to keep it together, as her mom joined her at the stove. Her dad and Jackson were talking about cars or something manly in the living room.

"Sophia? What is it?" her mom offered, putting an arm around her shoulder as Sophia lifted the pan of Cornish hens out the oven.

"Nothing, I'm great." Sophia plastered a huge smile on her face, probably overcompensating.

"I can see it on your face. You're thinking about Tim, aren't you?"

She stopped working at the stove, turning to look at her mom as she fought back tears. "Jackson's amazing. I like him a lot. I really do. He makes me feel safe." Her voice was barely a whisper.

"He seems great already. And I'm glad he makes you happy."

"I know. I just can't help but worrying I'm moving too fast."

"Listen, honey. Grief has no time limits. If you're ready to move on, then do it. Don't worry about a timeline or about what people are going to say. Worry about you."

"I know. But, Mom, how can I be sure I'm ready?"

"I don't think you can. Listen, I don't know what you're going through. I never lost my husband like you did, especially at your age. But I can say this. I think you need to be careful you're not just grasping for happiness. I can see the way you look at Jackson. I know you care for him. Just don't rush into things to try to avoid your grief. I don't think you can just cover it up. If you don't let it unfold at its own pace, if you try to rush it or to mask it, I think it's going to come back to you full force. I want you to do what's right for you, but I also don't want to see you rush into something new only to have the grief of Tim's loss come tumbling down on you later. Go at your own pace, but don't rush through it. Feel what you need to feel when you need to feel it. Everything else can wait."

Sophia grabbed her mom for a hug, holding her for several moments. Over her mom's shoulder, she saw Jackson laughing with her dad, saw his rugged smile lighting up the room. Her mom was right. She needed to be careful. She needed to take things slow, to amble on with care.

She wasn't completely ready to move on just yet. She wasn't ready to close the door on her grief, on her life with Tim. Nonetheless, as they sat down to dinner, Jackson across from her, she also wasn't ready to say never to the gorgeous man across from her who filled her with a peace she knew she wouldn't find anywhere else.

———— ————

"Seriously? Why would you do that?" Jackson asked as the whole family erupted once more in laughter.

"I was five."

"Still. That's ridiculous."

"Thanks, Dad." Sophia scowled as she took another sip of wine. After they'd settled into dinner and endured the customary questions, her dad had decided to tell the story about Sophia getting her head stuck in the deck railing.

"I think we might even have pictures," Martha added, also grinning.

"Okay, first, what kind of parents takes pictures of that? Weren't you worried?" Sophia asked, still scowling.

"Nah, it was nothing a little butter couldn't fix."

Jackson shook his head, forking another bite of chicken as he laughed.

"Trouble at five, huh?" he asked through a mouthful of food.

She groaned. "Okay, change of conversation. How's the trip to Paris coming along?"

"Oh, that's boring. Jackson doesn't want to hear about that. He'd rather hear about you," Martha said, winking at Jackson.

"Well, I'd rather not unearth any more horror stories from my childhood."

The night continued, playful bantering and wine passed around. The mood was relaxed and easy. Sophia found herself enjoying the food, enjoying the company, and enjoying the sight of Jackson at the table with her parents.

"So, Jackson, Sophia tells us you're working at the restaurant in town?" Martha asked politely once the laughter settled down.

"Yeah. I like it there."

"Quite a change from the army, huh?" her dad noted. There wasn't a hint of judgment in his voice—it was just an observation.

"Yeah," Jackson said, nodding. "I just wanted something completely different, you know? I like being in the kitchen. I thought seriously about becoming a chef at one point before I headed to boot camp."

"You know, when I worked at the high school, I was pretty good friends with the culinary instructor at the Vo-tech," Stuart added. "He actually went off to work at a pretty big restaurant in New York City. Maybe I could hook you up with his contact info sometime if you were ever interested in moving on."

"Thank you, sir. I'll keep that in mind. But right now, I don't have plans to go anywhere." He smiled, eyeing Sophia strategically across the table, and her heart fluttered.

Dinner came to an end, and before long, everyone was getting ready to head out.

"Tonight was great. Thanks for including me," Jackson murmured in her ear before reaching down to say goodbye to Henry, now fast asleep in front of the fireplace.

"I'll talk to you later," she said, leading him to the door.

Once he was gone, she turned around to say final goodbyes to her parents.

"He's a good bloke," her dad said.

"You just like him because he can talk cars with you," Martha teased. Her dad shrugged.

"Don't you like him, Mom?" Sophia asked.

"I do."

"But?"

"But, honey, I just want you to be careful. That's all. Don't let your heart get ahead of itself."

"I won't," she promised as she said some more goodbyes and exchanged hugs. "I love you guys."

"We love you, too. It's good to see you smile again So-So," her dad said, making her roll her eyes at the sound of her childhood nickname.

As she closed the door and headed to the couch to unwind, her mother's words reverberated in her mind. She did her best to squash them, basking only in the thought of Jackson's smile, his kiss, and his plans to stay in town.

Chapter Eighteen

"Hey, stranger. Good to see you," Stella teased when Sophia walked into the shop a few days later.

Sophia managed a weak smile. "You, too."

"You've been so busy after work, I barely get to see you. Stud muffin soldier boy's been keeping you busy."

"Sorry." Sophia felt herself blush.

"Hey, I'm not complaining. It's good to see you feeling happier again."

"And it's good to see Larry keeping you happy, too," she said, heading to her station to plug in her equipment and get ready for the day.

Stella tossed her a store-bought, prepackaged cinnamon roll, their go-to breakfast.

"You know, we should probably start eating like

thirtysomethings instead of twentysomethings," Sophia teased as she ripped open the package.

"A little curves never killed anyone," Stella said, running her hands on her hips as she laughed.

"You're full of yourself today."

"Yeah. Larry and I had a pretty good night last night." Stella gave her an overly dramatic wink, snickering at Sophia's creeped-out face.

Sophia winked back. "I won't ask for details. I'm sure it was pretty steamy."

"You better believe it." She stared at Sophia questioningly. Sophia stopped, mouth full of cinnamon roll.

"What?"

"Nothing."

"What?"

"Just wondering if your nights are getting steamier, too." Stella busied herself at her styling station, organizing some bobby pins as if she hadn't just asked an extremely personal question.

"Stella! Seriously?"

"Just saying. He's pretty gorgeous. And completely into you. And you're young, vivacious. What gives?"

"I can't believe I'm entertaining this discussion. Need I remind you..." She pointed to her wedding ring, still on her finger.

"I know, I know. But you can't keep it closed for business forever, you know."

"Okay, we're done here," Sophia joked, wiping her hands on her apron. "Next topic, please."

They chattered on about Larry's facial hair, about Stella's mom's new boyfriend, about Henry, and about the latest action on their favorite soap opera. They carried on discussing anything and everything until the first customer arrived at nine.

As Sophia busied herself with Mrs. Rally's permanent wave, her mind started to wander.

Stella's question had really made her uncomfortable, made her squirm. It wasn't, however, because she was a prude or because she didn't talk to Stella about such things.

It was because deep inside, she'd been thinking about Jackson's sinewy body in ways she didn't quite think were rated G.

And she hated herself for it.

———— —

The movie played in her head, over and over. Jackson taking her in his arms, wrapping himself around her, tossing her on the bed...

Then she jolted out of it. It wasn't her bed.

It was hers and Tim's bed.

She knew it was probably natural to be feeling... well... needy. It had been a long time. Jackson was sexy. Beyond sexy.

But this was disturbing. She felt dirty and awful. How could she be thinking about this? How could she be thinking about another man's body with everything that had happened?

She certainly wasn't ready for this. Just yesterday, she'd spent forty-five minutes bawling her eyes out because one of Tim's favorite shirts fell to the floor of their closet and Henry had chewed the sleeve. She still had her moments of searing pain, of debilitating hurt that made it hard to breathe.

It would creep up on her at strange times. In the grocery store, she would feel her chest tighten at the sight of the double stuffed Oreos, Tim's favorite. She would feel it on the way home in the car, when a song would come on that he used to sing crazily to. She would feel it when she couldn't manage to get the window open because it was jammed. She'd feel it when she went to laugh and to tell him about the crazy client who had come in today.

She felt his absence in every minute of her life.

Although the grief was tiresome, the relentless reel of their memories playing in her head drained her even more. The smallest incident, the tiniest trigger would set off a string of memories, of moments. They were moments of sheer happiness. She'd loved Tim, been crazy about him. He'd made her whole, made her Sophia.

Without him, she still felt like only a part of her former self.

Then came Jackson. He was kind and loving, understanding and empathetic. He was a straight shooter, never sugarcoating things. From the moment she heard him speak at the grave that day, she'd felt a connection to him. He understood her. He comforted her.

He was someone she could see herself with.

In truth, if she had met Jackson first, things might have been different. She could see herself falling for soldier Jackson, for pre-Chloe and pre-Tim Jackson.

These thoughts, though, incited the endless cycle of guilt and grief. Because when she thought about Jackson, she instantly thought about Tim and what he would think. She felt like a cheater, even if her husband was gone. She felt awful about the whole situation. She wished she could just feel nothing at all.

So after work, she did something she hadn't done in a few weeks, perhaps out of avoidance, perhaps because she knew the guilt was building up.

The sun was setting when she stood on the ground, a light layer of dirt coating the top of the stone. She brushed it off, stooping down to the headstone as she always did. She wanted to feel close to him, even if this stone was as close as she could get.

She was all alone in the middle of the cemetery, the only souls in sight the souls of the departed. She looked around, thinking about all of the company Tim was keeping. Babies. Elderly. Teenagers. Death didn't spare anyone, as she'd learned all too well.

Before Tim's death, she'd thought she could never be one of those unfortunate women. Other unlucky women—poor things—lost their husbands at a young age. Not her. Not Sophia. Not Tim. She'd fooled herself into the naïve oblivion of so many in their twenties and thirties. She'd felt immortal, like death happened around them and to others, but not them.

Then came the earth-shattering call. She'd been at Pink Lemonade when it happened. The words no one could believe, the words she thought she had dreamed.

———— ————

The horror story began a warm Tuesday afternoon, at exactly 11:19 in the morning. That was when her immortal world stopped turning, replaced by the shivering specimen of death.

It hadn't been a monumental day. There'd been no flashing signs telling her life was about to flip over on its side. She'd had a cup of Folgers with him, both relaxing at the island in the kitchen listening to the morning news.

"I have a meeting after work today," he reminded her.

"Okay. I think I'll make barbecue chicken for dinner. Is that okay?"

"Sounds good. Maybe we can head to Home Depot after dinner? We need some light bulbs for your closet."

"Yeah, okay. My last appointment is at four today, so we should have plenty of time."

He finished sipping his coffee, both basking in a long, quiet moment. Tim sighed, looking at his watch. "Guess I should get going. Have a great day, babe. Love you."

"Love you too."

They'd kissed. He'd left.

Then, at 10:47 in the morning, Tim died, all alone in his office, a pile of paperwork his only guide into the afterlife. The heart that had beat solely for her had stopped beating. He'd died, taking a piece of her heart with him, too. He'd torn out of her life in a flash, in a moment, in an unexpected blur. As effortlessly as he came into her life, he was gone, and she was left to fathom how it all happened.

She knew she was lucky to have had a final, calm moment with him. Some women in the grief group she'd attended the first month had horror stories of harsh, sour final words. Her last encounter had been the normal, routine encounter of their marriage. I love yous, a kiss, and an assumption they would see each other later.

She couldn't see it that way, though. It was just a painful reminder of how blindsided she'd been.

There had been the moments of shock that began at 11:19 that horrifying day. She'd slumped to the floor, zoned out, tuned out Stella's shrieks and tears. Everything blurred in a swirl of irrational thoughts and feelings, of both chaos and emptiness. In many ways, she felt like she was gone, too, an empty carcass being toted through the motions.

She barely remembered being transported home, the visits from loved ones, the phone calls, and relentless flowers. She didn't ask questions, didn't beg for details. She didn't hear the comforting words from friends and family, didn't stop to analyze what it all meant. The moments from the torturous phone call until the moment at the funeral were a hellish blur, a whirling cloud of black smog in her crushed heart. In reality, every moment after Tim was a hellish blur, *a distinct fight for survival from a girl who had once had it all.*

———————

Every time she stood here on this icy piece of earth, she was taken back to those moments, those moments of sheer hell, when her world had disintegrated beneath her feet.

Time will heal, everyone told her. *It'll all be okay.*

In a way, they were right. Time was making it more bearable. She didn't want to die every second of every day. She didn't wish every breath were her last.

True, she still had moments each day when she wanted to quit, when the pain of losing him was so torturous she wanted to suffocate.

She still missed Tim. She still loved him.

"I love you, Tim. I will always, always love you. I hate how you went away. But I'm trying to make a life for myself. I'm trying to carry on. I'm sorry if it hurts you that I'm trying. I'm sorry."

Sophia wished like the movies, she could hear a whisper of forgiveness in the wind or a rustling of the trees. She wanted a sign Tim was okay with her moving on.

There was just dead silence. She could only hear her own breath.

A part of her knew asking a dead man for permission to move on was ludicrous. She hadn't lost her mind or anything. Another part of her, though, felt like she owed it to the man who was her soul mate, her everything, to tell him what was happening.

A year ago, if you'd asked Sophia if she would ever fall for another man, she would have laughed in your face. She didn't even fantasize about other men like some women did. She didn't fantasize about Gerard Butler or anyone else of celeb status. The only man she saw when she closed her eyes or when she thought about forever was Tim. She'd known from the first time their lips had touched two weeks after the lasagna meeting he was it for her.

It had been a soft, slow, sensuous kiss, the kiss a woman only dreams about. There was no rain like in so many romance movies. Instead, the sky was a heavenly blue, not a cloud in the sky blocking out the sun's gorgeous rays.

A mariachi band played a festive tune as they stood on the sidewalk, waiting for Stella and her latest man crush to buy a funnel cake. Crowds of kids ran screaming through the streets of the annual festival as parents frantically chased after them. Fried foods passed by everywhere. Sophia hung back, standing near the lemonade stand as she waited for her friend. Tim stood by her, his toe tapping to the music.

They'd had a lovely third date, reconnecting with their inner-childhoods as they maneuvered the simple street fair. Cotton candy, a few corn dogs, and a lot of getting to know you questions had eased them into a comfortable place.

Now, he stood smiling, staring at her. She twirled a curl in her fingers self-consciously. "What?"

"I might be falling for you," he admitted without hesitation, staring directly in her eyes. He said it as if he were telling her his name was Tim or he loved pizza.

She felt her cheeks warm. "Okay."

"Are you falling for me yet?"

"You're forward." She grinned. She liked his honesty. She'd never been with a man who was so open, so willing to admit his feelings for her.

"Are you?" He took a step closer.

"I mean, I like you, but it's a little soon, don't you think?"

"No," he said, gently taking her face in his hands and leaning in to kiss her.

She'd thought about pushing him away, about saying it was too soon. Who was this guy? Kissing her already?

She couldn't, though. Because as soon as his lips touched hers, she realized this was the kiss she'd been waiting for. This was the kiss to make her believe in love, to make her fall for a guy she met over a plate of lasagna. His lips moved slowly, carefully, as if he were drinking in every second. He was gentle yet confident, smoldering yet playful. It was a kiss hinting at what they could be together. It was a kiss hinting Tim was right—it wasn't too soon, and she definitely could fall for him.

Tim and Sophia only pulled away when they heard a whistle and some clapping behind them.

"Nice!" Stella said, laughing as she stopped her clapping.

Sophia pulled away, wanting to admonish Stella for being immature. She couldn't say anything. Her gaze was glued to Tim, her lips tingling with the feel of his lips.

The only words that came to her were ones she would later regret. It was a comment Tim would mercilessly tease her for, would always bring up. Later, when they were in a heated argument or she was pissed at him about his socks lying on the bedroom floor, he would turn to her and say the words symbolic of their relationship.

As Tim, Stella, and Ricky waited for Sophia to say something romantic, intellectual, or just plain normal, all she managed to say was, "Hot damn!"

———————

Sitting on the ground now, Sophia smiled at the memory. "Hot damn," she said jokingly, knowing if anyone were around they would have her committed.

It was a ridiculous thing for her to say, but it was all she could think of. He'd knocked her socks off with the first kiss and every other moment in their time together. He was charismatic, charming, but he always made sure she knew she was the only woman for him. When they went to a party or wedding or a family gathering, she could always feel his eyes on only her, could see him looking at her with sheer lust and love. Their marriage had never undergone the seven-year itch or the boredom so many experienced.

Sure, they'd had their issues and fights. She hated how he left dirty laundry everywhere in the house. She hated how she had to beg him to pressure wash the house twice a year or to help her clean out the rain gutters. She hated how he never put the salt and pepper shakers back or how he left cereal in his bowl in the mornings. There'd been fights over money, over in-laws, over forgotten dating anniversaries.

Overall, they'd had a good run. Which only made his death even worse.

If Tim had lived until he was 109, she knew she'd have been by his side. She'd have never strayed, have never dreamed about another man in her bed.

Now, a daunting thought plagued her. Tim hadn't lived to see old age, and she just might.

As much as she wanted to rip her own heart out and leave it there on the gravestone, she couldn't. She couldn't stop her heart from feeling, couldn't close herself off completely.

Maybe she shouldn't want to.

Maybe it was okay to look for those feelings, to explore a life with Jackson. He would never be Tim. He could never replace their lemonade stand kisses, their late-night fights, or their dates in the middle of a snowstorm at the Chinese restaurant.

Maybe, though, she could find new memories with Jackson. Christmas walks, trips to the zoo, and new things to keep her alive, keep her feeling.

"I'll always love you, Tim. And I never want to say goodbye to you, not completely. I hope you understand I have to find a new kind of happiness. I love you. Always."

She rose calmly, quietly from the grave, put one hand on the stone again, and turned to go home.

Chapter Nineteen

JACKSON

"Are you sure you're ready for this?" Jackson asked as she put Henry in his crate.

"It's just some burgers," Sophia replied, but Jackson sensed a hint of tension in her voice, in her stance.

He'd been surprised when she'd called yesterday to tell him the plan to go on a double date with Stella and Larry. Now, as she stood before him in a simple pair of jeans, a tight red shirt, and a blazer, her hair billowing in soft curls around her face, he was filled with mixed emotions. It felt good to be on the same page, to be overcoming the guilt and the roadblocks on the way to... whatever this was.

The roadblocks, he'd come to realize, would probably always be there. A glimmer of hesitation on both of their ends would always hold them back; hers from the loss of her soul mate, and his from the way Chloe's affair cracked his heart. They couldn't start completely fresh with each other, not really. They would always be haunted by a tenuous past and by their connection through their mutual love for Tim.

As she smiled at him though, asking, "Ready?" that tension melted away. He was done analyzing and categorizing. He just wanted to feel, to bask in the softness of her face, the glow of her. She was radiant, not just on the outside. She was a soothing voice in a weighty storm. She was a reminder that life, no matter how tough, had elements of beauty.

"Let's do it," he said, leading her to his truck, opening her door.

"I can't wait to try this place," she said.

"You've never been?"

"Nope."

"Well, looks like we'll be making new memories, then."

"Yes, we will."

He put the key in the ignition, off to whatever Red Robin, a double date, and the future might hold.

———— ————

"What? It's not like I'm trying to fool you guys. You all know I like to eat," Sophia said as Jackson eyed her plate. She certainly hadn't held back, ordering a colossal burger, fries, some cheese sticks, and a chocolate shake.

"No, I like it. I like a woman who can eat. I just don't

think you're going to finish it all."

"Game on," she teased, as she reached to his plate for a French fry.

"How the hell do you stay so skinny?" Stella asked.

"Oh, stop," Sophia grumbled back.

It's been a good night so far, Jackson thought as he downed some fries, dipped in his milkshake of course.

He'd hit it off with Larry, both sharing a love of video games—to Stella and Sophia's chagrin—and an interest in classic cars. They'd chatted about engines and rims until Stella finally interrupted them.

And then she turned the conversation to hair and makeup, to the guys' utter dismay.

It had all been fun, despite the gender-slanted conversations. The four of them found common ground, a common sense of humor, and a common sense of comfort at the table at Red Robin. He couldn't remember feeling so connected with a group of people he'd just met. He liked Stella's bold observations and Larry's calm demeanor.

Mostly, he liked Sophia. He liked the feel of her against him in the booth. He liked joking with her about her appetite and her mispronunciation of Gouda cheese.

He liked being the man beside her.

When she finished her burger and moved on to the cheese sticks, she turned to him. "Still think I can't finish my food?"

"Nope."

"Bet me?"

"You're on. What do you want to bet?"

"Hmm," she said, twirling her hair. "If I win, you have to take me to see a chick flick tonight. My pick."

"Okay, and if you lose?"

"And if I lose, we'll see the gross action flick you two were raving about."

"You're on." He shook her hand. He'd been hoping for a bet a tad more lascivious, truth be told, but he couldn't be picky.

"You better eat up," Stella instructed Sophia. "I do not want to see a nasty old actor. I need some good eye candy to look at."

Larry raised an eyebrow at her. "Besides you of course, dear," Stella said, wooing him with her smile.

Over the next ten minutes, Larry and Jackson's dreams of guns and explosions waned as they watched Sophia devour every last morsel on her plate.

"I win." She winked. "Sappy love story it is."

Jackson pretended to be upset, to be forlorn. Deep down, he knew he was the real winner, getting to take this hot, burger-eating woman to the movies on his arm.

———

"That was such an amazing movie," Sophia gushed as he pulled into her driveway.

"I know. It's definitely in my top ten," he joked. It hadn't actually been too bad, mushy kissing in the rain scene aside. He obviously wouldn't risk his masculinity and admit it, though.

"Oh stop. You laughed a few times."

"At the cheesiness of it."

She undid her seat belt, and he looked over at her, not quite sure how to handle the goodbye. He didn't want to move too fast.

So when she turned to him, eyes twinkling, and said, "Do you want to come inside?" he was surprised—in a good way.

"Okay."

He turned off the truck and followed her. As she rustled for the key in her bag, he put his hand on the doorjamb, feeling their closeness acutely. He could smell her soft perfume, feel her breath near him.

Stop it. Take it slow. Don't ruin this, he told himself.

"I'll just be a minute. I want to take Henry out," Sophia said. "Make yourself at home."

He took a seat on the couch. Glancing around, he saw relics of Sophia's life with Tim everywhere. Pictures on the mantel, pictures on the wall. Trinkets from their trips and vacations. Furniture they'd picked out.

I didn't plan on this happening, he said to Tim in his mind. *I promise I'll take good care of her, though.* Jackson wasn't a religious man in any sense of the word, but he'd hoped if there was an afterlife and if Tim could see them, he would forgive him.

He didn't have too much time to think about it, because before he could second-guess everything, Sophia was back, settling on the couch beside him with two glasses of wine.

Henry clambered into his bed on the floor, a growth

spurt perhaps making him more tired than usual. They lounged for a few moments by the empty fireplace, sipping on wine, reflecting on the evening.

"I had a great time tonight," Sophia whispered. He looked into her eyes and saw something there he hadn't expected. A need, a lust. A complete trust in him.

"Me too," he said back, taking her hand in his. "Are you still okay with all of this? I don't want to make you feel guilty or rush things."

She set her glass on the end table, taking both of his hands in hers. "I want you to know I will always love Tim. He will always be right here," she said, putting a hand over her heart. "But I know he's gone. And I know he would want me to be happy. I've done a lot of thinking these past few weeks, a lot of rationalizing. I've tried to talk myself out of us, out of being with you. There are twenty reasons why this isn't right, why we shouldn't pursue this. There are twenty more reasons why we should. You make me happy. I feel empty when you're not around. I don't know where this is all headed or if it's heading anywhere at all in the distant future. I do know life is short and fragile. We have to seize everything that makes us happy."

He leaned in to punctuate her words with a kiss. He ran his hands through her hair, kissed her passionately, his heart leading the way.

Their kissing quickly intensified, the heat from their bodies smoldering between them. Their bodies grew hungry for each other, their fast motions and passionate touches leading the way to a path he knew all too well.

He didn't want to stop, wanted to succumb to passion with her.

His conscience screamed at him to stop.

He pulled back, looking into her face, painted with confusion. "What is it?" she whispered, her voice cracking.

"We can't. I don't want to do something you'll regret."

She sighed, running a hand through her hair. He waited for her to agree, to say he was right.

Instead, she leaned closer, wrapping her arms around his neck. "No regrets. I want this."

He knew he should be the rational one, knew he shouldn't let this continue. He worried she'd have guilt and regret swirling in her heart the next morning.

But God, she was so damn sexy, the way she was nibbling on her lip, the way she was looking at him as if he were the only man in the world.

"Are you positive, Sophia? I'm okay with taking this slow."

Her only response was to slowly, meticulously pull his shirt over his head, her hands finding his abs within seconds. He groaned, knowing he was all hers.

He threw her back on the sofa, and they fell prey to the passion that had crept between them. He moved past the insecurities and the doubts, the fears of regret. When he collapsed into her later, burying his head in her neck, he felt complete.

He felt like the man he'd once been.

He felt like he never wanted to let go of this moment, of this woman, no matter how complicated the pathway to her was or would be.

Chapter Twenty

JACKSON

As one would expect, the night that began at Red Robin and ended with Jackson and Sophia in each other's arms had marked a crucial turning point in their lives, both individually and together.

For one, Jackson noticed an unarguably cheesy quality to his every move. Suddenly, he wasn't so angry in the morning when the alarm clock went off, leaning over to his nightstand to check his texts first thing, smiling when he saw one from her. Work was no longer about escaping to a mentally neutral state—it was a time to think about Sophia, to think about the next time he would see her.

Even his family had noted a change in him.

"What the hell is up with your stupid grin?" Gretta asked him on the Sunday after his night with Sophia. "Who is she?"

"No one," he denied, shaking his head, trying to look stoic.

"You're not back with Chloe, are you?"

"God no," he'd said.

"Bring her to dinner next week," his mom chimed in.

"Guys, I haven't even admitted to seeing anyone."

"You don't have to," Jonathan added, joining the interrogation.

Jackson rolled his eyes, a smile flooding his face, contradicting his feigned annoyance. "Fine. I'll bring her next week. Promise not to hound her, though, okay?"

"It's Sophia, isn't it?" his mom asked, savvy to her son's life even when he was trying to be evasive.

"How'd you know?"

"I knew you were crazy about her from the first time you talked about her." She winked. "Ask her what she likes for dinner, and get back to me."

"Okay, Mom."

"And I'm glad to see you happy, honey. She's a keeper in my books already."

Sophia and Jackson had become inseparable in the days following their commitment to one another. Breakfasts, lunches, dinners—they squeezed in time together whenever they could. They took Henry for late-night walks reminiscent of their Christmas walk. He took Sophia ice-skating for the first time, holding her tight so as to not let her fall. They went to new restaurants, new movies, and they went on another double date with Stella and Larry.

They tried to go to places she'd never been, tried not to

tread on Tim's old stomping grounds too often. He wasn't trying to erase Tim from her life or to ignore the elephant in the room. He simply wanted their relationship to be built on new memories. He wanted Sophia to think about him without having memories of what once was.

Not that the memories didn't creep in from time to time. Plenty of moments reminded them of just how tricky their relationship was, how time hadn't quite healed all of her wounds.

———————

It had been a simple date only three days after their sexual encounter that had reminded Jackson she wasn't quite healed.

He'd expected some regrets, some tears the morning after their night together. Instead, he'd been met with a smiling Sophia, breakfast, and plans for the weekend. He'd been met with warm stares, soft kisses, and promises she was glad they'd committed to each other.

The tears came three days later in the middle of Café Amor, a small, romantic diner an hour outside of town.

They'd been eating some pasta and sipping on wine, talking about work, the weather, and her trip to Jackson's family dinner on Sunday. There'd been no warning, no signs of impending doom. Her tears had come like a flash flood, catching him off guard and threatening to tip the delicate balance they'd found.

"I'm sorry," she said, tears falling as she put down her fork.

"What's wrong? Did I say something?" He was confused, racking his brain for any signs of triggers.

"No, it's silly, I'm sorry."

"It's okay. Tell me." He reached across and put his hand on hers.

She wiped her tears away with the back of her hand before cautiously proceeding. "It's not you. Really. I'm excited to go to dinner with you at your mom's, I am. It's just... talking about Sunday dinner with your family, being here together. It just hit me. I'm starting a new life without him. It used to be Tim across from me who would tell me we had dinner plans at my in-laws. He used to be the one to reach across and sample my plate. It's not that I wish he were here instead of you. But, I guess in a way I do. I miss him. I'm sorry. I know this hurts you." She balled her fist in her hair, the pain painting itself in her expression. She was clearly a conglomeration of mixed emotions, of confusion. Maybe even, regret.

He shook his head, squeezing her hand. "Stop. It's okay. Don't apologize. I know you still love him. I knew that going in."

"I just feel awful. I feel like I'm constantly between the two of you. Which is stupid, I know. He's dead. But I feel guilty for always bringing him up, for making you feel like you're a rebound or second fiddle. And then I feel guilty if I don't."

"Hey, you don't have to feel guilty. I knew what I was getting myself into. And I wouldn't change it. Tim was my friend, too, you know. I don't mind talking about him. We don't have to pretend like he doesn't exist. I know if he were still alive, you'd still be with him. I know that."

She looked at him then, relief in her eyes mixed with sadness.

"I just want to feel better. I want to stop being haunted everywhere I go. I hate how I'm always crying. I'm always ruining these moments for us."

"You're not ruining anything," he assured her. "Cut yourself some slack."

Her face was solemn. Her eyes told him she was far away.

He paused before saying, "We can slow down, you know. If you feel like it's too soon. I'm not rushing you."

"I know. I just... I don't want to feel like I'm sitting around waiting for it to be okay to be happy. I don't want to rush, either. It's just..."

"Messy?" He finished her sentence for her. He knew exactly what she was feeling. He felt the same contradictory feelings, the same back and forth of emotion. This wasn't easy. It wasn't conventional.

Looking at her face, spending time with her, he knew it was worth it, no matter what happened. She made him feel alive again. They were good together. They just needed to be patient with each other.

And most of all, with themselves.

She smiled. "Thank you."

"For what?"

"Being you. Being understanding. Helping me maneuver this. I couldn't do this with anyone else. I wouldn't want to."

"Same here. You make me a better man, Sophia."

"And you make me better, too."

They went back to their dinners then, tears slowly drying as they talked about Henry's crazy shoe-eating antics this week and his sister Gretta's overt bitchiness that she should be prepared for.

There were no magical I love yous that night or a promise to forget about Tim. There was no wave of a magic wand to right everything.

He knew this would always be complicated, but it was okay.

He wouldn't want to be anywhere but beside Sophia, tears and all.

———

"I *love* your sister," Sophia said as they waved to his family and headed down the road back to her place.

"Are you serious?"

"Yeah, why? She's straightforward."

"Some would call it bitchy."

"No, I like her. She's just looking out for you."

Jackson wasn't so sure. Between Gretta's comments about Tim and her discussion of some of Jackson's less than lawful times during high school—vandalism incidents involving an enemy's car—he was quite sure Gretta was just trying to ruin his life. Or at least tear Sophia away from him.

All in all, it had gone better than expected. Over a

dinner of stuffed pork chops and mom's homemade apple pie, Sophia had graced his family with her witty charm, her spunk, and her smile. His mom loved her from the first moment, talking hair and nails with her and promising to stop by the shop later in the week. Gretta, too, gave her the unwritten stamp of approval, complimenting her killer shoes and asking to see pictures of Henry.

Everyone was taken with her, which wasn't surprising. Sophia was a perfect fit in his family. She was sweet enough to win over his delicate mother but sassy enough to stand up to the loudmouthed Gretta. She'd even won Jace over, playing Legos with him for a half an hour after dinner.

She was perfect.

"My family loves you already, I can tell. You've probably replaced me in the will." He winced. "Sorry."

"I'm fine. Please stop apologizing every time you say death or hint at it." She glanced out the window, seeming peaceful. "It was nice to be there with your family. It felt right."

They drove back to her place, and he pulled in the driveway.

"I had a great time tonight," she said.

"The night's not over yet."

She raised an eyebrow. "What do you have in mind?"

"Go get Henry. We're heading back to my place."

"Why?"

"Just trust me."

"This is how all horror films start."

He shook his head. "Really? A pork chop dinner with

the crazy family and then a murder in his apartment—with your mastiff puppy? What kind of B-rated movies are you watching?"

She laughed. "Let me get a few things and I'll be right back."

———————

"Should I be nervous?"

"Terrified actually," Jackson said as he checked his watch, mentally noting it would be there any minute, as long as Sebastian was on schedule.

"I just don't understand why we're standing outside in this brisk weather with Henry."

Although spring was certainly on its way, tonight was one of those nights that flashed them back to the winter months; that hinted spring wasn't quite ready to take over.

"Would you please just be patient?"

"That's not my thing."

"I see that."

He tapped his foot, starting to worry this would all fall through. Just as he was about to text Sebastian, a friend of Evan's brother, he saw it coming down the street. Actually, he heard it coming before he really saw it, the familiar clomping and slight squeaking the telltale sign his plan to sweep Sophia completely off her feet was back on.

Henry let out a pathetic woof as Sophia turned her head to the right to gauge what was happening. "What the?" was all she could manage. Jackson smiled.

"Ms. Clawson, I do believe your chariot awaits," he said, happy to have made her speechless.

"A carriage ride? Here? Now? How did you manage?"

"A man never reveals his secrets," he said as he pulled on her hand, leading her and Henry to the curb.

"Can Henry come?"

"Why not? It'll be his first carriage ride, too. You did say the other week you'd never been on a carriage ride, right?"

"Yes. But I didn't think you'd go about setting one up for me. I sort of feel like Cinderella."

"Good. Just don't label me your fairy godmother. That would get a little weird."

The carriage stopped in front of his house, and the driver gave a command for the horses to stop. Henry let out a few more barks, but the horses, beautiful white creatures with manes that truly did look fairy-tale inspired, didn't move.

"Thank you so much," Jackson said to the driver, dressed in a tux.

"My pleasure."

They crawled into their places, Henry between them, looking perplexed but intrigued at the same time.

The carriage slowly took off, leading them down the familiar streets of their hometown, letting them see it from a very different vantage point. A light wind blew as the stars sparkled, creating a scene straight from a movie. Sophia looked entranced.

They sat for a few moments in silence, taking in the scene, his arm stretched across the back of the seat and resting on her shoulder.

"How did you manage all of this?" she asked with an air of apparent gratitude.

"Evan's brother is friends with Sebastian, the owner of the carriage company. With the holidays long gone, it's sort of a slow time, so it was pretty easy to book a personal ride."

"This is so special. I can't even tell you," she said, leaning on his shoulder over Henry as the carriage rolled on, hooves clomping the only sound on the silent street.

"I hoped you'd like it. I remember you talking at dinner about how much you wanted to go on one."

"I can't believe you remembered."

"I remember everything about my time with you." He knew if Evan were here, he would be poking fun at him for the cheesy line, but Jackson didn't care. He meant it. He cherished every moment, every memory with this beautiful woman.

For a while, he'd tried to avoid this feeling, the shame of the situation barring him from his own heart. He'd since realized what a gift it was she had come into his life. Maybe in a strange way, fate had brought them together when they'd needed each other the most.

Before Sophia, life had been dismal, no hint of happiness on the horizon. He'd felt empty, focusing on his losses. He didn't see a way out of the gloom.

Sophia showed him a different path. She made him feel as if things would be more than okay, no matter what happened. The situation with Chloe, with Logan, and everything in between seemed survivable. With her by his side, he could muster the courage and faith to get through anything.

She turned to him, her eyes fully engulfed in him. "I don't want to move too fast. I know I said I wanted to be careful. But Jackson Gauge, I think I love you."

His heart froze, the words an unexpected gift on this night. "I *know* I love you," he replied confidently, leaning in slowly, savoring each second of the magical moment between them. He kissed her then, a soft, careful kiss, as if he were afraid of tainting the magic around them. The clopping of horse hooves lulled them into a whimsical state. Even Henry was quiet, still, as if revering the atmosphere of the carriage.

Things weren't perfect between them, and they probably never would be. The start of their relationship would always be marked by a seemingly insurmountable tragedy, a heart-wrenching loss.

Nonetheless, through the wreckage of the sadness, through the feelings of emptiness, they had managed to resurrect something breathtaking, something worthy of a romantic carriage ride in the brisk night.

"Thanks again," Jackson said as he tipped the carriage driver, Sophia heading into his apartment. He followed her, his hands numb from the plummeting temperatures.

Once inside, he walked to the kitchen and he retrieved the bottle of wine from the fridge.

"I had a great time," Sophia said, setting Henry down on the floor. The pup turned in a circle five times, plopped on the floor, and conked out.

"We're not done yet," he replied, pouring two glasses and then carefully handing one to her. He clinked glasses with her softly before saying, "To new memories."

"I like it," she nodded. "To new memories."

They both sipped, and he put his glass down. From the living room, he picked up a wrapped box he'd stowed behind the couch before returning to Sophia.

"And I'm also toasting to the preservation of them. Here." He handed Sophia the box, and her eyes again twinkled.

"You're just full of surprises tonight, huh?"

"Are you complaining?"

"Heck no. Keep them coming."

She set the box on the counter to open it. He came behind her, wrapping his arms around her waist as he put his head on her shoulder to watch the process.

When she unwrapped the box and lifted the lid, she grinned. She turned to face him, and they were nose to nose. "What's this for?"

"Us. Our memories."

"I love it."

"Open to the first page."

She complied, and found a page with a blank spot in the middle. Underneath the blank spot, he'd written *Our first carriage ride.*

"I wondered why you were so adamant about taking a selfie."

"What, did you think I was just vain?"

"Sort of."

He tickled her and kissed her neck. Spinning her around in his arms, he leaned her gently against the counter. "I know these past few months have been hard. I wanted tonight to be about us making new memories, memories you could think about that just contained us. I want us to never forget our past. Seriously. But I also want us to start to build our own album, our own moments. That's what this is about. I can't wait to fill the pages with you."

"Thank you," she said, tears flooding her eyes.

"Don't cry. I didn't want to make you cry," he smiled, kissing her on the cheek.

"You're beautiful," she said to him.

"I was thinking the same thing about you. But I think it's more acceptable for me to call you beautiful."

"I mean you're a beautiful person. Thank you." She kissed him, a soft, gentle kiss. They ignored their wine and she led him backward toward his bedroom, toward the sanctuary and privacy of his room.

That night, there wasn't the hungry passion between them they'd found once before. It was a sweeter, more sensuous experience because they knew without a doubt both of their hearts were in it.

Lying in bed with her in his arms, Jackson felt like he'd finally found peace in his life, like nothing could possibly go wrong. Things would work out, his life was back on track, and he had the most amazing woman in his arms.

Chapter Twenty-One

JACKSON

"If you need anything, you know, like a gorgeous hunk to scrub your back, let me know."

Sophia rolled her eyes. "I thought you were making lunch?" she asked, as she prepared to step into the shower.

"I could be persuaded to join you. I mean, it would be tough, but I could be convinced," he teased, eating up the sight of her and not hiding it. She shook her head playfully and stepped into the stream of hot water, shutting the curtain to block his view.

"Okay, okay. I'm off to make the pizza."

They'd spent the morning lounging in his apartment. Other than taking Henry outside for a bathroom break, they'd basked in the solitude, perhaps not wanting the real world to break into the magic of their past evening.

He meandered to the kitchen to scrounge up the ingredients. He'd promised to make her his famous white sauce pizza for lunch before they joined the real world and both headed to their responsibilities. He felt himself almost dancing around the kitchen, an unfamiliar jauntiness to his step. They'd turned a corner, and everything had changed—in a good way.

There was a knock at the door, which, although puzzling, wasn't uncommon. He figured it was one of his neighbors who had locked themselves out or a mailman delivering something.

When he tossed the door back to appraise the visitor, though, his jaw literally fell open. His stomach lurched. This couldn't be good.

"Chloe? What is it?"

She was smiling at him demurely. It was unlike her to seem so shy, so calm. For the past several months, he'd only met fury or condescension when he dropped Logan off after his weekend visitation.

She brushed straight past him into the kitchen, not waiting for an invitation.

"Is Logan okay? Where is he?" Jackson's head raced with worries.

"He's fine. He's with my mom," Chloe calmly said. "I wanted to come see you alone."

She smiled at him, which made his stomach lurch even more. What was going on? What the hell could she possibly want?

"Okay, so what is it? What couldn't wait?"

She leaned against the kitchen island and took a breath. "I'm here because I want to say I'm sorry. I messed up."

He almost laughed out loud, sheer shock making him pause long enough to appraise the look on her face. She wasn't kidding. She was serious.

"What the fuck are you saying?" he said, emboldened by the ludicrous behavior of his ex-wife.

"I'm saying I still love you, Jackson. I messed up. Seth and I are over. I want to come back."

There was a pause, both Jackson and Chloe weighing each other, staring at each other. Jackson waited a few breaths, determined she was serious, and then exhaled with a hint of nervous laughter.

"Are you kidding me? You still love me? Funny way of showing it, Chloe. Taking Logan away. Making bitchy comments to me. Keeping my son from me every chance you get. What's this really about?"

Her gaze didn't waver. "I do still love you, whether you want to believe it or not. I know my behavior has been crazy lately. But I want to come back. I do. Things are over with Seth. I want to be with you. I just... I was out of my mind. I hit a low spot. I've realized I wasn't the woman I want to be. Without you, I'm not even close to the woman I want to be. Think about it, Jackson. I know you're still mad at me, and rightfully so. But we could live together again, as a family. I know it won't be perfect. In time, maybe you could forgive me. We could raise our son together, like we always wanted. We could give him a gift—two parents in one house."

He stared at her, uncertain how he could ever have gotten to this point. When she'd told him she was pregnant, he would've never imagined someday they'd be here.

"Chloe, this is crazy. You know we're over. You've burned me too many times."

"So you're willing to give up your son?"

"No. I'm not. I'm going to fight for him. I'm not going to move in with you to have him back. That's not fair to anyone."

"I know you still feel for me. We were so good together. We could have it all back."

"Chloe, no. This isn't going to happen. You're crazy if you think I can forgive you for what you've done."

"Like I said, I know it's not going to be easy. Please think about this. Think about what a good thing this could be," she said, walking toward him, resting a hand on his chest. He looked into her eyes and saw a glimmer of the woman he had once loved.

The glimmer faded away quickly. This was surreal. Unbelievable. How could she expect to just walk back into his life? Behind the confidence, the apologetic woman, behind the sliver of the woman he once loved, Jackson saw something else.

He saw a desperate woman, a woman he could never love again.

He loved Logan and would do anything to have his son back.

But not this. This was too much.

"You need to leave, Chloe," he hissed, feeling something

for her he hadn't felt before.

Pity.

She was obviously not in a good place in her life to be here like this, begging for him. It wasn't like her.

Tears formed slowly in the corner of her eyes. "I'm not giving up on us." She turned to leave.

He wanted to scream at her, say she'd given up on them when she cheated on him, when she fought for sole custody. She'd given up every time she made rude remarks to him, looked at him like he was scum.

He didn't, though. No matter what Chloe did to him, no matter how much she'd hurt him or how ridiculous and insulting her behavior was now, she'd always be Logan's mother. He would always have some sort of place for her in his heart.

"If you need anything, call me. We'll talk later."

She scurried out the door, off to her car. He took a deep breath, weighing what had just happened, still shocked, enraged, and confused. He looked up, ready to return to his cooking, to push the whole encounter out of his mind, when he saw Sophia standing in the hallway, dressed in the same clothes from the night before.

She also had the suggestion of tears in her eyes. She eyed him cautiously but with a peaceful look on her face.

"I should go," she said, somberly turning to get her things.

"Sophia, wait. Why?" He rushed to her side, spinning her around. The tears were flowing.

"You should go back to her, Jackson. You'd get to be with

your son. You can't throw that out."

"How can you even suggest that? I love you. We're just getting started. I don't love her anymore."

"Think about Logan. Isn't this what you wanted? To have him back? Isn't that more important than whatever this is between us?"

He was taken aback by her words, surprised by how hurtful they were. "Whatever this is? What's that mean?"

"It means, Jackson, we've had fun, sure. But do you really think we can be something more than... this? How could we ever make this work, especially now? How could I be with you knowing if it weren't for me, you could be with your son? I won't come between you and him."

"Sophia, this is ridiculous. I'm not going back to Chloe. We can be together and work out things with my son."

"I won't do this. There's too much at stake. We knew this was a bad idea from the beginning. We both tried to fight it because we knew it was wrong. Here's another sign, another reason, we shouldn't be together."

He tried to stop her, to pull her back to him both literally and figuratively.

She was already gone.

"What's happened? Just a few minutes ago, we were great, more than great."

She dropped her gaze to the floor. "Things *are* great, Jackson. I meant every word. I love being with you. I love you. But this, this is just a bad idea. We can't make this work in the long run, not with Chloe, and my feelings for Tim, and everything working against us." She fiddled with the hem of her shirt, avoiding his gaze. When she finally looked up at him, tears in her eyes, she spoke so softly he could barely hear her. "Thank you for everything," she said as if he were a grocery store clerk who had just finished ringing up her order instead of the man she'd professed to love just a few hours ago.

"Sophia, wait," he begged as she grabbed Henry from the sofa and headed out the door, chin up and footsteps confident. She'd made up her mind.

He slammed his fist on the counter, rage taking over. Chloe had fucked everything up in his life yet again. He'd lost the shard of hope he'd just found, and for what?

Last night, he'd made a breakthrough with Sophia, had finally helped her settle into the idea of a life with him. Now it was gone. Like a wisp of a dandelion in the merciless hands of a reckless child, the safety of their relationship was gone, with the whirlwind of Chloe's reappearance.

His heart undoubtedly belonged to Sophia. But the doubt he'd worked tirelessly to help her overcome was revived, and he didn't know if he could combat it this time. He felt like he was standing in the middle of a swinging blade, recklessly flying back and forth between "yes" and "no" with Sophia.

Now, the blade lowered, ready to land right on the neck of its victim.

Maybe Sophia was right. Maybe they just weren't meant to be.

Chapter Twenty-Two

SOPHIA

You did the right thing, Sophia told herself when she arrived home to the empty house. She'd only been gone a day, but it smelled stagnant like an abandoned property. It felt cold and lonely.

Better get used to it, she thought.

She hadn't wanted to eavesdrop, had felt completely inappropriate doing so. She'd just turned off the shower, basking in the happiness of the night. She'd finally felt at peace in her heart, in her soul. For a long time after Tim's death, she'd felt like she'd never be okay again. Love was certainly not a consideration. Her heart had blackened with death when she saw his casket lowered into the ground.

Jackson, though, had changed that. It wasn't just his

killer looks or his sexy stubble. It wasn't the way his muscular arms made her feel safe or the tender way he kissed her. It was in his heart, in the way he saw what she needed before she even did. It was in the way he respected her past while also wanting her to see the future.

It was just him.

As she'd towel-dried her hair in his bathroom, she smiled, thinking she'd turned a corner in grief. She knew she hadn't come to the end of the long, tenuous stretch of road called grief. There would still be many more turnarounds and potholes. Still, she felt like with Jackson by her side, she would get through. She could survive the loss of Tim.

She could love again.

She had thought she'd heard Jackson talk to someone, but dismissed the idea as she dressed. She heard his voice rising, though, heard someone in the kitchen, and her curiosity was piqued. She'd cracked the bathroom door slightly, her ear to the crack to listen and to gauge the situation.

That's when she'd heard her. A woman.

She still hadn't jumped to any conclusions. In fact, she'd thought about closing the door and primping for a while, giving him his privacy.

She couldn't. Because she'd heard the word, the pesky four-letter word she'd recently said to Jackson.

Love.

So she listened in, assessing the situation. As she did, the peaceful calmness surrounding their relationship subsided to something else—the resurgence of uncertainty panging in her heart.

Tears threatened to form, but she told herself to stop being ridiculous. She had no claim to Jackson other than a few romantic date nights and some promised I love yous under the false pretense of romance. True, there was certainly something building between them, something promising to bring both of them out of the darkness. True, she did love him, a love she hadn't expected, a love she'd refused to recognize at first.

But here was the offer to truly resurrect Jackson's life. This was what he wanted, what he needed more than he needed her.

His son back.

He'd loved Chloe once, from what she gathered. Here was the promise Logan's custody could stop being in limbo, that Jackson could get back the thing that rightfully mattered most—his son.

She inhaled deeply, knowing what she had to do. Her heart pounded with the loss already, her chest heavy with a different kind of grief than before.

So this was what a broken heart felt like, one not caused by the grasp of death but by the grasp of another's heart instead. In truth, it wasn't a whole lot different. Except at least in this case, she knew Jackson would be happy.

We might not have worked anyway, she convinced herself, reaffirming her steadfast decision to walk away. *This could have just been a rebound fling for both of us. It was fun while it lasted.*

Even as she said the words internally, she knew they held no merit. This was not a rebound or a fling. This was not a cheap excuse for a relationship. This, her heart told her, was the real deal, as real as her love had been for Tim.

It didn't matter. She had to walk away.

Slumping on the sofa, alone, only Henry there to comfort her, tears drenched her cheeks. She'd done the right thing. It didn't mean, however, her heart had to accept it as the right thing.

She closed her eyes, the pain surging now for two lost men.

For the millionth time since Tim died, she felt utterly lost and hopeless. She felt, as she did on the day she watched her soul mate buried in the unforgiving ground, as if she wanted to curl up and die. Deciding this wasn't healthy in any way, she did what she always did when she was hurting, or lost, or confused.

––––––––

"Hey, Chica, what're you doing here? You have the day off," Stella said as she held up a curling iron on a middle-aged woman's head. The salon had a few customers waiting in the front area, but it was relatively quiet.

Sophia painted on the chipper, fake smile she was used to. "Oh, you know, I was bored. Wanted to come in and get some stuff organized."

Stella frowned. "What's wrong?"

"I'm fine. Really," Sophia assured, busying her hands at

the front desk.

Stella didn't argue, continuing to work on the lady's hair. Sophia fiddled with the appointment book, offered some lemonade to the waiting customers, and just generally kept herself busy.

A few hours later, Stella had finished working on the final customer. After he left, Stella almost burst.

"Okay, spill," she demanded, handing Sophia the bag of Swedish Fish and motioning to the chair.

"Jackson and I are over," she whispered, figuring there was no use lying to her friend. Stella was relentless when she wanted information.

"Why? What happened?"

"I ended it."

"Are you crazy? You finally seemed happy. Head over heels, obnoxiously so. I thought you guys had finally rounded a corner? What happened?"

Sophia stared ahead, shoving a few pieces of the familiar candy into her mouth. She chewed the sticky fish, swallowed, and then told Stella the entire sordid tale.

Stella sat, speechless, once she'd heard about the carriage ride, the scrapbook, and finally, the Chloe situation.

"Well?" Sophia asked, looking at her friend who was rocking side to side in the salon chair.

"Well, I think you're nuts."

"What do you mean? Don't you understand?"

"No. Not at all. Because obviously he doesn't want to be with her, Soph. He loves you. I mean, come on, a carriage ride? What kind of man arranges that if his heart isn't in it?"

"It's not a question of whether or not his heart is in it. It's that it can't be, not if he wants a life with his son."

"There are other ways to see his son. The appeal, remember?"

"I don't know, Stella. I just didn't want to be the one to mess up his life."

"So you mess up his life by walking away from the great thing you have going?"

"He'll be fine."

"You're not giving yourself any credit. You think Jackson is helping you. You can't see how you're helping him, too. So by walking away from him, you've hurt him in the worst way."

"No. I gave him a chance to have a normal life back."

"Normal is overrated. Trust me."

"I just wanted to do the right thing."

"I think you just didn't want to be happy."

"Excuse me?" Sophia scowled now.

"You heard me. You're sabotaging yourself. You're afraid to be happy because you think it'll mean your relationship with Tim meant nothing. So you're using this as an excuse."

"No, I'm not. You have no clue what you're talking about."

"Soph, it's me. I've known you for years. I've seen you lie to clients about hairstyles looking good on them so long I know your tell."

"And what is my *tell*?"

"You tap a hand against your leg."

Sophia looked down. Her hand was tapping a quiet

pattern on her thigh.

"Dammit."

Stella smiled. "What are best friends for, huh? Now stop being a damn idiot. Go tell him you were stupid, and get him back."

Sophia shook her head, exhaling in frustration. "I can't do it." Tears threatened Sophia's eyes again. "You're right. I was happy with him. And you're right. This isn't about Chloe. I can't just move on with him. Chloe was a good excuse. But how can I move on with him when my husband's in a hole in the ground? Why do I deserve to have love again, a full life, when Tim doesn't get any of that?"

Stella rose, embracing her friend. "You're right. Tim didn't deserve to die. But Soph, you can't change that, and you can't just give up your life, too. He wouldn't want that."

They embraced in silence for a long moment.

"That's it. I'm tired of this sob fest," Stella said, heading to her bag to get her phone. She dialed a few numbers, held the phone to her ear and said, "Hey, I can't make it tonight. I'm having a girls' night."

Sophia furrowed her eyebrows, trying to decode Stella's actions.

"I love you, too," she continued, then hung up the phone.

"Stella, what are you doing? Why are you canceling on Larry?"

Stella held up a finger, dialed her phone again, and waited for the party on the other line to answer.

"Yes, I would like a quart of chicken broccoli, a pint of lo mein, and an order of your wonton soup, please. Uh-huh. Yep. Stella Major. Yep. See you in ten."

Stella smiled and her huge, toothy grin told Sophia she had plans.

"Get your stuff together. We've got Chinese food to pick up and movies to watch."

"What are you doing?"

"We are having a girls' night. No talk of boyfriends and sappy crap. Just you, me, some *Bruce Almighty, The Hangover,* and maybe even some *American Pie.*"

Sophia wanted to argue, to tell Stella she shouldn't be canceling her date just for her. But the thought of a night of funny movies, Chinese, and her best friend warmed her heart. She couldn't resist.

"Sounds amazing. I love you," she said as she lifted herself out of the chair, tossing the empty Swedish Fish bag in the trash.

"Love you back. Now, let's get moving. I can't wait to get my hands on that handsome little man Henry. I hope he sits with me."

"He will if you give him some lo mein."

They headed out the door, locking up Pink Lemonade. Sophia had known a trip to her shop would cheer her up. It always did the trick.

Chapter Twenty-Three

SOPHIA

The weeks passed. Despite Stella's pleading with Sophia to talk to Jackson, she refused. She was doing the right thing, even if it didn't feel like it. Her heart ached for Jackson, but she wouldn't give in. This was what was best.

Jackson hadn't given up on her yet, his stubborn nature underscored by his incessant attempts to contact her. There'd been at least one phone call or text each day from him. There had been a night when he'd knocked on her door.

She'd practically had to tie herself to the couch to resist answering it.

She'd been strong, though, knowing eventually he'd give up, he'd give in, and he'd get his son back. He'd go back to Chloe, and his life would be smooth sailing. She would be left alone to wallow in her grief, just like she should be.

A few weeks after her split with Jackson, she did something unexpected. She went back to the grief circle she'd quit a few weeks after Tim's death. She'd felt overwhelmed by it then, disgusted by the prospect of talking about her loss. She didn't want to have warm faces pitying her as she told her tale. She didn't want other women who thought they understood nosing around her business, analyzing her grief. She wanted to do it alone.

She realized it was a good thing to go, if not for the companionship, for the simple fact it was a way for her not to forget about Tim. She didn't want to slip into a routine and let her memories of him disintegrate. As grim as it sounded, she wanted to soak in the pain of his absence so she felt like she could appropriately work through it.

She had to admit, the group was easier with more time having passed. The anguish, although still palpable, was not as malignant, as fresh. She could stand at the podium and talk about Tim now, and she didn't feel the need to shred someone's eyeballs when they winked at her with a conspiratorial *I know where you're coming from* wink. In fact, she found herself actually connecting with a few women her age, actually sticking around for the cookies and punch after the weekly meetings to socialize.

See, you weren't in love with Jackson, she actually convinced herself. It seemed like life without Jackson was possible. She did miss him, especially at night when the stars were out and she'd think of their strolls through the neighborhood. She missed the smell of his cologne, the feel of his warm, scratchy hands on her.

She missed him.

But she could get through this. She could survive in a life without Tim or Jackson. She didn't need love. Her heart was dead, after all. She would never feel that way again.

She plowed right through the workweeks, smiling more, talking more with her customers. She went out for drinks with Stella a few times, and she even joined a spinning class to get back into shape. She worked with Henry, teaching him basic obedience. Time marched on, and as the days rolled by, she felt confident she was going to be okay.

And then it happened.

A few words, a gleaming smile, and a shining gemstone threw her off the path to recovery, turned the glittering of the spring sunshine into a demonic black hole.

———

"I'm so happy for you, Stella! That's amazing! Give me a hug."

These words instinctively flew from Sophia's lips to her best friend's ears. They were the words she knew she had to say, words she wanted to feel.

In her gut, though, as she hugged her best friend who was stamping her feet in a weird jig due to excitement and giddiness, bile rose.

"Isn't it gorgeous?" Stella said, flashing a delicate, shiny rock on the telltale finger.

"Of course it is," Sophia said, grinning while flashing a lot of teeth. She needed to play the part, to be the supportive friend.

She was happy for Stella. Larry was a great guy. He grounded Stella without stifling her. He made Stella want to settle down, to settle in. He accepted her, pink hair and witty remarks. He loved her. It was obvious.

And Stella was crazy about him, too. Sophia had been there through many relationships, breakups, and mistakes. She'd seen Stella be infatuated for the wrong reasons only to end up heartbroken. She'd known this was different from the beginning. Larry and Stella had started as a slow burn, igniting in a careful, contained way. Their relationship was the thing marriages were made of, Sophia knew. She recognized the signs, the sparkle in Stella's eye, the visions of the future.

Now, a wedding was certainly in her future.

"How did it happen?" Sophia asked, again following the customary questions.

"It's kind of silly, actually. So you know how my favorite animal is a dolphin, right?"

Sophia just nodded. Clearly she knew this.

"Well, he took me to the aquarium, which I'd been wanting to go to. And then, by the dolphins, with screaming kids and old people walking around, he just dropped to one knee and proposed."

"That's sweet."

"It was definitely different. But I loved it. We're actually thinking of saying our I dos right there."

"At the aquarium?"

"Yeah, why not? Conventional is so overrated."

"You don't say," Sophia teased. "Does this mean I'll be wearing flippers and scuba gear?"

"No. Obviously not. But a dolphin broach might not be out of the question."

"Whatever makes you happy."

She turned, heading to the fridge to get some beverages, trying to busy her hands. This was what she hated most about the loss. The grief was a stealthy stalker, waiting until a certain moment, a certain word, a certain event. Then it pounced, threatening to strangle her in pity, in jealousy, in anger. Love circled her. People were happy all around her, and she didn't want that to change.

But why couldn't she be happy, too? Why couldn't her heart be bursting with excitement for the future? Why did hers have to be blackened by death, corpse-like in her chest?

"Hey," Stella said, coming up to her in the kitchen. Henry trailed at her feet, biting her toes. "I'm sorry."

"Don't, Stell. This is your time."

"I know. But this can't be easy. I was insensitive. I'm sorry."

"Stop! I'm tired of everyone tiptoeing around me like I'm some selfish wench who can't hear about other people's happiness. Just stop." The anger gurgled and bubbled, flowing out in an inferno of words. Stella stood silently, seemingly sensing Sophia's need to vent.

Sophia closed her eyes, exhaling loudly, putting down

the wine bottle as she spoke. "I'm sorry," she whispered. "You're right. I *am* upset. It's not that I don't want you to be happy. Really. I'm glad you have Larry."

"You just feel like it's not fair you have to be so unhappy." Stella eyed her seriously, a look telling Sophia she truly got it.

Sophia nodded, admitting to her friend what she'd been trying to hide.

"Soph, I get it. I do. Your world is still in limbo. It's natural to feel angry when everyone else is moving on, but you don't have to be in limbo, not forever. Stop constricting yourself. Stop being afraid to feel. Grief has no time limit, it's true. Standing still isn't going to bring Tim back. Pretending you don't feel something won't resurrect what you had."

They stood, the words simmering between them. It should have been an awkward moment, one of those friendship-defining moments that pulled two people apart. It wasn't.

Sophia, not really knowing where to go with the conversation, simply said, "So what does Larry think about the Flipper-themed festivities?"

"Does it matter?" Stella smiled. "Plus, I mean, the man proposed to a pink-haired, mismatched sock wearing woman who eats SpaghettiOs on a regular basis. He probably knows the white dress, church wedding isn't really in the cards."

"Well, he's damn lucky to get you. Seriously. You spice him up. An engineer. I would've never guessed."

"Me neither. But that's the thing about love. It's not really logical, huh?"

"Neither is life."

The two plopped onto the sofa to talk wedding gowns and cake flavors, sipping a bottle of wine as they chatted.

It would only be later, alone in bed, that Sophia would let her mind travel where Stella had stopped it from going.

———

It was a Tuesday, and the night of their four-month dating anniversary. Sophia was dressed in a knee-length dress Stella had deemed too conservative—although anything was probably conservative compared to the damn miniskirt she'd let her borrow on the night she met Tim. She headed to their regular spot. She and Tim went to "their" restaurant at least once a week, the call of the lasagna, Tim's immense discount, and the memories of their first meeting beckoning them back.

Pink Lemonade had been up and running for a couple months. It was a hectic time. With Tim back in school and Sophia absorbed in the day-to-day running of a new business, it seemed like there was never enough time.

One thing that wasn't crazy and chaotic, however, was them.

Ever since the encounter at the restaurant the first night, Tim and Sophia had been inseparable—and Stella certainly noticed. She was always teasing the two about their googly eyes, their sweet sentiments, and the fact Sophia constantly talked about Tim.

Sophia had her share of heartbreak and crazy ex-boyfriends to know her connection with Tim was something special, something magnificent really. It wasn't because of outlandish romantic gestures or unguarded passions between them. It was the ease of their connection, the way she could tell him things she didn't think possible. It was because in just the four months they'd been together, she trusted him. She trusted him enough to tell him about her father's secret fight with mental illness and her own troubled moments during her teenage years. She trusted him enough that she was able to open her heart, to show her vulnerabilities and fears. She trusted he would never see her differently.

Sitting at their regular table as Tim told his coworkers that no, he couldn't bus table fifteen because he wasn't working, Sophia smiled as she set her purse on the floor and settled in. Within a few minutes, Kenzi, Sophia's favorite waitress, came to get their orders.

"I'm guessing it'll be the usual?" she asked, getting out a tablet and looking at them expectantly. They nodded, and Kenzi smiled. "I'll tell you what. You two are adorable." She winked then, looking conspiratorially at Tim, who winked back.

"How are things going?" Sophia asked, ignoring the odd feeling stirring from their wink and turning the conversation to Kenzi. She always chatted up the friendly brunette when she was in.

"Good. Joe's taking me to Paris next month, which is

pretty exciting. It's our ten-year anniversary."

"How awesome! Congratulations," Sophia said, truly happy for the woman.

"I better get back to the kitchen."

"Oh, wait. Can we have the appetizer now?"

Kenzi nodded. "Sure thing."

Sophia gave him an odd look. "We don't usually order an appetizer."

"True. But we have a new appetizer, and last week when I was working, I told Kenzi I wanted to try it."

Sophia nodded, not quite believing Tim. He seemed calm, sipping on his water as he looked at her.

"How's the client list coming?" he asked, changing the subject.

"Good. We've added about thirty in the past few weeks, which is awesome."

"And the lemonade? Still a hit?"

"Of course."

He looked at her, his warm eyes dripping with some type of unidentifiable emotion. He looked like he wanted to say something, like he was just buying time. She couldn't shake the feeling things were off, but she couldn't imagine what. Things had been great with him. She was crazy about him, and from the night they had last night, he was crazy about her. What could possibly be wrong?

Before she could think too much, Kenzi returned with the appetizer.

"What's that?" Sophia asked as the waitress put down a beautiful pink plate of strawberry cheesecake, Sophia's *favorite, and two glasses of pink lemonade. "What kind of appetizer is this?"*

Kenzi smiled, clapping her hands as she backed away, trying to give them privacy. She didn't go very far.

Tim took a deep breath. Then, he began speaking in a low, confident voice. "It's been four months since you walked through the door and asked me for a pink lemonade. From that moment, I knew there was something about you. I'm not naïve enough to call it love at first sight... but it was certainly something. The way you smiled, the way you blushed, everything about you—I had to know more. The past four months have been some of the best times of my life because I've been lucky enough to get to know you. I've learned just how amazing you are, from your talents at running a business to your compassion. I've seen your interactions with others, from the time you stopped to give a homeless man fifty bucks from your wallet to the time you gave a stray cat a bath last week. I've seen so many amazing things about you that have made me fall more and more in love with you. But it's not just the good I see, Sophia. I see your flaws too. I see your short fuse when it comes to slow drivers. I see your tendency to talk too fast and your inability to stop buying shoes."

Sophia had been tearing up, but now she looked at him in confusion. "Thanks... I think?"

"My point is, I don't love you for this perfect image I have of you. I know you're human. I love you, good and bad, perfect qualities and flaws. I love every single piece of you, and I know I will for the rest of my life. I know this is crazy.

I know it's only been four months. I know you might say no. I'm a future lawyer. I don't take risks. I'm taught to not take cases I can't win. For once in my life, I'm taking a risk, going against the rational thinker within me. I'm going to lay it all out there. Because you're worth it, Sophia. I would do anything for you."

He stood, other patrons now alight with excited murmurings. The scene, though, started to whir around her. She felt excited and nauseous at the same time. She hadn't seen this coming, not at all. On one knee, Tim pulled out a ring box and presented it to her.

"You're my best friend. I love you. Will you marry me?"

She looked at him, unsure of how to react. In the movies, girls cried, or gasped, or screamed at this moment. They leaped into the arms of their lover, sometimes tumbling down in a cute and clumsy display of affection.

Sophia did neither.

She sat, stunned, silently appraising the situation. The ring, the restaurant, the eyes on her... it was all too much.

"I don't feel well," she said, standing as she fanned herself. She felt really hot all of a sudden, a scorching sauna lifting from under her skin.

"Sophia?"

"I'm fine. I just..."

And then there was nothing.

Sophia woke to a crowd gathered around her, a woman

shouting she was a nurse pushing her way to her. She felt the strange woman's hand on her wrist. Everything was blurry, but then it came into focus.

"What happened?"

"I don't know. I think you blacked out. Just stay there." A woman's hands were on her head, pushing firmly. She tried to brush her away.

"I'm fine. My head just hurts a little." She started to sit up, wooziness overpowering her. Tim and the woman pushed her back down gently.

"The ambulance is on its way," another voice shouted.

"Tim, I'm fine. This is silly."

Suddenly, she felt something sticky on her forehead. She pulled her finger in front of her eyes and saw it—blood. Hot, sticky blood.

Then there was nothing again.

———————

The next thing she remembered was opening her eyes from a hospital bed, bandages partially blocking her eye. Tim was pacing around the room, and her parents were there, too.

"Mom? Dad? What's going on?" she croaked. They ran to her bedside.

"Oh, honey. You're fine! You just took a spill."

"What?"

"Do you remember?"

She thought, rummaging through her mind for the appropriate memories. It came back to her in bits. The ring, feeling very warm, and then nothing. Then the blood... and nothing again.

"What happened?"

"They ran some tests. They think you just had low blood sugar from not eating all day," Tim said. "You passed out, but I couldn't quite catch you in time. You fell in an awkward way and cracked your head on the corner of the table. You got some stitches."

"Well, your fiancée isn't quite the graceful woman she claims to be," her dad added, and Sophia's heart stopped. Of course! The proposal. The ring. She had never said...

"It's not fiancée yet," Tim said, looking at her expectantly. "Although after this whole scene, I'm not so certain about her answer anymore at all."

He approached her, taking her hand in his.

She smiled at him, despite the aching in her head and her exhaustion. "Yes, Tim. I was going to say yes."

"Really?" His grin was goofy, like a small boy who found a five-dollar bill on the ground.

She nodded gently, and he let out a cheer. "Hallelujah!" He reached in to kiss her, vigorously brushing his lips against hers.

"Ow," she said.

"Sorry," he sheepishly apologized. "We're getting married! Let's set a date."

"How about we get me out of this joint first," she teased.

Their toast wasn't quite the adorable, memorable pink lemonade toast he had planned for them. They didn't get to enjoy the celebratory cheesecake either, hospital Jell-O *having to serve as a substitute along with some ginger ale.*

Despite the chaos and the bandages, the impromptu trip to the hospital, the pain, and the mild concussion, it was all worth it.

She was marrying Tim. She had found the one, her Mr. Right, the man she would spend forever with. At that moment, hospital bed and all, Sophia was happier than she ever dreamed she could be.

———

At the time, stitches from a fall were the worst thing Sophia and Tim could imagine in their life together. They hadn't been able to foresee, to even consider life would throw them an even harsher, unbearable blow. A decade of happiness, of flashbacks to their memorable proposal would be scarred by a sudden loss, a devastating blow to their relationship. Forever wouldn't be as long as either of them had planned.

Stella's ring had brought visions of that first proposal, but in truth, they'd brought visions of another proposal, too. Sophia wanted to block this second one out, to pretend her mind wasn't going there.

But it was.

Because when she saw Stella's ring, she had also been considering what it would be like to have Jackson ask her to marry him, to have him say sweet, tender words to her on a carriage ride, reminiscent of their first real moment together. She had thought how the name Sophia Gauge flew sweetly off her tongue.

Tears welled, and her heart ached. She missed Tim. She hated herself for wanting Jackson. Most of all, she hated the aching pierce of her lonely heart.

Chapter Twenty-Four

"I'm sorry I missed last night, Mom. I couldn't get off work." Jackson handed his crudely wrapped gift to his mom, who was leaning on the counter.

"You've been working a lot lately, honey," she replied, reaching for the package. "We missed you last night."

"I know. I'm sorry." He led himself to a stool at the island as she unwrapped her birthday gift.

"Do you want some leftover cake?" she asked, setting down the package to reach for a plate.

"No, I'm good."

She started cutting him a piece anyway. She handed him the cake before returning to the gift.

He sighed, deciding the chocolate cake with peanut butter icing did look amazing.

His mom crumpled the paper, putting it on the counter as she opened the box to reveal the bracelet he'd picked out—this morning, but she didn't need to know that.

"Honey, it's gorgeous. I love it," she said, heading over to hug him after she put it on her wrist. "Thank you."

She kissed him on the cheek as he shoveled cake in his mouth.

"So, how are things?"

He swallowed a glob of icing before replying. "Okay. Busy."

"Yes, I know. I've barely seen you this month."

He eyed her, trying to mask the despondency on his face. "It's been hectic at work."

"Jonathan told me the appeal was approved and you're going to court soon."

"Yep."

"Aren't you happy about that? It's a good sign."

He shrugged. "I'll probably lose anyway."

"Jackson. What is this? You're so negative and down. I'm worried about you."

"Mom, I'm fine."

"You're not fine. You haven't been fine since she left. Stop pretending you haven't been around because of work."

"I told you, I've been working a lot."

"Not last night."

His cheeks reddened and his gaze fell to the floor. "How'd you find out?" he mumbled, ashamed.

"You know I have eyes everywhere."

"Gloria."

"Yes, Gloria found out from her son who knows Joe, your coworker."

"I'm sorry."

"Honey, I don't care about you missing my birthday party. I'm an old hag. My birthday doesn't even matter anymore. I'm more concerned about you. You're slipping away, Jackson. I see it on your face."

He put his head in his hands. His mother was right. She was always right.

He hadn't wanted to admit how close he was to the edge again, how close he was to slipping back into the Jackson he had been after Chloe left him. He didn't want to own up to the fact that the bottle was calling his name, that suddenly the sunshine felt like it was melting his skin. He found himself, more and more, craving the solitude of his dingy apartment and he felt the mindless television gaining room in his life. He found himself sinking slowly away from the man he'd become.

The man he'd been with Sophia.

Gone were the days of laughter and optimism. He didn't even know the man who thought he could win Logan back. He looked in the mirror and he saw sadness, loneliness.

He saw a broken man.

But he wasn't one to ask for help. He wasn't one to admit it. Instead, he'd been slipping away from everyone, from everything. His days were again overrun by work and sleep.

He snapped out of his thoughts when his mother put

her arms around his shoulders.

"Jackson, get it together. It's not too late to get her back."

"Mom, stop. I've tried."

"Well try harder. It's not like you to give up so quickly. God, all those years growing up, you were a stubborn ass. Now, you find the woman who makes you happy, and you just let her go at the drop of a hat? What the hell are you thinking?"

He turned to look at her, and she smiled.

"Wow, Mom. Way to be subtle."

"I don't have time for subtle. Neither do you. Don't let that woman slip away. Fight for her. Fight for Logan. Fight for your life back, Jackson."

It'd been a hard few weeks. He hadn't felt any glimmers of hope. The turned down phone calls, her insistence it was over. A few annoying visits from Chloe, a few violent outbursts when he swore up and down it was still over. Nothing seemed hopeful.

But leave it to his mom, the crazy, sometimes foul-mouthed lady who loved to stuff him with food, to reignite his views of the future.

She was right. What the hell was he thinking?

He wasn't ready to let her go. He didn't think Sophia was ready to let go either, no matter what she'd convinced herself.

"I love you, Mom," he said, kissing her on the cheek. "Happy belated birthday. I'm so sorry I wasn't here to see you blow out the candles. I hate to run, but I have somewhere to be."

His mom smiled, clapping her hands together. "I knew that candle was lucky."

"What?" he asked as he stood from the stool.

"That candle Gretta brought. She found this birthday candle shaped like a cat, so naturally she bought it for me. I made a wish when I blew out the candles yesterday—not that you would know since you lied and skipped my party." She grinned, showing she was teasing. "Anyway, I made a wish. And I think it's about to come true if you're heading where I think you are."

"I'm heading to the graveyard."

His mom furrowed her brow. "Okay, well, that wasn't my birthday wish."

Now it was his turn to grin. "Well, maybe not. Hopefully not. But I think, in a roundabout way, this is going to make your wish come true."

"Okay, I'm done asking questions, you weird boy. Now, get out of here. Thanks for the bracelet. I love it. Oh, and next time you decide to lie to your mother, at least make it a convincing one."

"What's the point? I thought you have eyes everywhere."

"True. Always have."

"I know. I found out the hard way."

"Not my fault you thought you could hide cigarettes."

"Yeah, or kiss Becky after we skipped class. Or swipe a chocolate bar from the general store."

"Wow, I forgot what a terrible child you were. Maybe Sophia was right to get away from you."

"Really, Mom?"

"I'm kidding. Now go. My show's starting in fifteen minutes."

"You know you could get a DVR."

"Your father doesn't want the government spying on us."

"Okay, I'm seriously out," Jackson said, shaking his head.

His family was, in fact, crazy.

He truly loved them for it.

Chapter Twenty-Five

JACKSON

Headlights passed by the cemetery, blinding Jackson with their ricocheting light. They lifted the graveyard out of the uncanny, celestial glow from the stars.

Most would be frightened by the prospect of standing in a graveyard this late, but Jackson wasn't. The blackness, the stark silence seemed more fitting than the daylight visits.

He didn't really know much about daylight visits, in all honesty. It'd been a while since his feet had plodded on this plot of ground. He'd been, in reality, avoiding this area.

He didn't want to forget Tim. He couldn't even if he'd wanted to. The man had been such a fixture in his life, even when he wasn't actually there. He'd been a part of almost every single one of Jackson's childhood memories and moments.

The situation with Sophia, though... well, it did sort of make graveyard visits a bit different. He understood Sophia's guilt over their budding relationship because it was, in many ways, his own. You didn't covet your best friend's wife; the commandments even made that clear. Did that rule apply now, though? His rational sense said no. But the part of him that would always see Sophia like he had the very first day—on Tim's arm—said maybe.

He wanted to believe Tim would be okay with this. Tim had been such a selfless man. He'd always been. He knew Tim would want both Sophia and Jackson to find happiness in a world without him, no matter what that meant. Jackson had to believe Tim would understand it wasn't planned.

Still, when he'd realized how right his mother was, Jackson felt an instant pull to come here. His mind made up, he knew he needed to clear the air, if not for Tim's sake—obviously—then for his very own. He needed to be here, to feel Tim's presence. He needed to feel close to him, to feel in a way as if they were settling things. It was an odd feeling, an odd request. Then again, nothing from the past year was conventional or expected.

Jackson lowered himself to the ground, a bit soppy from a light afternoon sprinkle. He felt chilled, the night air still not committing to full spring temperatures. It didn't matter. All he cared about, all he needed, was to be present in this moment, to reflect, and to figure things out.

He sat in silence, thinking about a lot of things, twirling

a blade of grass between his thumbs. He thought about Sophia, about seeing her at the mall months before Tim passed. He thought about the sorrow on her face at the grave.

He thought about their memories, though, too. He thought about the feeling he tried to push out of his shattered heart, the feeling that pulled his heart back together. He thought about her laugh, about the way she said his name, about the way she blew her bangs out of her eyes.

Looking at the gravestone, his mind traveled back to a time long ago.

A time when Sophia wasn't his or Tim's.

A time when Tim was the brother he'd never had.

"Jackson, just spill. What is it?"

Jackson shook his head, anger churning inside. Sitting on the sofa where they usually played games, he felt his fury erupt as he crushed his soda can, the metal crumpling.

"Nothing."

"Just tell me. You've been stewing all afternoon."

Tim and Jackson were partaking in their usual Friday night tradition—video games and pizza. It was their junior year. They'd been friends for a while. They'd been through the awkward junior high years, a prom, a few girlfriends, a few kisses, and a few trips to third base. They'd been there for each other through a few breakups, a few mistakes. Tim had been there for the loss of Wade, and Jackson had been there for Tim through an intense cancer scare.

But Jackson had never really felt like this.

"It's Terra, isn't it?"

Jackson didn't reply, gritting his teeth at the mention of the name.

He felt like a damn fool, an idiot for getting this upset over a girl. He'd lost his brother. He'd been through hellish ordeals. What was wrong with him? How could he let this get to him so much?

"Hey, listen. I get it. She was important to you," Tim offered, putting the controller down to focus on Jackson.

"I'm over it. She's a bitch," he said, his immaturity shining through.

In truth, he wasn't over it. He'd loved her. He'd thought it was the real deal. At sixteen, love was viewed through some pretty jaded glasses, and every breakup was like a million glass shards stabbing into your chest.

Terra, though…Terra's betrayal of him was like a million glass shards mixed with an atomic bomb.

"She is a bitch. I agree. But listen, you have to let this go, man. She was an idiot. You'll get over her. You will."

"Easy for you to say. You're not the joke of the football team."

"Well, yeah, doesn't help that she left you for the most sought-after dude in the school. But it's okay, he'll get his. Someday, you'll get the chance to beat his ass."

Jackson shook his head. "You were the one who held me back yesterday."

"Well, it wasn't the right time." Tim shrugged. He was always the logical one.

"I just"—Jackson grabbed the rim of his hat, bending it—"God, I fucking loved her. I thought she was it, you know?"

He turned his gaze to Tim, who was just looking at him, shaking his head.

"I know. Pathetic," Jackson said, exhaling in an attempt to calm himself, fists clenched.

"No. Not really. I get it. She was hot. And pretty okay. Until the cheating thing, of course."

"Yeah, well, I'm done. I'm done with chicks. Not worth my trouble."

Tim shook his head. "You're so not done. I give it a week."

"What's that supposed to mean, asshole? Just because your nerdy ass has his head in the books all of the time doesn't mean I have to."

"Truth. Honestly, man. You're not done. Not even close. Now you know what you had with Terra, well, it wasn't the real deal. Now you'll know what it's like when you find it."

"Okay, Shakespeare. What do you think the real deal is like?"

"I don't know. Never found it yet. I just think when you find her, Jackson, you'll know."

"How?"

"Because when you find her, you won't be sitting on a couch eating pizza if you two argue or break up. Your ass will be getting her back."

"So you think I should take Terra back?"

"No, idiot. I'm saying when you find a girl you're willing

to fight for, a girl you're willing to fight to get back no matter what baggage she comes with or what mistakes you made, then I think you've found her."

Jackson grimaced. "You're getting all poetic on me here. I need some beef jerky and some football. Let's man up a bit here, please."

Tim shook his head, grabbing his controller. "You're on. Let's see who's the real pussy here."

To Jackson's true disappointment, he earned the title when Tim kicked his ass five games in a row.

"I think I found her, Tim. I do. And I think you're the one who helped me realize it."

Jackson smiled, wishing he could go back to the sofa and talk to his sixteen-year-old self. He wanted to tell the smug troublemaker Terra definitely wasn't worth his time—she was now in jail for drug dealing—and to enjoy his time with Tim a little more.

"I don't know if you'd approve of this, buddy. I hope you would. The thing is, I've found her. I've found the one I'm willing to fight for. The one I can't let go. I hope you understand."

He clambered to his feet, slapped the gravestone, and turned around.

No stars fell from the sky. No whispers carried on the wind.

But Jackson knew.

He knew in his soul Tim would be nodding.

———————

"Mommy says you don't want to be with me," Logan said, playing with his stuffed kangaroo in his car seat when Jackson picked him up the next day for his visit.

"Buddy, you know that's not true. I'm here now." Jackson peered in his rearview mirror and caught Logan frowning.

"Mommy says you won't come live with us. Mommy says you won't be with her."

Jackson sighed. Leave it to Chloe to turn their son into a weapon. "Logan, it's not like that. It's complicated."

"I miss you, Daddy. Why won't you live with us?"

"I miss you too. But Daddy and Mommy have a lot of issues."

"Do you hate Mommy?"

"No, I don't hate Mommy."

"Why does Mommy hate you?"

"She doesn't."

"Yes, she does. She tolded me she hates you. She said I should hated you, too."

Jackson slammed on the brakes at the stop sign, resting for a moment to calm his anger. He turned around to look at his son.

"Listen. Sometimes grown-ups say things they don't mean. Mommy is just upset about things. I love you. We're best buds, right?"

Logan leaned up to give Jackson their traditional fist-bump. "Buds. I don't want to hated you. I told Mommy that."

"Okay. Enough talk about hate. It's not a nice word. Let's talk about what we're going to do this weekend, okay?"

The car behind him honked, forcing him to turn back around.

He let the anger recede. He would not let Chloe get to him, would not spend the weekend thinking about what a bitch she was. He would enjoy their time together this weekend. He would call Jonathan to see if the trial for the appeal could be moved up.

Then, after the weekend, he would start getting his life back in order.

He had a plan, and Chloe's inappropriate comments wouldn't derail him. He just had to do a few things, make a few calls, and then he could get Sophia back.

Once Sophia was back, he knew everything else would fall into place. It just had to. It was about time the universe conspired with him instead of against him.

"Daddy, is your lady friend coming with us again? The pretty one you kissed?"

Jackson was shocked, but then he let out a laugh. "Not this time, buddy. But next time. I promise."

It was probably not the wisest thing to do, but he felt an air of confidence. Jackson did not make promises to his son he could not keep.

He knew, though, Sophia would be back in their lives. She just had to be.

She was the one he would fight for. He would do whatever it took.

Chapter Twenty-Six

SOPHIA

Sophia rocked, back and forth, back and forth, trying to lull herself into a state of peace. The solitude of the room, this room in particular, irked her. The rocking chair creaked, its white paint chipping. Even though it wasn't very comfortable, she kept rocking, silence giving her more time to toss the thoughts around in her head.

Her gaze traveled along the walls. All around were pictures of her time with Tim. There was a photo of the two of them at Kennywood, her stuffing her face with cotton candy. They were laughing, glowing in a childish way. There was a picture of them on their honeymoon, a picture of them at Christmas. All around, his image called to her, beckoning her to what once was.

She kept rocking, bouncing her feet gently off the floor,

tears rolling down her already tear-stained face. She felt comatose, frozen in place. She felt like maybe she was going a bit mad. Maybe she was.

Running her fingers against the smooth armrest, she thought about the symbolism in this moment, in this chair. At one point, this chair had brought her so much sadness, so much disappointment. It was from a time she thought she would be building her family with Tim, when they still had hope for what was to come.

───────────

"We're here!" her mom shouted as she burst through the door, and Sophia grinned. She knew she couldn't stay away.

"Mom, Dad! You didn't have to come over right away." She pulled Tim toward the door, the two abandoning their dinner.

Last night, she'd made the call to share the news. She knew her parents would be ecstatic, knew a visit would be coming. But she hadn't expected them tonight, not really.

"I couldn't stay away. We wanted to congratulate you in person," her mom said, running over to sweep Sophia into her arms. She squeezed her girl for a long moment, gripping her tightly. "I am so happy for both of you."

Sophia's dad shook Tim's hand, giving him a pat on the back. Sophia's parents were beaming. She was sure their expressions were mirror images of her own face.

Sophia's mom patted her tummy. "Hello, in there. It's Grandma," she said. Sophia rolled her eyes.

"Mom, it's a tad early."

"It's never too early. How many more days?"

"A lot. I have an appointment tomorrow. I think I'm like five weeks."

"Oh, I'm so excited."

"I can't believe you guys came all this way. Are you hungry? We just ate. If I'd have known..."

"Don't be silly. You go rest."

"Mom, I'm pregnant. It's not tuberculosis or paralysis. I can make you something."

"Stop. Sit. We have a present for you anyway. Stuart, go get it, would you?"

"A present already? I could get used to this."

"Need any help?" Tim asked, always the gentleman.

"I've got it. Sit down."

A few moments later, her dad returned with the gift. Sophia teared up.

"Are you serious?"

The white rocking chair sat in the kitchen area. Sophia walked over to touch it, emotions and hormones mixing into a potentially dangerous explosion.

"Of course, darling. I always knew someday I'd pass it down. Grandma would want you to have it."

"It's beautiful. Thank you," Tim said, hugging his mother-in-law.

Sophia took it all in. The rocking chair had been her grandmother's, her mother's, and now hers. She felt her hand go instinctively to her stomach, imagining all the times she would rock their little one to sleep in the chair that had *raised two generations so far. She took in the sight of her husband with her parents, all the important people in her life gathered in one room. It was a picture-perfect moment, a memory she knew she would cherish.*

After her parents had gone and Tim had moved the rocking chair to what would eventually be the nursery, she had sat in it a long time, rocking back and forth, thinking about their future.

"I love you," he'd whispered, sneaking into the room to find her there an hour later. He kissed her cheek. "I can't wait for this baby. I knew it would happen."

"I love you more," she replied, slowing her rocking. "It just feels like a miracle."

They'd been trying for thirteen months, had started to feel like giving up.

And it happened. God had answered her prayers. They were starting a family.

Rocking back and forth, she saw visions of them as the perfect family—dance recitals, spelling bees, playing catch in the yard. She couldn't wait to hear the word she'd been wanting to hear.

Mom.

———

The tears picked up in intensity as she rocked, just like she had years ago. She felt a flashback to the warmth she felt on the first day the rocking chair came into the house. She felt a pang of the hopes for the future, for what could've been.

Five weeks later, those dreams were crushed under a

word she'd never expected to hear.

Miscarriage.

The single word had shredded her, body and soul, in a thousand ways. It had ripped the dream right out from under it. She had returned to the rocking chair only to feel herself gripping the armrest, her nails shredding the paint.

Her parents, Tim, Stella, they had all told her to be patient, with time she would be okay. They told her it was unfortunate, but these things happened, and they would just try again.

She'd tried to believe them, tried to pick up the pieces. Eventually, the sorrow dulled to a soft jabbing pain. They tried again.

And again.

And again.

Another rocking chair moment never came. There was never another beautiful family moment of her parents congratulating her.

Slowly, the dreams of being a mother dimmed.

They had turned to the thought of adoption, had decided it was their route. She'd been okay with that. The rocking chair sat still, waiting for her to rock her baby in her arms, even if it wasn't biological. She still held out for the word "mother."

And then Tim. The heart attack, the death, the pain even worse this time.

The rocking chair sat empty. The word "mother" vanished completely from her thoughts. She would never experience that. The perfect dreams of dance recitals and playing catch were incinerated. The pictures on the wall of their planned nursery suddenly became horrendous, flashing reminders of all they'd lost. She had shut the door the week after the funeral, not wanting to step foot in a tomb of what could've been.

Except today. Today, she'd creaked open the door, inhaled the dusty, shut-in smell. She'd run her fingers over the glass of the pictures on the wall, realizing they'd never really left her mind. She lowered herself into the rocking chair, simultaneously numb to the reality and painfully aware of it.

She rocked. For hours, she rocked, Henry curled in a ball at her feet, thinking about the madness called life, thinking about how everything changed. Thinking about how sometimes wishes and prayers were answered in ways unimaginable.

———————

"Honey, what are you doing?" Stella asked as Sophia looked at her in the doorway of the room. Stella crossed the rough hardwood floor, tripping on the edge of the area rug. Sophia didn't try to wipe away her tears or hide her state. She was too tired, too confused to be anything except honest.

"Sophia, what's going on? Are you having a hard day? What's the date? Is today a significant day?"

Sophia didn't say anything, just stared as her friend knelt down to be eye level. She stopped rocking. Sitting motionless felt odd after the hours of rocking. "No. It's just a regular day."

"Then, honey, what's going on? I was worried when you didn't show up for work and didn't answer your phone. Just overwhelmed? Thinking of Tim?"

"Always."

"What can I do?"

She dropped her gaze to the floor. There was no point keeping up the façade, not with Stella. "I'm pregnant," she whispered, her voice sounding scratchy. She didn't cry, and her tears had dried. She was empty, empty of emotion, empty of tears, empty of everything.

"What?" Stella asked, her voice underscoring her shock.

"I'm pregnant." She turned her head back to Stella, staring into her deep blue eyes. She waited for judgment. She waited to see how Stella would react. She waited for Stella to tell her how to react, how to feel.

Because she was just so damn conflicted.

There was the guilt. She felt like she'd cheated on Tim, abandoned him for a dream with another man. She felt all of those reasons pulling her back into sorrow. She also felt foolish. She'd been so adamant she should end things with Jackson, but she ended up pregnant. She should have been more careful with her heart and with her body.

In spite of all those negative feelings, though, she also felt happy. A baby. She'd always wanted this. Suddenly, she realized there would be someone in her life, someone there. Someone to live for, to get out of bed for. Suddenly, she didn't see her life as a string of dates on a calendar.

Most of all, she was terrified. The last time she was pregnant...

Plus, she was terrified about how people would react. What would Jackson say?

Everything had been complicated. Now it was just more complicated.

"Soph, that's great. How far along are you?" Stella took her hands in hers.

"Six weeks."

Stella hugged her. "This is good news."

"Yes. I guess." Stella pulled back to look Sophia in the eye.

"I know it's not how you imagined it."

"Not at all."

"I know. But it's a miracle. It is. And Jackson loves you. He only left because you made him. He's going to be ecstatic. It's not too late, Soph, to get your life back with him. You're going to be so happy, even if you can't see it now."

"I don't want to be with him just because of this."

"You won't be. I don't care what you say. You never stopped caring for him. And he still loves you."

"This is just all so messy. I didn't expect this. I miss Tim. I love him. I wanted this dream with him."

"I know."

"You're right, though. I do love Jackson, too. I do. But how can we just move on together? How can we forget that this was once my dream with Tim? How can I just replace him?" Suddenly, the tears she thought were gone came back. Stella held her for a long time.

"Shh, it's okay. It's okay. It's all going to be okay."

"I don't know."

"I do. Listen. Life, it's fucking crazy."

Sophia paused, grinning a bit at Stella's typical bluntness. She wiped the snot from under her nose as Stella continued.

"It's chaotic and weird and strange and unexpected. But you can't sit here feeling sad and sorry for yourself. You can't let your sadness overshadow this amazing news. A baby, Soph. You've always wanted this. I know you're scared and worried. I know this isn't how you pictured your life. But that's the thing. This is your life. Roll with it. Soak it in. Be happy. It doesn't mean you've forgotten Tim. It doesn't mean you're moving on completely and forgetting him. It means you're going to live your life and be happy. He would want that for you. And honestly, if he had to pick someone for you to be with, don't you think it would be his best friend?"

Sophia scrunched her eyebrows. "Um, no. Think that might be a bit much."

"Okay, okay, you're right. Too far." Stella laughed, putting her hands up. "Seriously, though. You're having a baby with a guy you love. No one can judge you for that. And if they do, I'll kill them."

Sophia laughed, nodding. "Maybe you're right. I can't change things that have happened. I *can* decide where my life's going. And I want it to be happy."

"Okay. Great. So when are you telling Jackson?"

Sophia blew her bangs out of her eyes. "I don't know."

"What do you mean? What happened to the carpe diem attitude?"

"I'm serious. I don't want us to reunite just because I'm pregnant. I don't want him to feel obligated."

"You're ridiculous."

"I will tell him. Eventually. But I want to think some things through first."

"You're so damn frustrating."

"So are you."

"I'll take it as a compliment. Now listen, go brush your scuzzy-ass hair, wipe off your mascara, and get some real clothes on."

"Why?"

"We're going out to celebrate. I'm going to be a godmother. This is big news. Let's go get ice cream. Don't preggo women like that? Do you want pickles with it?"

"Oh my God. You're ridiculous."

"You love me."

"God help Larry when you're knocked up."

"Ha. That'll be the day."

Sophia shook her head. She suddenly had an image of Stella holding a pink-haired baby dressed in a black lace shirt and a studded necklace.

She smirked.

"What?" Stella asked, appraising Sophia's weird expression.

"Nothing. Just hoping that wasn't a vision of the future. Let's go get ice cream. But no pickles just yet."

"Deal."

She ran a brush through her hair, feeling better about everything.

Good friends did that for you. They made you realize when you were being ridiculous, told you when you looked ratty. Most of all, they told you it was okay to be happy.

For the first time in a while, Sophia believed it.

"Will you be wanting pictures?"

"Absolutely," Sophia replied, exhaling deeply as she tried to calm her nerves. The table beneath her was cold, and the technician was even colder, staring at the screen intently.

Sophia's heart was full and warm. The clinical feel of the room, the oatmeal-colored walls couldn't bring her down.

She was going to see her baby for the first time.

It had been a little over a week since she'd broken the news to Stella. A week to get used to the idea, to let Stella's reassurance sink in.

A week, though, to decide she couldn't tell Jackson, not just yet. She would eventually. She wasn't the kind of woman to keep it to herself, to hide something this important. But, as she had told Stella, she also didn't want to be the kind of woman to make their relationship about a baby, to make him feel obligated. She wanted to do this on her own, for the time being, to figure it out, to find the right way to tell him.

So there she was, her first sonogram.

Granted, the baby would probably look like a grain of rice on a splotchy screen at this point, but it didn't matter. She was going to get the first look at her child.

Her child.

It hadn't taken her as long as she thought to get used to the idea. Sure, things were still a mess—hence her attending the first sonogram alone, as the technician aptly pointed out, *several times*, when she asked, *several times*, if she was sure no one else was coming for this moment.

Looking at the ceiling—also oatmeal colored... these people needed a lesson in interior design—she thought briefly about the fact she was all alone.

"The baby's there," the technician grumbled, pointing to a dot on the screen. This lady was clearly unhappy with her job.

Sophia couldn't bring herself to care about the technician's harsh tone. All she could care about was that she wasn't here all alone; she wasn't alone at all.

Her baby. The baby growing every day, the baby she would raise, would love, was on the screen.

Her eyes teared up. "Hi, little one," she said.

The technician gave her a look as if to say *Crazy*.

Sophia grimaced. "You know, my pregnancy book says babies can hear and determine their mother's voices in the womb," she said pointedly.

The technician, true to her mousey nature, said nothing.

Sophia's gaze returned to the screen. She couldn't stop staring.

Looking at the scaly, scratchy picture, though, her heart ached a little.

Actually, her heart ached a lot.

She realized she did want someone else to be here, to be by her side, holding her hand, making her laugh in the face of this horrid technician. She wanted someone else with her to break up the oatmeal color, to radiate with her at the sight of the baby.

It wasn't just anyone holding her hand she wanted, no needed, now.

It was one person. One man.

Jackson.

She smiled, a wide, toothy grin.

She didn't have to go this alone. She didn't have to feel guilty. The answer, the one she'd been looking for, was on the screen. It was in her heart.

She was ready to say hello to this new life, to shout carpe diem after all. She was ready to crawl out of the black, dark hole of grief and let joy come flooding back in.

Chapter Twenty-Seven

Sophia scratched her nose with the back of her arm, sneezing as she did. In her rolled up purple sweatpants from high school—which had a mystery stain on the thigh—and a holey, red T-shirt, she was quite the sight.

Call it early nesting, call it being in a good mood from the sonogram appointment, call it realizing her house was a freaking disaster; it didn't matter. She was spring-cleaning, organizing, and just plain getting the filth out of the house—and she wasn't looking very good doing it. She wasn't a domestic goddess, although she never had been.

Tim had made fun of her for her lack of domestic charm. He wasn't sexist, doing his share of laundry and dishes, too. He just loved to tease her about her cluelessness in the cleaning aisle, by the washer, and in front of the stove.

Now, she was determined to make the place shine, even if it was just for her and Henry. She was in better spirits today even though she typically hated cleaning. Pandora blasting in the background, she continued on to the living room with her yellow duster, prepared to tackle some dust bunnies in hibernation.

When the doorbell rang, she thought nothing of it, yelling, "One second," as she headed to her wallet for some cash. Her stomach grumbled in anticipation of the General Tso's chicken waiting for her at the door. Hey, she was in a better mood, but she wasn't crazy. She wouldn't tackle cleaning the whole house without some amazing Chinese cuisine to get her through.

Adele came on the station, and Sophia was tempted to belt out the first note. She reminded herself Mike—she did frequent the Chinese takeout restaurant quite often, elevating them to a first-name basis—was at the door and probably didn't need or want to hear her off-tune rendition of the singing goddess. She flung the door open, a ten-dollar bill in hand.

But Mike wasn't at the door, and her General Tso's chicken was nowhere in sight. Instead, a familiar face, lined with stubble, greeted her. Her heart clenched in icy panic. What was he doing here?

And shit, she was wearing the mystery stain pants in the grape hue with her red shirt.

And she hadn't washed her hair in a few days.

And she was covered in cleaning solutions.

"Um, hi, do you need something?" she asked, stumbling

over her words, taking in the sight of him, the scent of his cologne floating on the breeze toward her.

He had a handful of daisies, her favorite. She couldn't help but ogle them.

Her chest clenched again. What was he doing here? Stella had to have told him. She must have spilled…

"Can I come in?" He interrupted her thoughts, grinning, his eyes sparkling. He was the same Jackson she'd said goodbye to a month or so ago. Somehow, though, he was different. It was more than the stubble. It was the confidence in him, the chin up feel of him. It suited him, she had to admit.

At the moment, all she could think about was how this was a chin down moment for her. She wasn't sure if she was ready to face everything just yet, despite her sonogram revelations. She was just starting to feel okay; she was just convincing herself of this. She was just looking for one day of mindless dusting and belting out tunes before approaching the father of her unborn child.

However, looking at him in his jeans and Johnny Cash black T-shirt, she realized she did want to talk to him. She wanted him here, wanted him looking into her eyes. She missed their walks, their deep conversations. She missed the feel of his hands on her.

She gestured toward the living room, Adele still blaring in the background. God, this was a long song. And the symbolism in it couldn't be ignored, to her chagrin. She hoped he didn't notice.

He smirked. "This seems fitting, huh?" he said. Yep, he noticed.

He walked into the kitchen, heading toward the cupboard with her solitary vase. He pulled it down, put the daisies in, and filled it with water. It was natural but intimate. It was the move of a man who lived here.

"So," she said, trying to assess where this was going, not really believing he was actually here.

"So." He took a few steps toward her, and she was again reminded of how gross her hair was and how she looked terrible. "We need to talk."

"Okay." Her heart danced in her chest. Her palms and armpits were sweating as if she were a high school girl about to be prom-posed to.

"I'm a military man, right? So I don't believe in pussyfooting around. I'm going to get straight to the point. This, Soph, is goddamn ridiculous."

She was taken back by his harsh words. She didn't know what she'd been expecting, but she knew she hadn't been expecting this. She froze, afraid to speak, wondering where the hell he was going with this.

"I love you. I know you love me. I don't care what you say. I don't care if this is complicated, hard, and guilt-ridden. It's all of those things, I know. But, Sophia, I love you. No, I didn't expect this. I didn't want this, not at first. I just wanted to be there for you and, selfishly, I wanted you there for me. I felt like you were the only one who understood me, who knew what it was to lose everything. Then, when neither of us was looking, it blossomed into something else. I hate how it took a tragedy for us to find each other, I do. But we can't change it. No matter how it happened, I love you. I want to be with you. Not Chloe.

Not anyone but you. This past month has been the worst month of my life, and I've been through a lot of stuff. I've given you space. I've given myself space. But I'm done. I know what I want. I want you, every single piece of you. The broken shards, the guilt-ridden pangs, the memories, wishes, and what-ifs. I want the girl who loves Swedish Fish, the girl who prefers sneakers to high heels. I want the girl who watches *Bridesmaids* once a month, who cannot sleep with socks on. I want every single part of you. And dammit, I'm here to get you back, whether you want me to or not."

Her breath quickened as tears stung her eyes. His words spun in her head, and they made sense. They did. But then they didn't. Back and forth, that's where she'd been for the past few months. She'd wrestled with right and wrong. She'd worried about what made sense, what was right. She hadn't listened to her heart.

Now, her heart tugged her toward him, pulling her out of her head, out of her questions.

Instead of answering him, instead of arguing, instead of trying to rationalize what she should do, she finally did what she'd been wanting to do.

She listened to her heart.

She stepped forward, bridging the small gap between them. She threw her arms around his neck, her arm brushing against his stubble. She leaned up on her tiptoes, pulling his head toward her, taking his lips in her mouth, and kissing him like she'd been wanting. She kissed him like she was starved for him, like she had a month to make up for—which she did.

Soon, he took the lead, just the way she liked it. His strong hands were folding into her hair, his lips moving ravenously on hers. His tongue found hers and moved expertly, sending heat through her entire body.

She slowly crept backward, leading him through the hallway. Her mind threatened to stop her, to tell her she shouldn't, not in the bed where she and Tim…

But he stopped her first. He pulled back, all smiles, his voice raspy. "Listen, I want to. God, I want to. But I have something to show you first."

She winked playfully. "Oh yeah?"

"Yeah. So let's… God… okay… let me get my breath. But later, oh later, I'm picking up right here." He nuzzled her face with his nose, kissing her cheek gently.

Calmed momentarily by their break, she got to thinking. *It didn't matter,* she thought. But she just wanted to know.

"Have you talked to Stella?"

"No, why?"

"No reason."

Her smile widened. This was genuine. This was about the two of them. This wasn't about guilt or duty or doing the right thing. This was about Jackson's heart needing her just as she needed him. Why had it taken her so long to realize it?

It was okay, though. These things took time.

Time didn't push the past away or make the future less certain. It did, however, offer clarity. It softened emotions, allowing the truth to shine through.

"You ready?" he asked.

"I am now."

When Mike finally arrived with her Chinese, she didn't even care that it was fifteen minutes late and a bit cold. It didn't matter anymore.

All that mattered was their lives were heading in the right direction—together.

After putting the Chinese food in the fridge for later, she let Jackson take her hand and lead her out of the house.

"I don't get it." Sophia gazed at the Lanzel property, which was about two miles from her current house. The familiar redbrick house had belonged to the elderly couple since she'd moved here. It was a quaint house, a 1950s style charmer. Jackson had stopped his truck in front of it, but she wasn't getting it. Had he gone mad?

"This past month, I've been thinking. About us, about you, about where I wanted my life to go. I just realized we were both going about this whole thing wrong. We were trying to meld the lives we had into one solid future. But maybe what we both need is a fresh start. I'm not suggesting we forget the past, and I don't want to pressure you. But I want this to be a turning point for both of us. I want us to start carving out a new path. Life hasn't gone as planned for either of us. I lost Logan, got divorced, and lost my best friend. You lost your husband and best friend all in one go. It's time, though, Sophia. I think together we can find a new way, a new happiness."

"I think you're right. But why are we here?"

"I want to start fresh. So I bought it."

"Wait... you what?"

"Yep. The Lanzels are retiring to Florida. I pulled some strings, scraped together a down payment, and made an offer. They accepted yesterday. This is mine."

"That's so great," she exclaimed, smiling genuinely for him. This was a big step.

"Yeah. And the appeal is happening soon. So if all goes well, maybe I'll be able to let Logan help decorate his room."

"He's going to love it. I'm so happy for you."

"That's the thing, Soph."

She turned to him, sort of knowing where this was going but wanting to hear the words officially.

"I don't want to pressure you, and it's okay if you're not ready. I know your house is full of memories, good memories. But I want you to know, whenever you're ready, if you're ready, this place belongs to you, too."

She caught what he was saying. He didn't have to elaborate.

She stared at the brick walls, gazed at the rockers on the front porch. She squeezed Jackson's hand.

She hadn't thought about moving out of her home. She never considered it because it hadn't made sense. It still didn't quite feel right. She wasn't ready to let go of all of it, of the entire dream. She wasn't ready to let go of their belongings, of the life they'd built, not completely.

Baby steps, she told herself. Grief took its time. It wasn't a logical road.

She was ready to see where this thing with Jackson could go, was ready to open her heart again.

But she wasn't ready to move in with him, to let go of the past completely. Not just yet.

"I love you. I want a life with you. This is a big step, a huge one. I'm not quite ready, not yet. I want us to take some time to really date, to build a relationship sans guilt. But when I'm ready, and I know someday I will be, you'll be the first to know."

He smiled and nodded. "I thought you'd say that. I did. I just wanted you to know the offer is there. I can't wait to make new memories with you, Sophia. I don't care if they're here or at your house or if they're in a box. I just want you to be happy."

"I am."

"Okay, so you can let me know when you're ready?"

"Yeah. But I think I know when."

He furrowed his brow. "But I thought you said…"

"I said not quite yet, which is true. I need some time to take things in. We need some time to date, really date. But I think, as long as you don't get sick of me, I think in about, oh, seven and a half months we'll be ready to move in with you."

"That's great. But very specific."

She smiled again, putting a hand on her stomach. "Well, might be a little less. I mean, we might want to get the nursery situated."

He froze, a dumbstruck look on his face. "Wait, are you saying… what?"

"I'm pregnant."

He sat, silent, his hand momentarily covering his smile as he sat in disbelief. "Seriously?"

"Seriously."

He reached across to grab her, to kiss her, to celebrate.

She let herself celebrate too. She hadn't planned on this all happening so fast. But that was Jackson for you. Intense, to the point.

Passionate.

"This is amazing," he whispered, pushing a piece of her bangs out of her eyes. "Why didn't you tell me sooner?"

"I was still working on my heart, sorting everything out. I just… I didn't want you to feel obligated."

"Are you kidding? Are you blind?"

"Okay, Mr. Hot Shot. Not all of us are super egotistical. I just wanted to make sure if you wanted to be with me, it wasn't out of moral obligation."

"I'm with you out of love. And maybe a touch of carnal obligation." He winked.

"So are you seriously okay if I don't move in right away?"

"Hey. Seriously. Take all the time you need. We've got a lifetime."

"Okay."

"But one thing."

"Yeah?"

"We can maybe, I don't know, put sleepovers in the cards as possibilities?"

"Yeah, I think."

"Okay. Deal."

"Deal."

They kissed again. "Sophia, I'm so happy. Seriously. I know this all happened so fast. But I'm glad it did."

They took one last look at the house, the two of them taking in all of the twists and turns from the past hour. Then, he drove away.

He pulled back in front of her house. "So, where did we leave off?" he asked as they got out of the truck.

"Well, I believe we left off between 'let's be lovers again' and 'we're having a baby.'"

"Well, what do you say we explore the middle a bit?"

"I'm game. But only if the middle involves eating some Chinese. I'm starving."

She succumbed to him, body and heart, as they headed inside to reheat the Chinese takeout. She let herself feel the happiness she'd been afraid to feel. Suddenly, the future seemed more than survivable.

Chapter Twenty-Eight

JACKSON

Jackson was a bundle of nervous energy, but he wouldn't have it any other way. He sipped on his third cup of coffee—perhaps this had something to do with his ceaseless pacing—and then jaunted to the back bedroom, just to eye up the furniture one more time.

He had made the executive decision to go with green, Logan's favorite color. He hoped it wasn't a mistake now.

He didn't have time to think about it too much because the doorbell rang. Jackson covered the distance from the back bedroom to the front door in record time.

"Daddy!" Logan exclaimed when Jackson opened the door.

"Hey, buddy," Jackson said, stooping down to give his son a hug.

Chloe stood on the doorstep, a few of Logan's suitcases in hand.

"Here." She practically flung the suitcases at Jackson. Logan ran past him, heading to check out the house.

"Do you want to come in?" Jackson offered civilly.

Chloe snorted. "Fuck you." She turned, sunglasses hiding her face, and stomped toward her car.

"Chloe," he called after her. Despite everything, his heart panged a bit. He didn't want it to be this way.

She stopped at her car, scowling at him.

"Chloe, I want things to be okay with us. It's not good for Logan for us to be fighting."

"You should have thought about that when you appealed."

"My son needs me in his life."

"Don't count on it," she said. "He better be on my doorstep in two weeks at exactly nine."

With that, she slammed her car door and peeled out of his driveway.

He sighed, shaken from the encounter. Even Chloe's foul mouth and attitude, however, couldn't kill how happy he was.

Logan was back. His son was back.

Granted, it was shared custody. Every two weeks, Logan would flip back and forth between Chloe and Jackson. It wasn't ideal. It was going to be tense until they all settled into a routine. But it would be okay. Logan had both of his parents in his life, which was what every child deserved.

"Logan, come check out your room. I started decorating

it, but we can pick up some new stuff today."

Logan raced back down the hall, and Jackson followed.

"Dinosaurs!" the boy shouted, heading to jump into his dinosaur-themed bed.

"Do you like it, buddy?"

"I love it. Do I get to sleep here?"

"Yep. It's your room."

"Cool."

Jackson couldn't think of any better word to describe what he was feeling.

Life was back on track.

———————

"Hi, Logan," Sophia said when she came in the front door the next night bearing pizza and ice cream.

"Hi. Want to see my dinosaur?" Logan asked, handing her his stuffed animal. Sophia smiled.

"Do you remember Sophia?" Jackson asked.

"Yep. The lady you like."

Sophia and Jackson looked at each other and smiled.

Sophia had been worried about overwhelming Logan. She insisted she should stay away these two weeks, give him time alone with his son. But Jackson disagreed.

"Soph, you're a part of his life now. You're going to be having his brother or sister. We need to start building a relationship between you two."

"Chloe isn't going to like it."

"Chloe doesn't like anything."

"I don't want to tell him about the baby, though, not yet."

"Deal. We'll wait a little while. Plus, I should probably tell Chloe first."

"That's going to be a fun conversation."

Jackson had grimaced, knowing she was right.

The appeal had been even uglier than he anticipated. Chloe's lawyer pulled out all the stops, from Jackson's struggles with alcohol to his near breakdown after he returned from Iraq. He'd been forced to talk about things on the stand he didn't want to talk about—he rarely broached the subject of his time in the army with anyone.

Sophia had sat beside him holding his hand when he needed it, being a shoulder to cry on when he felt like it was hopeless. She never judged, never pushed him. She was exactly what he needed.

Sophia, Jackson, and Logan headed to the kitchen table to eat pizza and Henry sat under Logan's seat hoping for a pizza crust—Logan quickly obliged. Logan animatedly talked to Sophia about his new room, the puppy he saw at the park yesterday, and his favorite cartoon. She smiled the entire time, a genuine smile. She was going to be an amazing mother, to both their unborn baby and his son.

Sitting at the table, Jackson felt like a new man. All of the heartaches he'd dealt with, first in Iraq, then with Chloe, then with the loss of Tim; they felt miles away. He looked around the table and he saw happiness, he saw his future. He saw everything he ever wanted.

The three spent the evening and several more that week doing what families do—going to the movies, watching television, walking to the park.

By the end of the two weeks, Logan was holding Sophia's hand more than his. Henry was already Logan's best friend, according to the boy—the two were inseparable. Jackson was more than okay with it. They were becoming a family, a family with baggage, but a family nonetheless.

———

On the weeks Logan wasn't home, Jackson felt like there was a hole in his heart. The custody agreement was certainly better than what he'd had, but it would never be perfect.

Still, he made the best of the situation. He used the weeks without Logan as weeks to build his relationship with Sophia, to make new memories.

That first Saturday without Logan, he headed to Sophia's house, handing her a box.

"What's this?"

"Open it, woman," he teased, nodding toward it. She smiled coyly but obliged.

Inside, she pulled out an orange bikini.

"What's this?"

"Your attire for our first surprise date."

She raised an eyebrow. "What are you talking about?"

He walked closer, taking the bikini from her hands and setting it on the counter. "Well, you said you wanted to give this whole dating thing a go before you even consider being ready to go to the next level. So I figured a woman like you needs some pretty mind-blowing dates to be impressed."

"Yeah, clearly, I'm super high-class."

"Well, I'm not taking any chances. I am going to impress you if it kills me. So you see, I've planned twelve surprise dates. Twelve."

"Twelve?"

"I figured twelve was a respectable number of dates to impress you enough to move in."

"You think twelve dates equals moving in status?"

"No. But I think twelve amazing dates with *me* might equal moving in." He flashed his killer smile. She just shook her head.

"Well, that might be true, but listen, if you're going to impress your pregnant girlfriend, shoving a bikini in her face probably isn't winning any points. I don't even want to think about putting this thing on, let alone going anywhere in it."

He nuzzled against her cheek. "Stop. You're gorgeous. And while it is tempting to keep you here all to myself in this bikini, we do have somewhere to be. So go put that on, put something over it, and meet me in the truck in ten minutes."

She sighed, but the sparkle in her eye told him she was enjoying this surprise thing, bikini or not.

"This is the best," Sophia said, lounging in her inner tube.

"Agreed. See, I told you I was going to wow you."

They floated down the lazy river at Great Wolf Lodge, inner tubes tied together, hands joined. There were kids splashing and other couples linked together nearby, but Jackson barely noticed them. All he was focused on was the beautiful blonde floating down the indoor river with him.

They'd driven three hours to the indoor water park, Jackson figuring a lazy river was a perfect way to end the week, a perfect new memory to make.

He'd been right. They spent the next few hours laughing, lounging, and floating their worries away.

When they were completely waterlogged, they dried off, putting some clothes over top of their swimsuits. They found a coffee shop and bakery inside the lodge, both getting the biggest cupcakes the shop had along with some herbal tea.

As they shoveled in the glorious pink frosting, talking about the date and how they would have to bring Logan back sometime, Sophia grew serious.

"Can I ask you something?"

"Yeah," he said, wiping chocolate crumbs from his mouth.

"Why don't you ever talk about Iraq?"

This had sort of come out of left field. He paused for a moment, catching his breath and contemplating how to respond.

"Sorry. Mood killer," she said, wincing.

He shook his head. "No, it's fine. It's just... it was a rough time. I saw some stuff no one should have to see. I lost some people. It's just not something I like to dwell on."

She shook her head. "Fair enough."

"Really? You don't need to know anything else? You're not curious?"

She put her spoon down. "No. Jackson, I love the man in front of me, no matter what happened in the past. Your past can stay there. I want to live here, in the moment. Whatever you went through, it made you the amazing, strong, sexy man you are today. That's all I need to know. When you're ready to tell me more, I'll be here to listen."

He nodded. "You're amazing, you know?"

She shrugged playfully. "I mean, yeah, I am." She winked, finishing her last bite of cupcake before leaning in for a kiss.

Chapter Twenty-Nine

JACKSON

As the weeks passed, their connection morphed into the relationship Jackson knew they could have. He continued to surprise her, to date her, to get to know her.

The more he found out, the more he found to love. He loved the way she laughed hysterically at certain commercials, especially the one with a monkey in it. He loved the way she ate mustard on her French fries. He loved every piece of her, the sexy, the smart, the sassy, and the broken.

He just loved her.

Over the weeks, he continued taking her on surprise dates. He wanted to make sure they had a lifetime of memories, new memories, memories free of guilt. They went to another water park, they went fishing to a new fishing spot he'd never been to. They went on a picnic. They went to a drive-in. They took Logan to DC for a weekend, to a book fair, and to the aviary.

They ate fancy dinners. They visited mom and pop restaurants. They went shopping, swimming, ice cream eating, and all sorts of things in between. They did all of the cheesy dating traditions he, not long ago, had sworn off.

Things weren't rosy. There were still moments of melancholy, dates that hit her hard, dates that hit him hard. There were moments of indecision, moments he wanted them to move faster, moments she needed to slow down.

They were navigating tricky waters, but he wouldn't have it any other way.

He came with his own share of baggage, too. Chloe was none too happy when he told her about the baby. There were screaming fights, attempts to sabotage his time with Logan, and copious amounts of expletives. But they were navigating those waters, too.

Together.

"Are you nervous?"

"No. I'm excited. Why would I be nervous?"

"Gretta. I'm sure she'll have something to say about it."

"First, I don't stress about my sister and what she thinks. Second, she's going to be thrilled. She loves you. Are you nervous?"

"I mean, a little. I just don't want to curse us."

Jackson reached over to squeeze her hand, one hand on the steering wheel.

"You're not cursing anything. It's fine. The baby's going to be fine."

"I know it's silly, but I just feel like the more people we tell, the more we press our luck about this pregnancy. I've already lost a baby. I'm so scared."

"We're not losing this baby. I promise."

Seeming content, she shifted the package on her lap, the silver wrapping paper crinkling.

"You're right. I'm sorry. This is a good moment, and I don't want to put a damper on it."

"You could never put a damper on this. Baby, I'm so excited. Getting to share some good news with my family for once is such a godsend."

They'd already shared the news with her parents last weekend. Sophia's mom had embraced them both, tears dampening his shirt as she exclaimed how happy she was. He'd been worried about how they would react, worried they'd feel he'd taken advantage of the situation. They'd felt nothing but joy. They were thrilled at the prospect of a grandchild and at Sophia reclaiming her life.

Now, it was his family's turn. He'd told his mom he was bringing Sophia to Sunday dinner. She'd been animated at the news, talking a mile a minute about new casserole recipes she could try and Pictionary games they should play.

The only thing he was nervous about was that she

would literally explode with joy at the news. His mom loved Sophia, and she loved babies. Her heart was going to burst.

When they arrived, he put the truck in park. Sophia turned to him, handing the package over.

"You sure? This was your idea. You can give it to them."

"No way. This is your moment, your good news."

He kissed her hand as he took the present. "It's our good news," he corrected before they got out of the truck and marched toward the front door.

———————

Inside was the chaos typifying Jackson's family. His dad and Jonathan were playing poker at the kitchen table, Jackson's mom barking orders at them to vacate, so she could set the table. Jace ran around with a marker, Gretta chasing after him, pleading with him to drop it.

"Sophia! Jackson!" the boy exclaimed, running at them.

Jackson passed the present to Sophia and caught the boy in his arms, lifting him to the sky as was their tradition.

The boy, marker still in hand, doodled on the wall before anyone could stop him.

"Jace! Look what you've done!" Gretta shrieked.

The boy giggled. "I decorated way up high."

Jackson couldn't help but laugh, causing Gretta to give him a death glare.

"Wait until Grandma sees what you did," Gretta chided as Jackson returned Jace to the ground.

"Wait until Grandma hears what?" His mom said, turning from her food prep to saunter into the living room where the impromptu decorating had occurred. Her eyes followed everyone else's stares and landed on the drawing up near the ceiling.

She simply shrugged. "Oh well. Your grandpa needs to repaint in here anyway." She fluffed Jace's hair before the boy tore off into the kitchen, marker now mercifully in his mother's hand.

Jackson's jaw flew open. "If I had done that as a child, you would have murdered me."

"Yeah, same. What is this softening up stuff, Mom?"

Their mom just shrugged. "What can I say? He's way cuter than both of you were."

They both scowled but eventually agreed. Sophia laughed.

"Now will everyone just simmer down. We're going to scare Sophia away," she said, leaning over to hug her. "What's this?"

Sophia pulled from the hug and handed the box to his mom, eyeing Jackson. Jackson nodded.

"It's a gift for you and Dad."

"For what?"

"Just open it, Mom," Jackson ordered.

The whole crew ushered themselves into the bigger, airier kitchen. Everyone gathered around as his parents carefully pulled the silver paper off the box. Jackson held Sophia's hand, squeezing it.

His mom opened the box and pulled out an elegant

silver picture frame.

It was engraved with the words "World's Best Grandparents."

"Does this mean?" his mom questioned, looking at Jackson. He nodded, beaming. His mom practically leaped across the table, rushing to squeeze both Jackson and Sophia into the tightest hug accompanied by shrieks at a dangerous decibel.

"I'm so thrilled. This is the best news! I knew you two were going to get together."

Jackson felt himself blush. His mom continued to squeal. Once she let them up for air, the rest of the family gathered around, and congratulations flew.

In that moment, Jackson's heart almost imploded. To see his family so joyous over the news, to see them rallying together to congratulate him and the woman he loved, it took his breath away.

He'd been through so many obstacles in the past months. He'd had so many dejected moments, so many times his family had to help scoop him out of the gutter.

Now, looking around, especially at his mom, he saw sheer happiness. His life was turning around. Good things were coming his way.

The woman he loved was standing right beside him, carrying a baby who meant everything to him already. His baby.

He fought back a tear, knowing Gretta would never let him hear the end of it if he started crying. As his mother continued her interrogation of Sophia about baby showers, baby names, due dates, and everything else baby related, he leaned down to kiss Sophia on the cheek.

She'd brought happiness back to him, to his family. She'd handed him redemption and hope when his world was nothing but bleak.

Looking at her here, with his family, he saw a lifetime of happiness, of kisses, and of chaotic family gatherings before them.

He was happier than he'd ever been.

Chapter Thirty

JACKSON

It was on a Thursday about two months after Jackson had moved into his house when it happened.

Life changed again. If he weren't careful, he'd get whiplash.

Sophia showed up at his doorstep at six o'clock, unannounced, dressed in jeans and a T-shirt. She carried a picnic basket.

"Hey," he said after kissing her on the cheek. "You know you don't have to ring the doorbell, you weirdo."

"I wanted to."

He eyed her suspiciously. "Everything okay?"

"Yep. It's all good. You busy?"

"Well, I was thinking of watching the baseball game, eating steak, and drinking beer. You know, the bachelor life. But I guess I could squeeze in some time for you."

She punched his arm.

"That freaking hurt."

"Wimp. Come on. I have a surprise for you better than steak and beer."

She grabbed his hand, and he let her pull him out the door, into the muggy summer night.

The sun was warm on his face as he walked beside Sophia. He offered to take the basket from her, but she swatted him away.

"Hands off."

"Hope that's not the motto of the entire night." He nudged her. She nudged him back.

They strolled, silence filling the void between them. They walked casually like they had so many times. She leaned on his arm. It felt easy.

When they reached their bench—they probably should get a plaque for it at this point—she paused, ordering him to sit. He obliged, and she sat beside him, setting the basket on the ground.

He stared at her expectantly. She just smiled. She pulled two champagne glasses and some grape juice from the basket. She poured them each a glass as he eyed the label.

"Hazards of dating a pregnant lady."

"Hazards I'll gladly accept. What's this?"

"This is us celebrating. Official date thirteen."

He smirked. "I'm the one who is surprising you."

"Yes. And you delivered as promised. You gave me twelve amazing dates. You gave me so much more, though,

Jackson. You gave me time. You gave me time to move on, to really, truly move on. You gave me time to be certain about all this."

"I'm patient when I want to be. Plus, it wasn't really a punishment, you know."

He clinked her glass and took a sip of grape juice, his gaze still locked on her.

"The thing is, when you brought me to this bench for the first time, I was a broken woman. I couldn't manage to see past my own driveway, let alone into the future. I thought it was over for me. I wanted to just cease to exist."

His face tightened now with the memory of that time. "I was a broken man, too. I was in the same boat."

"I know. But somehow, together, we sort of crawled our way out of the hole, huh? We crawled back to life, with each other. And it's been crazy and unexpected and messy. We've gone back and forth. We've tried to quit this. But we can't. Because Jackson, together, we're so much better. We're better people. We're better versions of ourselves. And this baby, well, this baby has just made everything even clearer. I didn't want Tim to die. I didn't want to lose the life I had. But with you, Jackson, I've realized I haven't lost my life completely. I've found a way to look past not only my driveway, but past myself. I can see happiness again in a life with you."

"Me too, Sophia. I love you."

"I love you, too. So much. Therefore, date thirteen is a simple date."

"Oh yeah?"

"Yeah. Date thirteen is us sitting here, talking, sipping grape juice."

He blinked.

She laughed. "I know, you think I'm crazy, right?"

"No. I think it's fine. I'll sit here on this bench for eternity with you."

"Really?"

"Can I get to at least second base while on this bench?"

"No."

"Then I retract my statement."

"Well, let me finish. We sit here on this bench. Then…"

"Yeah?" he asked.

"Then we go home. To our home."

He smirked, wanting to make sure he heard her right. "Our home?"

"Yes. Here," she said, reaching back into the basket. She pulled out a picture frame.

In the frame was the picture from their special night, the carriage ride when they first really admitted this was going somewhere.

"I thought it would look good on our mantle."

He took the picture from her, knowing without a doubt she was in it for real. He set the picture on the bench seat beside him, put his glass on the ground, and took her face in both his hands. He kissed her long and hard. He kissed away the grape juice from her lips. He kissed away so much more, too. He kissed away all the doubts, fears, and denials they'd lived through. He kissed away the pain of loss.

He kissed away the Sophia and Jackson they had been

up until a moment ago. He kissed them right into their new life together.

When they were breathless, she silently reached down, dumped out their grape juice, and tossed the glasses haphazardly into the basket. He grabbed their picture and offered her his arm.

They strolled peacefully down the street again, silence returning. There was nothing to say in this moment, this perfect moment. They were on the same page, finally.

He was ready, so ready, to start living his pages with her.

Chapter Thirty-One

SOPHIA

The sun's rays danced around the room, imploring Sophia to wake up. She slowly opened her eyes, the brightness of the summer day contradicting what this day now symbolized.

Death. Loss. Grief.

Sheer tragedy.

Her chest heaved with the weight of the date, with the remembrance of where she had been exactly one year ago today. The phone call. The debilitating news. Life forever changed.

Tears welled, a sign of how today would be. She hadn't expected any less. Everyone told her the first anniversary was the worst. Still, how did you prepare for something like this? How could you possibly get your emotions ready to face the day everything changed?

A year ago, she'd thought she'd wanted nothing more than to curl up and die, too. She'd been cloaked in the blackness of the news and of the gloomy outlook of a life without Tim. Her life was over, in her mind. She would never smile again, never get rid of the stabbing pain threatening to bowl her over.

The past year had been a windy road of sadness, overwhelming depression, and recovery. Swiping at her eyes, she felt Jackson stir, his arms pulling her in tight under the quilt. The warmth of his body soothed her, even if just a little. She was glad she wasn't waking up alone.

At one point, this mere thought would've brought waves of guilt. On the anniversary of Tim's death, waking up with another man would have horrified her.

So much had changed.

The love she'd found with Jackson had changed her.

In a seemingly impossible situation, he'd brought light back to her life. He'd opened her cold, dead heart again to possibility. He'd radiated life through her veins when she'd wanted nothing but nonexistence.

It was going to be hard, there was no doubt about that. She'd cry a lot. She'd think about all they'd lost, think about all Tim had lost. She'd drown herself in memories of Tim, of a life they thought was untouchable.

She still loved him. She always would.

Still, Jackson had taught her it was okay to love Tim and move on. Her heart didn't have to be mutually exclusive. Giving her heart away again, finding happiness with

Jackson didn't mean she was disrespecting Tim or letting him go completely. She'd learned over the past year the heart was flexible. It could wrap itself, twist itself in ways unexpected.

She hadn't expected to wake up with Jackson's arms around her, hadn't planned on falling for him. The heart, though, was sometimes an uncontrollable entity driven by passion, chemistry, and connection—things she and Jackson definitely shared.

She put a hand on her growing belly, stroking it as she did every morning. After a long moment, she rolled into Jackson, kissing him softly, tears still rolling down her cheeks. He groaned, sleepiness wearing off and awareness taking its place.

"Hey," he whispered, kissing her forehead.

"Hey," she said, her voice cracking.

They didn't say anything more. They didn't have to. They both knew what the day was, knew how momentous it was. They both knew there was nothing Jackson could say to ease the burden. It would be awkward for both of them, a day to remember the past.

But Sophia knew they'd get through—together. Yesterday, Jackson had offered to give her the day to grieve in private. She'd wanted nothing of the sort, though. She knew Jackson was as essential to her survival of the day as anything. She needed him by her side. She needed him to talk about Tim, to remember.

She needed him, plain and simple.

They spent a long time just basking in each other's arms. No words, no suggestive touches passed between them. They simply reveled in the comfort of each other, understanding between them unspoken.

"Are you ready?" Jackson whispered a while later, his voice wistful.

She nodded, doing the thing she thought she'd never do on a day like today.

She got out of bed.

She rose to face the day, the unspoken mission ahead of her. They dressed, both in black, and walked through their morning routine. When they were both ready, he took her hand and they sauntered outside into the bright day.

———————

"Do you want some time alone?" Jackson asked after they'd each placed a white rose on Tim's grave. They were sitting in the grass, side by side, cross-legged like innocent schoolchildren. Sophia played with a rogue dandelion growing beside the grave.

She glanced at him, his steel-gray eyes both pained and comforting.

"No," she whispered. "Stay."

Jackson nodded, putting an arm around her. They sat for a few moments in silent reverence of the grave, of the day, of the memories.

Finally, the words came to her, the words she needed to say.

"I miss you, Tim. I miss you so much. I hope wherever you are, you're doing okay. We're doing okay here, in spite of everything."

Tears stopped her, choked her up. She had so much more she wanted to say, so much more she wanted to confess. She wanted to tell Tim about the baby, about Jackson. She wanted to talk about their memories, revisit the past. She wanted to apologize for things she was still clinging to, fights they'd left unresolved, moments she hadn't appreciated him. She wanted to talk about her life now, tell him the details of how she was getting it together.

The words failed her, the heaviness of the day weighing on her. She couldn't say the words, couldn't say any more.

Jackson put an arm around her now, pulling her in. She cried on his shoulder.

"He knows, Sophia. He knows you love him."

They were words a man should be jealous of, words most men wouldn't want to hear or admit. Yet Jackson, the selfless man he was, could say exactly what she needed to hear. He always recognized what she needed. No matter how hard it might be to admit the woman he was in love with still left a piece of her heart here at a gravestone, he said the words she so desperately needed assurance of.

"I love you," she said, turning to him. She knew today would be tough, but she hadn't realized how debilitating the resurgence of pain would be. Thankfully, she wasn't alone.

Tim was gone. That fact still remained true. However, in Jackson she'd found a man she could see a new forever with, a man who helped her dream again.

They sat for a while longer, Sophia lost in memories. They didn't verbalize their stories. This wasn't the place.

They sat, hand in hand, remembering the man who had touched both of their lives.

Then, after a while, Sophia swiped at her tears and stood. Jackson followed suit.

"Are you ready to head home?" Jackson questioned, kissing her on the forehead. "No rush, of course."

Sophia took a step closer to the headstone, stooping down to touch the cold, hard stone. She contemplated the idea in her head for a moment. It was what she wanted to do. It was what she needed.

So she turned to Jackson after straightening back up. "Can we stop somewhere first?"

"Yeah, baby. Wherever you want."

"I thought we could go to Mama's."

Jackson froze, clearly not sure how to respond. "Honey, I don't know…"

She nodded, taking a deep breath. "I haven't been there since Tim died. It's a place of so many memories. I don't want those memories to die. I know it's sort of strange asking you to go with me. But I want to honor Tim. I want to know I'll never let go of that part of my life completely."

"Sophia, it's not weird. I'm not hesitant because of how I'll feel. I'm just worried it will be hard for you."

"It will. But I don't want to spend my life avoiding places, memories. I want to remember Tim, but I want to move on, too. Will you go with me? I don't think I could go there alone. With you, I think I'll be strong enough."

"Whatever you want."

She nodded. She knew it was a strange request, taking

Jackson to the place that symbolized her life with Tim. In a way, it was fitting. Mama's was where her life with Tim began. She wanted to start a new tradition, a new start with Jackson.

She would never say goodbye to her memories with Tim, but she would say hello to new memories. She would march toward the future, a mix of the woman she had been before and the woman she was now.

Jackson and Sophia went to the restaurant. Her heart was heavy when she walked in, and she was teary when she saw the booths that reminded her of those monumental times.

But over spaghetti and lasagna, she and Jackson did the best thing they could have on a day like today. They talked about Tim. They shared in memories. They toasted to the man who had meant so much to both of them.

They walked out, leaning on each other, moving on together in a world without Tim, a world that a year ago had seemed impossible to survive.

Chapter Thirty-Two

"You sure you don't want to change your mind? I don't want you regretting this."

"If not wearing a veil is my biggest regret, I'm golden," Stella said, blowing a piece of her pink hair from her eyes. They were in the tiny bathroom, putting the finishing touches on their makeup. Sophia stood in her turquoise, skin-tight dress—for the first time, she had to completely comply with Stella's wardrobe choice for her—and her dolphin earrings. She looked… well… interesting, especially with the dress clinging to her bulging belly bump. There was nothing left to the imagination, and she felt a little bit like a bloated whale in the dress. But Stella was happy, which was all that mattered.

"Are you sure you're going to be okay?" Stella said,

turning to her. Even on her wedding day, she was still worried about her.

"Are you kidding? It's your freaking wedding day. I'm thrilled!" She leaned in to hug Stella. The thing was, she *was* thrilled.

A year ago, the scene would have been impossible. She wouldn't have been able to handle it. Now, she knew she could brave it. She could more than brave being maid of honor in her best friend's wedding. She could enjoy it.

Part of it was time. Time didn't heal wounds, but it did make them a little duller. She still missed Tim. Some days were harder than others. Some days, she was still angry the universe had ripped her perfect life apart. Some days when she saw his favorite television show or smelled a whiff of his cologne, she almost fell apart.

But the "some days" were getting farther apart and more bearable.

Part of it was time, but a big part of it was something else.

Jackson.

He didn't replace Tim. He never could. She wouldn't want him to. But he did remind her life was for living. He made her smile. He made her excited.

Hand resting on her belly bump, she smiled. Life was moving on. There were so many beautiful moments to grab. She was ready to grab them.

"I think we should go. Jackson just texted to say Larry is ready," Sophia said after her phone buzzed. Jackson was a groomsman, and Larry's brother was the best man.

"Okay, let's do this," Stella said, not an ounce of nerves apparent.

They marched out to the lobby area, a red rose in each of their hands. Stella's sister and parents were waiting in the lobby as well, ready to walk down the makeshift aisle.

The aquarium was eerily quiet. Larry had paid extra to have it shut down for the wedding. At first, the aquarium wasn't sure how to handle such a request—they probably didn't have many couples beg to get married there. But, after some coaxing, they complied.

So, here they were. A group of thirty of Stella and Larry's best friends and family ready to watch them say vows by the dolphin enclosure.

Sophia wouldn't expect anything else.

With a backdrop of noisy, splashing dolphins, Larry and Stella said their own vows. Stella promised to be faithful to Larry despite his love of pleated pants and kale. Larry agreed to love Stella despite her hatred for organization and her love of the Pittsburgh Penguins. The ceremony was quirky, down to earth, informal... but it was moving.

It was moving to see the love radiating from Stella and Larry. Stella's smile was never as wide, as beautiful as it was when she was with Larry. They completed each other, balanced each other. They were good for each other.

When Stella and Larry leaned in for their first kiss, Sophia couldn't help but wink at Jackson. She felt her heart leap a little.

Not long ago, this would have been agonizing. Not long ago, she had burst into tears at the thought of Stella getting married. Now, she was hanging on to a vision of tomorrow. She could see a life for herself that, like Stella, was filled with her best smiles.

Despite the layers of pain and worry, despite all of the what-ifs and maybes, she saw something. She saw herself, one day in the future, standing with Jackson, a preacher telling him to kiss his bride. For the first time, the thought didn't make her feel guilty or scared. It just made her look forward to what was coming.

That night, after Jackson and Sophia headed home following an evening of cake, dancing, and toasts to the happy couple, after they had celebrated the romance in the air in their own way, Sophia lay beside Jackson in bed. His arms around her, she nestled in against him.

"Today was nice," she said against his bare chest. He played with her hair with his free hand.

"It was. They make a great couple. And despite the unconventional locale, it was a beautiful wedding."

They basked in a silent moment.

"Jackson?"

"Yeah, babe?"

She paused, hesitant. But then she decided to go all in.

"Do you think someday that could be us?"

He shifted to look at her. "You mean married?"

She nodded, feeling her cheeks burn. "I mean, not now or anything. Just someday."

He smiled, leaning in even closer. He was very serious. "When Chloe stomped on my heart, I said never again. I vowed to never, ever marry again."

Her heart sank. "Oh." She turned away. She was stupid for saying this.

He took his hand and grabbed her chin, turning her to face him. "Then you came along. You changed everything. Absolutely everything. You talk about how broken you were when we found each other, but you don't see how I was broken, too. I thought I'd never say hello to a new relationship. I thought I'd never let go of the hurt and the mistrust. But one look at you, one walk with you, and it all changed. I knew I could leave behind the man I was, the man Chloe made me."

Sophia's heart reignited. She hadn't realized how much she needed to hear this until now. She put a hand on his stubbly face.

"I love you."

"I love you, too," he replied, softly kissing her lips. "So yes. Yes, I see us married. Just like the dating and moving in and everything in between, it's on your terms. Whenever you're ready."

She knew in that moment, without a doubt, that with Jackson, it was possible. With Jackson, she could love again, marry again.

She could, in fact, be ready to let go.

Epilogue

SOPHIA

"Are you sure about this?" she asked hesitantly, examining her lipstick in the visor mirror. It wasn't that she needed to look good. She was just filled with nervous energy, excitement... and anxiety, too.

"Hey, stop it right there. We talked about this."

"I know, but I feel bad."

"Well stop it." He reached for her hand, and she turned, looking at him.

She was so lucky. He was gorgeous, and he understood.

He understood her through the good days, the laughter. But he understood her when the sadness crept in. There wasn't a hint of jealousy or anger or frustration. He let her be her. He let her grieve. Jackson acknowledged grief wasn't a straight line.

He loved her anyway.

When the car slowed to the spot all too familiar, she inhaled.

"Do you want me to come?"

She turned to him. "Would you mind if I went alone?"

He nodded and smiled. "Take your time. I'll be here."

"I know." She gave him one last smile and rubbed his hand before getting out of the car, being careful not to step in the mud puddle in her sparkly shoes.

She softly walked through the wet grass, sunrays cascading and bouncing around the headstones.

When she reached the familiar spot, she stopped.

It had been two years since the ground had accepted Tim. It had been two years since the widowed woman in all black tried to toss herself in beside him.

It had been two years since she saw her life as though it were as dark and musty as the cold earth Tim had been lowered into.

The years had been strange, no doubt. She'd gone through the cycle of grief and back through it. She'd woven in and out of the sorrow, the anger, the guilt, the anxiety. She'd cried herself to sleep. She'd cried herself awake. She'd gone numb, gone lifeless, gone limp.

Somehow, she'd remerged from the grave. She'd come back to life. Her parents, Stella, they'd played a role.

But it was Jackson, the man in the car waiting for her, who had really made her see life wasn't over. He'd crept his way in slowly and surely. He'd found her heart before she even knew it still existed. He'd made her reconnect with life.

Two years ago, she'd never have seen herself here. At the time, two years didn't seem like enough time to figure out how to move on. She'd known women who lost their husbands and died single, grieving for decades. She'd known women who took five years to gain the courage to date again. For Sophia, it had taken two years and finding love in an unexpected place. Grief was like that, she realized. It moved at its own pace, in its own way. It wasn't something you could generalize, even though people tried.

She'd had plenty of stares, plenty of whispers in the grocery store. She'd heard words of "slow down" and "how could you move on" and "I could never." She'd heard all the judgment. It wore on her sometimes, it did. She hated how people assumed they knew her, knew her situation, knew her heart. She was getting better. Stronger. She no longer worried about the grocery store gossipers.

She knew she had to do what was right for her.

She was different now. She wasn't the woman she'd been with Tim. She was hardened, a little wiser, a little leerier than that woman had been.

It was okay, though. She knew now she would never be the Sophia who was on Tim's arm. Life had taken that from her. It wasn't fair. It was still awful.

But she could survive it. She *had* survived it.

She stood staring at the only physical remnant of the life he'd lived. The man who had been the love of her life, who had seen her through her twenties. It still hurt to imagine him there, to realize this was all that was left of him now. It always would hurt.

This wasn't all of him that was left, though. Tim had been a great man. He'd left his mark on so many lives. He'd left his mark on her life, had embossed her heart with his words, with their memories.

A gentle smile crept over her face. This was where she needed to be. It seemed odd at first. It was probably the last place most would go. She knew she needed to, though. She needed to find closure, to find a sense of peace. At first, she'd felt guilty, the pull between two men always a struggle. Jackson, though, was the first to let the pull go, to snap his end of the rubber band and let her feel free from the wrath of guilt.

When she'd looked at him, doughy-eyed an hour ago, he knew. She didn't have to say a word... which was good because she wasn't sure what the right words were.

"Soph, we can stop there. You know we can."

"Won't it be weird for you? I don't want you to..."

"Hey," he said, wrapping her in his arms. "We've talked about this. I love you. You love me. But Tim will always be an important part of your life, a part of you. I'm not taking that away from you."

So here they were. Here she was, doing what she needed to do.

This life would never be easy. There would be pulls back and forth. There would still be moments when she felt sadness, felt guilt creep in. But with Jackson, she knew it would be okay. They would be okay.

She moved across the grass, sitting down on the stone, running her hand over the smooth top. She let her mind go back to a foreign yet familiar place. She didn't tell herself she shouldn't be thinking of this or that it was weird. She, as she had learned over the past few months, just let herself go, let herself feel what she needed to feel.

Her hands were shaking, the yellow daffodils clearly showcasing her nerves.

"You okay?" her dad asked, tapping her arm.

"I will be. I don't know why I'm so nervous." She looked down at her sparkly white ballet flats—Stella had insisted she needed a shoe with pizzazz, especially if she were wearing a knee-length dress. She looked up now, seeing her best friend making her way down the makeshift aisle in the middle of the field. She wore a bright yellow tea-length dress, her pink hair vibrant against it. She wished Stella could come back, could help her down the aisle. She needed Stella to help her snap out of it, to remind her it was all good.

It was a small gathering, only forty of their closest friends and family. The white folding chairs were perfectly arranged in the middle of the field, the archway centered perfectly with wildflowers as a backdrop. It was magical; it was whimsical, like something straight out of a fairy tale.

The lone violin—a high school student Stella knew through a family friend—began to play the music.

"That's our cue, baby. You ready?" her dad asked. She took a deep breath, her hands still shaky.

"Yes," she said with certainty.

She was nervous, hell she was terrified. But not because of what she was about to do or because of any doubts in the man at the end of the aisle. Life was filled with uncertainties, but her love for Tim wasn't one of them. She couldn't wait to vow to love him forever because in her heart, she knew she would. No matter what.

She walked steadily, leaning on her father. She made eye contact with her mom, who was tearing up. She looked to Stella, who winked and gave her a thumbs-up.

Only then, when she was near the end of the aisle, did she let herself look at him.

The tears started instantly, just like she knew they would.

She looked at him, standing there in his gray suit, and she saw what she thought she'd never find.

Love. Security. Assurance.

A future, a certain future full of hope, love, and discovery.

When her hand found Tim's, she stopped shaking. She was still nervous, still full of energy from the momentousness of the day. But she was also calmed. With her hand in his, she knew everything would be okay.

"I love you," he said as soon as they were in their places and the music stopped.

The minister chuckled. "Not yet." Tim winked at him, and Sophia smiled.

Their ceremony was simple, beautiful, complete. When the vows came, Sophia said hers with assurance, looking in Tim's eyes, tears welling in her own.

But when his turn came and he was to repeat the "Till death do us part" line, he paused. The minister repeated them.

"I'm sorry. I can't."

Sophia's heart stopped, her palms becoming sweaty. She knew this was too good to be true. He was backing out. He'd realized she wasn't worth it.

Everyone sat, silently appraising the situation. "I can't say those words, because they're not true." He squeezed Sophia's hands. "The thing is, I don't want to think about our love ending, about it severing with our death. I love you so much, Sophia, that not even death is going to stop this feeling. I'll never say goodbye to you, Sophia. This love, it's not going to end with death or with anything else for that matter." She felt her face tighten as she beamed, looking into the eyes of the man who would be her forever.

They exchanged rings, a kiss, and were pronounced man and wife. Running down the aisle as a new bride, Sophia laughed as their family and friends cheered. Holding Tim's hand, she came to one conclusion, the sun shining in assurance her promise was true.

She would never, ever let this man go.

———————

"The thing is, Tim, I don't want to say goodbye. I never did. Back then, when we got married, we were just two naïve kids who thought we could choose our destiny. We thought love was a choice. But it isn't. Sometimes life makes the choice for us. I will never forget our love. I will never forget us. I will always, always love you. Always. But, I have to let go of the thought I can't be happy without you.

You loved me enough to make me believe I can be happy again. I've found that happiness. I found what I thought was impossible—a life without you. It was faster than I expected. It was different than I expected. But I guess that's what we learned, huh? Life never goes as we expect it to. It's crazy, it's messy, and it's awful. And then it's beautiful. And then it's confusing. It's all of these things rolled into one giant ball of madness. When you died, I thought I was done with it all. I did. But I've learned there's still good here for me. There's still so much to hang onto. So I'm not ready to say goodbye to my life, not yet. I'm not saying goodbye to you either. I'm just saying I'm okay. I'm more than okay. I'm happy. I love you."

She wiped the tears from her eyes, brushing her hand over the stone once more. Her heart surged. She'd needed to come here, needed to talk to him. A piece of her would always be here in this earth.

Walking back to the car, turning from the grave, she realized it was okay. It was all okay. Because the man waiting in the car for her would be there through everything. He would walk beside her, hold her hand. They would enjoy a life neither had imagined but one neither could live without, if they had a choice in it. They would raise Logan and Eliza. They would hopefully grow old together.

Life would test them. It might even try to wrench them apart. But she was strong. She knew the risk of love, the risk of loss, was worth it.

She wouldn't live the rest of her life tiptoeing around, protecting her heart. She would fall completely in, feel everything, and do the best she could to find happiness again.

As the sun's rays glinted off the tin cans hanging off the back of the car, she smiled, pausing with her hand on the car handle. She pulled down the hem on her short, white dress before getting back in.

"You ready, Mr. Gauge?"

"Only if you are, Mrs. Gauge."

And she was. She truly was....

Acknowledgments

A few short years ago, publishing a novel seemed like an unreachable dream. I had so many stories in me, so many characters, but I felt like they would never be shared. I have been so blessed, though, to get to travel this amazing writing journey. I am so grateful to everyone who has helped me on this path. I am still in awe that people are reading about characters I created, talking about stories I wrote. The surreal experience of seeing your book in someone's hands will never, ever get old.

I want to thank Hot Tree Publishing for believing in me and for helping give me a voice to share my stories. Thank you to Becky, Justine, Olivia, Peggy, and everyone else who works tirelessly to help shape and share my works. I am so blessed to be a part of a team of such dedicated women. I am also blessed to work with a publisher with so many talented authors. Thank you to everyone in the Hot Tree Publishing family for your support, your encouragement, and your friendship.

Thank you to my parents, Ken and Lori Keagy. You shaped my entire life path by teaching me what mattered most in life. You taught me to make education a priority. You taught me to be humble, compassionate, and motivated. You taught me that if you want something, you have to work for it. All of the life lessons you taught me have helped me achieve my wildest dreams. I am so blessed to call you my parents.

Thank you to my husband, Chad, my best friend. When we met at the art table in seventh grade, I had no way of predicting the path our lives would take together. I had no way of knowing that over a decade later, we'd be married with five cats, a huge dog, and be living out our dreams. There is no one I'd rather live out my dreams with. You make me laugh every single day. You are always there to push me when I feel like giving up. You believe in me, you support me, and you challenge me to be better.

I also want to thank all of the teachers who have shaped my path. Thank you Diane Vella, Sue Gunsallus, Tom Kunkle, and all of the professors at Mount Aloysius College. All of you taught me skills and confidence to pursue my writing. I would not be here today without all of the lessons you taught me.

Thank you to my friends, family, and coworkers for all of your support. A special thank you goes out to Grandma Bonnie, Christie James, Hannah Hauser, Jamie Lynch,

Kelly Rubritz, Sandra Corey, Kay Shuma, Alicia Shmouder, Lynette Luke, Jennifer Carney, Kristin Mathias, Kristin Books, Maureen Letcher, Mary Baker, and everyone else who has tirelessly supported me. All of you have been such an encouragement, whether it's coming to book signings, reading my books, buying my books, sharing my social media posts, or just offering kind words. I couldn't walk this road without all of you.

Above all, thank you to my readers. When I started this journey, I thought I would be lucky to have one reader. I have been so blessed to have so many fans and readers who believe in my writing and support my stories. My favorite part of this journey has been the opportunity it has provided to meet new people and share in the love of books with others. Thank you to readers everywhere. I love and appreciate all of you.

And of course, thank you to my mastiff Henry for cuddling with me tirelessly during the editing process and for waiting patiently to take your walks while I worked on this book.

About The Publisher

Hot Tree Publishing opened its doors in 2015 with an aspiration to bring quality fiction to the world of readers. With the initial focus on romance and a wide spread of romance sub-genres, they envision opening up to alternative genres in the near future.

Firmly seated in the industry as a leading editing provider to independent authors and small publishing houses, Hot Tree Publishing is the sister company to Hot Tree Editing, founded in 2012. Having established in-house editing and promotions, plus having a well-respected market presence, Hot Tree Publishing endeavors to be a leader in bringing quality stories to the world of readers.

Interested in discovering more amazing reads brought to you by Hot Tree Publishing or perhaps you're interested in submitting a manuscript and joining the HTPubs family? Either way, head over to the website for information:

WWW.HOTTREEPUBLISHING.COM

www.ingramcontent.com/pod-product-compliance
Lightning Source LLC
Chambersburg PA
CBHW032058180726
48284CB00002B/349